DRUMS AT DUSK

LIBRARY OF SOUTHERN CIVILIZATION

DRUMS AT DUSK

A NOVEL

ARNA BONTEMPS

WITH A NEW INTRODUCTION BY
Michael P. Bibler AND Jessica Adams

LOUISIANA STATE UNIVERSITY PRESS ✻ BATON ROUGE

Published by Louisiana State University Press
First published by the Macmillan Company in 1939
Copyright © 1939 by Arna Bontemps. Copyright © renewed 1967 by Arna Bontemps.
Introduction copyright © 2009 by Louisiana State University Press
Manufactured in the United States of America
First printing

Designer: Barbara Neely Bourgoyne
Typeface: Elegant Garamond
Printer and binder: Thomson-Shore, Inc.

The editors wish to thank Arna Alexander Bontemps for his interest in this project and for sharing his knowledge of his father and the rest of the Bontemps family. They also thank Cécile Accilien for her thoughtful commentary on the introduction. They would like to acknowledge the support of John Easterly at the Louisiana State University Press, Craig Tenney at Harold Ober Associates, and Dr. Jessie C. Smith at Fisk University. Finally, they are grateful to the Beinecke Rare Book and Manuscript Library at Yale University for helping them to access Bontemps's draft copy of "Purple Island," part of the James Weldon Johnson Memorial Collection.

Library of Congress Cataloging-in-Publication Data
Bontemps, Arna Wendell, 1902–1973.
   Drums at dusk : a novel / Arna Bontemps ; with a new introduction by Michael P. Bibler and Jessica Adams.
      p. cm. — (Library of Southern civilization)
   ISBN 978-0-8071-3439-9 (pbk. : alk. paper) 1. Haiti—History—Revolution, 1791–1804—Fiction. 2. Toussaint Louverture, 1743?–1803—Fiction. I. Title. II. Series.
   PS3503.O474D78 2009
   813'.52—dc22

                                                                    2008047175

CONTENTS

INTRODUCTION
RACE, ROMANCE, AND REVOLUTION

Michael P. Bibler and Jessica Adams

In 1939, Adolf Hitler's desire for a supreme Aryan empire sparked what would become the largest military conflict between nations that the world had ever seen, while in the United States, the film release of *Gone with the Wind* made millions weep nostalgically for the Civil War and the South's plantation past. In the same year, Arna Wendell Bontemps, an established and influential member of the African American literary community, offered a strikingly different perspective on race, war, and global politics with *Drums at Dusk,* a new novel about the 1791 slave uprising that began what is now called the Haitian Revolution. Unfortunately, even though this novel received some favorable reviews, it quickly fell into obscurity and has languished out of print for seventy years. This obscurity is no doubt partly due to Bontemps's distinctive—and, to his less favorable critics, disappointing—engagement with the issues of colonialism, African diasporic identity, and the fight for liberation from both slavery and imperialism.[1] It is probably also due to the prevailing tendency—until recently—to downplay or ignore works of American and African American literature written or set outside the boundaries of the United States. Yet these are the very issues that make the novel such a crucial and rewarding text for literary study, particularly as readers and scholars have become more aware of historic and cultural connections between the United States, the Caribbean, and Latin America, and how such hemispheric relationships are reflected in "American" writing. *Drums at Dusk* deserves a place among other major works of U.S. literature, African American literature, and, for its focus on Haiti's place in the Atlantic world, literature of the Americas. Concurrently, the voice of this extraordinary writer deserves an even greater presence in the ongoing debates about race, history, identity, violence, and humanity in the New World.

Although his name is not as widely known as those of some of his contemporaries, Arna Bontemps's influence on African American literature—and, by necessity, American literature—cannot be overstated. During the Harlem Renaissance of the early twentieth century, he won awards for his poetry and socialized with the likes of Countee Cullen, Carl Van Vechten, and A'Lelia Walker, and he remained lifelong friends with the poet Langston Hughes. By the time he wrote *Drums,* Bontemps had already published two novels for adults, numerous short stories and poems, and two books for younger readers, including *Popo and Fifina,* another story set in Haiti that Bontemps co-wrote with Hughes in 1932. *Drums* proved to be his last novel for adults, but until his death in 1973, he continued to write stories and novels for young people and children, as well as several important works of nonfiction. Furthermore, Bontemps arguably made his greatest contribution to the world of letters both through his work as the head librarian of Fisk University and as an editor and compiler of countless volumes of African American poetry, folklore, slave narratives, biographies, and autobiographies. Directly and indirectly, Bontemps has influenced the careers of innumerable writers and helped shape the study of African American literature and culture in the academy.

Given Bontemps's reputation and career, we can only speculate as to why *Drums at Dusk* quickly fell out of print. This novel is essentially a historical romance following the (white) French character Diron Desautels as he becomes forced to choose between his sympathies for the impending revolution in Saint Domingue (he is a member of the Société des Amis des Noirs) and his burgeoning love for the young, white Céleste Juvet. To a general audience smitten with the epic dramas of Stark Young's *So Red the Rose* (1934), Margaret Mitchell's *Gone with the Wind* (1936), and other popular plantation novels (both were huge best-sellers), this romance might have felt flat or melodramatic. For other readers, *Drums* might not have compared favorably with Bontemps's 1936 novel, *Black Thunder,* which fictionalized the 1800 slave uprising led by Gabriel Prosser in Virginia. Unlike in that earlier novel, Bontemps gives more attention in *Drums* to the fictional white characters than to a black leader (Toussaint L'Ouverture plays only a minor role here); and he depicts the events leading up to the revolution, not the revolution itself. On the surface, *Drums* seems less interested in the grand, complex scope of the revolution than in subtle dysfunctionalities embedded in the slaveholders' world, and the novel probably did not hold much appeal for readers hoping to see another account of a strong black character fighting—in this case, successfully—for the freedom of all people of color. At the same time, readers nervous about the instability caused by the growing war in Europe may not have wanted to find themselves reminded of war and instability in the nearby Caribbean. And for still other readers, the novel's violence could have been even more displeasing. Near the end of *Drums* the rebellious slaves exact a gruesome revenge on the decadent and cruel master of Bréda plantation, where most of the action is set, by blowing him to pieces with explosives. If some were nonplussed by the novel's apparent tameness, others might have been uncomfortable with its violent conclusion.

Why Bontemps chose not to reprint the novel later in his career is even harder to determine. *Black Thunder* enjoyed a resurgence of interest with the rise of the Black Power and Black Arts movements at the end of the 1960s, as the struggle over civil rights in the United States continued to heat up. Perhaps he felt that this new generation of readers would not receive *Drums at Dusk* with as much enthusiasm. Also, since this work marks his last attempt to write a novel for adults, it is possible that Bontemps viewed it as either a personal or an aesthetic disappointment not worth subjecting to further public scrutiny. Whatever the case, attention to *Drums at Dusk* is long overdue, not only for what the novel might teach us about Bontemps's remarkable vision of one of the most important events in the history of the

Americas—the Haitian Revolution—but also for what it reveals about the place of Haiti in the contemporary U.S. imaginary.

———•——

Like so much of Bontemps's work, this is a very readable novel that also deals with its subject matter in subtle and sophisticated ways. As the site of the only successful slave revolt in the Americas, Haiti served as an inspiration to blacks in both the northern and southern United States before the Civil War (Bontemps highlights Toussaint's influence on Gabriel Prosser in *Black Thunder*) and to other New World struggles for independence (Alexandre Pétion, president of the Republic of Haiti, provided both a safe haven and military aid to Venezuelan insurrectionary Simón Bolívar in his fight to liberate South America from the Spanish). In many other respects as well, Haiti has had a uniquely complicated history of relations with the rest of the Americas and the Atlantic world. However, one way to begin navigating this novel's engagement with the culture and politics of Saint Domingue at the eve of the revolution is to understand the personal significance that the revolution might have held in Bontemps's family. As the colony becomes engulfed by uprisings and rebellions at the end of *Drums at Dusk,* several white characters, including the sympathetically portrayed Bayou de Libertas, manager of the Bréda plantation, prepare to sail for New Orleans, which in 1791, though technically belonging to Spain, still had strong ties with France and its colonies. The city was a destination for many people across the racial and class spectrum

who were in flight from revolutionary upheavals between
1791 and 1804.[2] And although he could never say so de-
finitively, Bontemps felt that this New World history was
probably quite relevant to his own history as both a Louisiana native—he was born in Alexandria in 1902—and a
person of mixed racial heritage. According to Bontemps's
biographer Kirkland C. Jones, "The French family who had
first owned the Bontemps slaves had evidently emigrated
to Haiti from France. Once there, they acquired slaves and
began to intermarry with them." By 1821, "court, land, and
church records" in Louisiana identified people named
Bontemps as "homme de couleur libre" or "femme de
couleur libre," while census records listed them as W, Mu,
or B—white, mulatto, or black (some of those designated as
"W" may have been passing from persons of color to white
as they moved into a new social context).[3] This account
of Arna Bontemps's family history may not be entirely ac-
curate, but Jones's genealogical research is interesting for
the way it points out the particularities of French colonial
practices as well as immigration patterns in the Americas.
His observation about interracial marriage calls attention
to the fact that the French, unlike the English, advocated a
certain degree of assimilation in their New World colonies.
Although taboos developed against such marriages and it
is unclear how many actually took place, the 1685 Code
Noir (an edict meant to govern the treatment of slaves) did
endorse legal unions between masters and slaves in certain
instances.[4] It was through such cross-racial contacts and
other patterns of manumission and assimilation that the
class of free *gens de couleur,* or free people of color, emerged

in Haiti, Louisiana, and other French colonies. There is no evidence, however, that Bontemps's ancestors were actually members of this class, either in Louisiana or elsewhere in the French Caribbean, and Jones's conclusions about the family must ultimately be regarded as speculative.

Bontemps's parents, grandparents, and other family contacts were reluctant to discuss the family's origins, and so he never knew for sure whether any of his ancestors on his father's side—white, black, or mixed race—were in fact immigrants from Haiti. Bontemps was also unclear about his mother's ancestry, although he knew that his great-grandmother had been born a slave in the French Caribbean (he was never told where) and eventually brought to New Orleans to be sold. Although this side of the family was also racially mixed, in this case the mixture of races occurred in Louisiana between his great-grandmother and her English-born master, with no evidence that the two ever married.[5] Nevertheless, though Bontemps ultimately found few definitive answers, he saw the complexity of his own genealogy, as well as the uncertainty that prevented him from confidently tracing it, as expressing in microcosm the larger story of Africans and people of color in the Americas. He was dedicated to telling this larger story as an artist and a scholar, and the genre of the historical novel offered a particularly rich means for exploring the nuances of that story. Thus, while we cannot say that Bontemps's interest in Haiti was the direct result of a familial connection to the island, his history was nonetheless intimately connected with the multiracial narrative he chose to tell in *Drums at Dusk*.

Read in light of Bontemps's interest in the histories of the African diaspora, this novel is truly significant for the way that it concentrates more on questions of multiracialism and multiculturalism than on revolution. Although contemporary readers may have expected him to focus on the powerful black leader Toussaint L'Ouverture—as he had on Gabriel Prosser in *Black Thunder*—the protagonist of *Drums at Dusk,* the Frenchman Diron, actually follows a different set of characters from that earlier novel: the French Jacobins in Richmond who are sympathetic to the slaves. Thus *Drums* engages questions of black nationalism and revolution, albeit in different ways from *Black Thunder.*[6] But it also focuses most of its attention on the wide variety of ways that white people, especially sympathetic whites, interacted with slaves and free people of mixed race, or *mûlatres,* in Saint Domingue, and how they responded to the violence of the uprising. In *Drums,* in other words, Bontemps may be looking to Haiti to explore symbolically his heritage as a person with mixed racial ancestry—as well as the histories of interracialism that, in the United States, became so difficult to acknowledge as a result of legal mandates separating "black" from "white."

In fact, the novel meditates on the interlocking layers of colonial society by framing them in terms of partial and extended kinships. *Drums at Dusk* offers us no images of self-contained nuclear families and instead equates Saint Domingue's entangled social networks with family structures that are open and incomplete, their bloodlines fractured and indirect. Diron is staying with his uncle M. Philippe Desautels while his parents are in France. Céleste is living with her grandmother Mme Jacques Juvet while her dejected and alcoholic father, Hugo, hides from society in the city. Although Céleste is able to socialize at the margins of the elite, Mme Juvet had been an indentured servant at Bréda, one of the class of poor whites who came to be called *blan mannan* in Haitian Creole (a term that can be loosely translated as "white trash"), and who were considered just above the slaves in the colony's social hierarchy—their margin of superiority deriving only from their white skin. Thus Bontemps incorporates not three but four classes of colonial society, examining the contours of the bifurcated white world as well as those of the *mûlatres* and slaves. Céleste's romantic competition, Mme Paulette Viard, who is also a former lover of Hugo Juvet, attempts to seduce Diron and then tries to have him killed for his revolutionary beliefs, just as she did her husband Sylvestre. Even the owner of Bréda, Count de Noé, is absent from the text, living in France, far from the day-to-day workings of his plantation—as were a significant number of colonial planters in the eighteenth century. His proxy, his cousin Count Armand de Sacy, seems to be the owner, but is actually nothing more than a visitor who chooses to act the part of the sadistic master. The ties between people and between people and property blur as they stretch circuitously across Haiti and the Americas, reaching back to both Europe and Africa.

———•———

This focus on questions of multiculturalism and extended kinships in a novel about revolution does not mean that racial justice for African Americans and all people of color was not still an important issue for Bontemps personally. Rather, Bontemps's life and work clearly show his singular devotion to promoting the genius and value of African American literature and culture. In the early years of the twentieth century, his family left the climate of racial intimidation that shaped life in Alexandria, Louisiana, and moved to the growing city of Los Angeles. Educated in Napa Valley, Bontemps worked at the L.A. post office for a time, but moved from southern California to the place where black life was really happening in the 1920s—Harlem. Amid the creative ferment of the Harlem Renaissance, he taught at Harlem Academy and married one of his students, Alberta Johnson. Bontemps was an aspiring poet himself; but in 1927, realizing that poetry would never support his family, he turned to writing prose. When Harlem Academy closed in 1931, he took a position at Oakwood College in Huntsville, Alabama, located on the grounds of a former slave plantation. Bontemps was exhausted by his teaching schedule and unappreciated at a school he would characterize as "the world's worst," even as he and his family lived in the former plantation big house. "Andrew Jackson was a frequent visitor and sat at the fireplace that now warms my toes," he wrote in a letter to Cullen. "There are slave huts on the outskirts of the place, and on the adjoining plantation they say there are still slaves who do not know they are free."[7]

Soon after he moved to Alabama, Bontemps was confronted with a terrifying example of white supremacy and violence in nearby Scottsboro, where nine young black men were unjustly convicted and sentenced to death or long prison terms for allegedly raping two white women. These events gained international attention, and although one of the women later recanted the testimony she had given in a previous trial, it would take years before the so-called Scottsboro boys would go free. During this time, Bontemps himself became a victim of the racist fears and prejudices gripping Alabama—and, indeed, the nation—when the white president of Oakwood pressured him at least twice to burn his books and thus prove he did not pose a threat to the racist status quo. Bontemps refused to compromise himself or his sense of racial justice, and within three years he left Oakwood and Alabama for the Watts neighborhood of Los Angeles, where he completed work on *Black Thunder.*[8] By the time he was working on *Drums at Dusk,* the family had moved to Chicago. Bontemps had taken a position at Shiloh Academy, where he taught from 1935 to 1938. He then accepted a Rosenwald Fellowship for creative writing that, just as he was finishing *Drums,* enabled him to travel to the Caribbean.

Bontemps found his main inspiration for *Black Thunder* in the slave narratives he discovered in the library at Fisk University.[9] For *Drums at Dusk,* he drew mostly from secondary historical works such as C. L. R. James's *The Black Jacobins* (1938).[10] It may be because of this lack of access to primary accounts of the Haitian Revolution that *Black Thunder* views historical events through the lens of the slaves' inner thoughts and lives, while *Drums* subsumes historical events within the framework of a historical romance. Whereas Bontemps "empowered the fictional conspirators [in *Black Thunder*], especially Gabriel, to speak

for themselves," as Mary Kemp Davis argues, the super-
ficially less radical *Drums* dwells more on the local and
global political forces that helped precipitate revolution
than on the actors who seized the opportunities created by
those forces. This key difference offers a reason for Bontemps's decision to portray Toussaint L'Ouverture more as
an archetypal figure than a real person, as Mark Christian
Thompson reads him, just as it helps explain Bontemps's
greater ambivalence in *Drums* about the violence playing
out on both sides of the insurrection.[11] In any case, making
sense of Bontemps's emphasis on broad historical forces
still requires some understanding of the racial and social
complexities of life in Saint Domingue in 1791, of the revolution itself, and of the dynamics of race, migration, and
national identity that the revolution helped spawn.

———•———

To begin unraveling the historical subtext of this novel, we
must start with its central character, Diron Desautels, the
young, idealistic Frenchman who has spent much of his life
in Saint Domingue. Diron joined the Société des Amis des
Noirs while in Paris the year before the action of the novel
begins, and when we meet him he has rushed back home,
anxious to put his political ideals into practice. Founded in
France in 1788, Les Amis des Noirs had gained new promi-
nence with the French Revolution. The 1789 Declaration
of the Rights of Man—which included the provisions that
"men are born and remain free and equal in rights" and that
"the aim of all political association is the preservation of
the natural and imprescriptible [*sic*] rights of man," namely

"liberty, property, security, and resistance to oppression"—
inevitably highlighted the presence of hundreds of thousands of slaves laboring in French colonies. Moreover, a
conflict quickly appeared between this statement of revolutionary ideals and the existence of free men of color living
in Saint Domingue, Martinique, and Guadeloupe, who
were not, in fact, treated equally with white men despite
the Code Noir's provisions. In response to these discrep-
ancies, Les Amis did not include abolition as part of its
agenda, but instead advocated social equality for free *gens
de couleur* and the end of the slave trade, "disclaim[ing]
any desire to interfere with slavery" itself.[12] But the orga-
nization still drew a number of French intellectuals who
became more and more sympathetic to the antislavery
cause, including Jacques Pierre Brissot, the Abbé Grégoire,
the Marquis de la Fayette, the Marquis de Condorcet,
the Comte de Mirabeau, and Léger-Félicité Sonthonax.

In his capacity as a member of the commission charged
with preserving Saint Domingue as a French colony in
the wake of the 1791 insurrection, Sonthonax would go
on to declare slaves in Haiti's northern province to be
free French citizens on August 29, 1793—though this by
no means ended the conflict. Indeed, Sonthonax would
eventually be forced off the island for good by Toussaint
L'Ouverture, who in 1797 "suddenly accused him of plot-
ting to make Saint Domingue independent." (Toussaint's
accusation may have concealed his own desire to become
the leader of a free Saint Domingue; he "play[ed] the role
of a loyal servant of the French Republic" while systemati-
cally neutralizing those who might oppose him.)[13] As Les

Amis involved itself in one way or another in the struggle for equality on the island, however, white colonists saw the notion of equality between whites and any people of color as anathema. The slave population of Saint Domingue had increased exponentially in the century leading up to the revolution, as new slaves were imported "continually" to compensate for their brutal usage on colonial plantations; a slave's average life span in the New World was just seven years.[14] By 1791, there were approximately 30,000 whites in Saint Domingue, about 27,000 *mûlatres,* and nearly half a million slaves.[15] The whites' power depended on upholding the principle of white supremacy, and in their view those questioning it were guilty of treason.[16] This background alone explains why Diron is compelled to keep his affiliation secret throughout the novel, and it reveals how the intrigue surrounding Les Amis would already lend the novel some of the tone of a swashbuckling adventure, an aspect of the text criticized by a few of Bontemps's early reviewers.[17]

In strong contrast to the idyllic image of twentieth-century Haiti that Bontemps and Hughes offered in *Popo and Fifina,* both *Drums at Dusk* and a 1948 nonfiction book, *Story of the Negro*—in which Bontemps devotes three chapters to the Haitian Revolution—focus explicitly on these tensions and hostilities simmering between Saint Domingue's stratified populations at the end of the 1700s. While both texts recount in detail the systematic brutalization of the enslaved Africans, they also call attention to the status and the actions of free *gens de couleur.* In *Drums,* Bontemps notes that "many of these had inherited vast wealth from the profligate noblemen who sired them. In fact, one-tenth of

the plantations were in the hands of these mulattos. They
owned slaves. Their children were educated in France. A
year earlier, when they had offered a petition to the National Assembly in Paris, they had been able to accompany
their request with a token of $1,200,000" (36). In *Story
of the Negro,* he lists the contributions made to Western
culture by "a number of outstanding geniuses" arising
from this wealthy class, including the three generations
of famous men named Alexandre Dumas, as well as John
James Audubon.[18] Interestingly, however, despite the precise
attention Bontemps gave this elite class, none of the central
characters in *Drums* come from their ranks. In an early draft
of the novel, the villainous Mme Paulette Viard is identified as a quadroon (a person with one-quarter African ancestry), but Bontemps chose to make her white in the final
version. This change creates a number of notable effects: It
softens the presence of interracial desire and sexual contact
in the novel; it removes any suggestion of an ulterior motive
behind Diron's political sympathies as a "friend of the blacks";
it keeps inattentive readers from misinterpreting Paulette's
villainy as somehow tied to her racial difference; and it
prevents any association of her with the literary type of the
"tragic mulatta" or "tragic octoroon"—the usually sympathetic mixed-race woman (in the latter case, with one-eighth
African ancestry) who dies before she and her white suitor
can consummate their love. On a broader scale, Bontemps's
decision not to include any individual member of the *gens de
couleur,* fictional or otherwise, as a major character in *Drums*
makes sense in the context of the revolution as a whole. For
although this class played a crucial role in the events leading

up to the 1791 insurrection, that insurrection was still primarily a slave uprising that caught both the whites and *mûlatres* off guard. In keeping with his attempt to address the full complexity of this moment in Saint Domingue's history, Bontemps carefully asserts the importance of the free *gens de couleur* as a major faction within the larger historical narrative of the Haitian Revolution, but he does not overstate their role in the specific events that gripped the island during the brief span of time represented in his novel.

As Bontemps reminds us early in *Drums at Dusk,* the greatest contribution that the *gens de couleur* made to the revolution's beginning actually came a year prior to the slaves' rebellion of 1791. Wealthy as white men, some almost appearing "white" themselves, *mûlatres* in Saint Domingue chafed at restrictions imposed by those who could have been, or perhaps were, their own parents. In March of 1790, the French National Assembly declared that "all persons" aged twenty-five and older who were property owners in the colony, or who at least had been taxpayers for a minimum of ten years, had the right to vote. Two *mûlatres,* Jean-Baptiste Chavannes and Vincent Ogé (a veteran of the Battle of Savannah who had fought on the side of the American colonists with the future revolutionary leader André Rigaud and future king of Haiti Henri Christophe), decided to force the issue. Ogé obtained funds from Thomas Clarkson, an English abolitionist in London sympathetic to the cause of Les Amis. Departing London for Charleston, South Carolina, he purchased American weapons and sailed for Haiti's capital on the northern coast, Cap Français (modern-day Cap-Haïtien).[19] Upon his arrival there on October 12, 1790, Ogé

Introduction   xxiii

petitioned the governor of Saint Domingue, the Comte de
Peynier, but to no avail. Peynier declared that it would not
be possible, in the current political climate, to implement
the Assembly's decree. Ogé and Chavannes then massed
gens de couleur in the northern province and, with a force of
three hundred men, "disarmed every white in the parish."
Rather than arming the slaves—whom the *mûlatres* did not
view as their social equals, and whose cause they were not
espousing—Ogé and Chavannes approached the capital
city in a company comprised only of mulattoes. Eventually they were defeated by a militia made up of 1,500 men
that included both whites and blacks. The two leaders then
escaped across the border into Spanish-held territory (now
the Dominican Republic), but the Spanish—whose political interests at this time did not include facilitating unrest
in French territory—returned them to the doubtful mer-
cies of the whites. The Colonial Assembly promptly con-
demned Ogé and Chavannes to be "broken on the wheel
in the public square," as Bontemps writes in *Drums at Dusk*
(47), and the sentence was carried out on March 9, 1791.[20]
Twenty-two other rebels were hanged. Rather than end-
ing the conflict between whites and free people of color,
however, these events only inflamed matters. The brutal
deaths of Ogé and Chavannes spurred the French National
Assembly to declare that free *gens de couleur* who had free
parents were fully equal with whites under the law. And
though the population in question was very small, this gesture produced new violent upheavals in the colony. Some
whites talked of secession as the newly elected Colonial
Assembly gathered in Cap Français. Peynier refused to ef-

fect the Assembly's decree, and free *mûlatres* began to arm themselves again in preparation for civil war.[21]

And so Saint Domingue in the summer of 1791 was seething. As Bontemps writes in *Drums at Dusk,* the "tension remained," and "the muddle grew more involved" (47). The rebellion led by the *mûlatres* had just ended, while the explosion of revolutionary violence on the part of the slaves was only weeks away. Thus, it is the "tension" of this moment—more than the spiraling revolution itself— that constitutes the focal point of the novel. To explore this tension, Bontemps concentrates mostly on the population with the most to lose: the elite whites, whom he portrays as complacent, decadent, and completely "unruffled" by recent events (47). He organizes the novel around a fête held at Bréda, historic home of Toussaint L'Ouverture, where the whites are almost completely absorbed in sensual pleasures. Here, even the sympathetic white characters are utterly unaware of the uprising being planned by the slaves, for the approach of revolution is only hinted at in the beat of the drums, "throbbing like the heart-beat of the earth," carrying messages across expanses of space to those who could understand them (118). Bontemps's readers know the revolution is coming, but by keeping us in the blinkered world of Saint Domingue's white population, the author forces us to recognize how the revolution is a response to an entire social system that is rotten to the core—not just to a few bad slave lords like the Count de Sacy.

Of all the white characters in the novel, Diron is the only one whom Bontemps allows to mix, even in a sense to socialize, with the slaves who are preparing to revolt. But, as Diron stirs up interest in revolution at secret meetings held while riding through the woods with slaves from the large plantations of Saint Domingue's northern province, he never learns of the uprising they have actually planned—or of the Vodou ceremony held on August 14, 1791, to mark the fact that the date of August 22 had been set for it.[22] Diron is the novel's heroic central character, but Bontemps does not allow him to become a hero of the revolution. Indeed, at his final meeting with this group of slaves, he tells them that he "won't be riding with [them] again" because he is going to try to bring freedom to the island through "other means." "Meanwhile," he continues, "I scarcely need to repeat that if ever you blacks feel strong enough to help yourselves, you will have the active sympathy of many *blancs,* including myself" (53). Despite his good intentions, Diron is an idealist who comes close to patronizing the slaves he wants to help. And yet he still understands that when the captive blacks finally take up the struggle for their own liberation, they will not need the help or inspiration of any whites. Bontemps presents the revolution almost entirely through the point of view of Saint Domingue's white ruling class, but he never lets us forget that the spirit and the force of the revolution will come, wholly and exclusively, from the black masses. Moreover, by keeping the build-up toward the revolution offstage, Bontemps maintains its mythic resonance and thus "allows [this] historically contingent event," as Thompson writes, "to create a space for all black revolutionary theory and praxis," then and now.[23]

There are other layers to Bontemps's subtle depiction of the revolution as a black response to white oppression. One reason Diron stops associating with the slaves is that he has become unnerved by the power and the growing anger of their leaders. And perhaps Bontemps himself was ambivalent about Boukman, a coachman on the Clément plantation and a *houngan,* or Vodou priest, whom Bontemps describes as "menacing," "squat as the stump of a tree," with "tiny eyes" (53). "All told, Boukman's was a fairly repulsive bunch," he writes. "Diron could, with a little effort, dislike them strongly. But he could not forget that the rabble who stormed the Bastille were mostly a tough and sinister lot" (54–55). With these descriptions, Bontemps appears to have grown more uncomfortable with the violence of retribution than he was in *Black Thunder.* But he also makes clear that the blame for such violence lies squarely with the white oppressor. When Diron takes his leave, he tries to explain to Boukman that "there are reasons why I shouldn't ride with you." Boukman then responds with a sarcastic remark that Diron takes at face value: "Yes. . . . I know. We're stupid. Slavery has made us stupid—like oxen" (54). The ensuing conversation unmistakably indicates Boukman's awareness that Diron is leaving because he fears the slaves will eventually see him as nothing more than another white face and rise against him, too—a fear that is also an implicit insult to the slaves' intelligence. Boukman's knowing sarcasm thus underscores the fact that the slaves of Saint Domingue were not actually undifferentiated or "stupid," but instead cultivated, as C. L. R. James observes, "a wooden stupidity before their masters"— much like Boukman's own gruff behavior—as well as a "profound fatalism" and a refusal to expend energy that allowed them to survive. Sometimes the slaves' ill treatment even hastened them toward suicide, a common occurrence according to James, and one that Bontemps himself addresses when twenty-four recently arrived Africans bought for Bréda hang themselves in protest.[24] Like that mass suicide, Boukman's words and actions in the novel cannot be read apart from this history of the various ways that slaves tried to cope with or escape their enslavement. And yet, at the same time, there is an element of truth to Boukman's words that Bontemps clearly does not want us to disregard. Saying that "slavery has made us stupid," Boukman is not commenting on the minds or characters of the slaves themselves. If slavery has turned them into oxen, the slaves' tendency toward violence is the result not of some natural ignorance, but rather of the dehumanizing treatment they have experienced at the hands of their white masters. If the violence of the rebelling slaves becomes excessive to the point of spectacle, Bontemps suggests, this is because such violence is inevitably the product of a violent system of oppression.

Nowhere is the example of this white culpability for the violence of the slaves more visible than in the grotesque murder inflicted on the gratuitously cruel Count Armand de Sacy. Early in the novel, when de Sacy visits the slave ship *Hottentot* to inspect its cargo, the vile Captain Frounier asks, "What's a good way to deal with bad slaves, Count?" The Count replies, "Burn a little powder in their hind-quarters. . . . Make examples of them" (41). At the end of the novel, however, the slaves manage to catch de Sacy out in the wilderness—apparently, not long after he has raped Céleste—and they strip him and pack his rectum with gun powder, exacting the same punishment on him that he had contrived for them. Bontemps writes:

> The slaves were beyond mercy or compassion. A leaping, screaming circle of them, intoxicated with their desperately won freedom, driven wild by the imaginings of their own hearts and the examples of cruelty they had learned from their masters, made a frightful circle in the carriage road. Torches flared. The moon silvered the tips of coconut palms. Finally, the preparations finished, silence fell upon the group. Someone bent over and touched a flame to the paper fuse. Then all withdrew a safe distance, waited breathlessly. A few seconds elapsed. Then the dull thud of the exploding powder aroused them to a second noisy demonstration. An unseen spatter of blood, tiny bits of flesh and particles of dung filled the air. (205–206)

The mindless violence in this passage shows that Bontemps does not absolve the "frightful circle" for their lack of "mercy or compassion." Yet, he also makes it clear that for all their savagery, these slaves are not savages, for they simply re-create "the examples of cruelty they had learned from their masters," taking revenge on the man not only for what he has done to them, but also, though they do not know this, for what he has done to Céleste. It is important to note, moreover, that Bontemps included these scenes only in the final draft of the novel. He evidently wanted to make sure that the text showed the slaves' violence to be just as much reactive as it was excessive, and nowhere does this become more apparent than in his addition of this final act of vengeance on the most reprehensible white man in the novel.

As Bontemps partially rationalizes the violence of the revolution, both this passage and the earlier, unflattering description of Boukman suggest that he also saw the rebels and their excesses as more or less distasteful. Yet, historically, the slaves who originated the revolt were among those most trusted and privileged by their white masters. For the most part they were "Creole" slaves, among those born in the colonies, and they held positions of authority on their respective plantations.[25] As a *commandeur,* or slave driver, and then a coachman on the Clément plantation, Boukman Dutty was poised to influence other slaves and develop the network necessary to mobilize great numbers of revolutionaries in a unified uprising.[26] The oral history of Haiti's nationhood also locates Boukman—elsewhere described as a huge man—at the site traditionally understood to be a key point of origin for the revolution, the Vodou ceremony held at Bois Caïman, or Caïman Wood, where he presided with a manbo, or Vodou priestess, named Cécile Fatiman or Fatima.[27] According to *houngan* Max Beauvoir, the invocation Boukman gave at Bois Caïman has been passed down among practitioners of Vodou for two hundred years: *"Couté la liberté li palé nan coeur nous tous,"* he said—"Listen to the voice of liberty which speaks in the hearts of all of us."[28] On August 22, Boukman gave the signal for revolution to begin, and eventually led 50,000 rebels who "seized control of the important Plaine du Nord for ten days." They killed 1,000 whites, but lost 10,000 of their own.[29] In November of that year, Boukman was killed in battle and decapitated. White colonists displayed his head on a pike in the main square of Cap Français.[30]

In keeping with his focus on interactions among black, white, and mulatto within the plantation system, Bontemps avoids any mention of the secret Vodou ceremony and instead locates the beginning of the revolution at the party at Bréda, where mulatto seamstresses have fashioned the white women's gowns and black men serve their wine.

Bontemps's decision not to foreground the role of Vodou in his account of the revolution breaks with most popular representations of Haiti at the time because it avoids sensationalizing that aspect of Haitian culture. Despite the real, significant influence of Vodou on slaves' ability to connect with each other across the barriers of plantation life, and despite its existence as a primary source of spiritual, emotional, and cultural inspiration, Bontemps seems to have decided that it would have been impossible to represent Vodou during the time in which he was writing *Drums at Dusk* without invoking garish and titillating images in the minds of his readers. Thus Vodou makes no more of an appearance in his novel than in the suggestive reverberations of the drums. This wish to avoid sensationalizing aspects of the revolution also explains why there are so few depictions of the tremendous violence and bloodshed that characterized the actual uprising. Modern readers accustomed to more graphic scenes of violence might see *Drums at Dusk* as rather tame. But when read in the context of the Scottsboro incident and the racial tensions of the 1930s, Bontemps's decision to push the real brutality of the revolution into the background makes sense. As a black writer clearly aiming to reach a racially diverse readership, Bontemps no doubt wanted to avoid any accusations that he was somehow glorifying (or even inciting) violence against whites by blacks, and to keep attention focused on the *causes* of the revolution rather than the various atrocities committed by forces on both sides.

Bontemps makes a further break from both historical and literary tradition in his depiction of another of the original

revolutionary leaders, Georges Biassou (he spells the name
Baissou). A gigantic man, Bontemps's Baissou is incongruous in the clothes of a servant as he stands behind the chair
of the effete Count de Sacy at the dinner table at Bréda. At
the appointed moment, however, Baissou literally springs to
life in his true character and signals the start of the rebellion:

> Suddenly a hush swept the room, and in the silence shouts of
> distant voices could be heard between the throbs of demoniacal
> drums. The stunned gasp was not broken till a moment of utter
> panic followed in which the massive satin-clothed black behind
> the count's chair sprang to the top of the table with a single leap,
> his boots crashing glasses, scattering plates and bowls, and raced
> toward the window overlooking the drive.
> "*Vive la liberté!*" he thundered. (121–22)

This scene highlights the dialogue between *Drums at Dusk*
and other works of plantation romance, especially two earlier, very influential texts of slave rebellion: Aphra Behn's
Oroonoko; or, The Royal Slave (1688) and George Washington
Cable's story of Bras-Coupé, which he had originally written as a short story and then included in his 1880 novel
The Grandissimes. These earlier texts romanticize the figure
of the captive African by making him a figure of nobility
who dies tragically as a result of his inability and refusal to
adapt to his status as a slave. In Cable's novel in particular,
the intractable and angry Bras-Coupé violently bursts into
the wedding dinner party of his master to demand more
wine:

> Leaving the table, [Bras-Coupé] strode upstairs and into the chir-
> ruping and dancing of the grand salon. There was a halt in the
> cotillion and a hush of amazement like the shutting off of steam.

Bras-Coupé strode straight to his master, laid his paw upon his . . .
shoulder and in a thunder-tone demanded:
  "More!"
  The master swore a Spanish oath, lifted his hand and—fell,
beneath the terrific fist of his slave, with a bang that jingled the
candelabras.[31]

Bras-Coupé then curses his master and the land of the plantation, and runs away into the swamp to fight any attempts
to recapture him. Thus his tragic demise is set in motion.
In *Drums,* Baissou's leap directly parallels Bras-Coupé's in-
trusion, even borrowing Cable's language with the sudden
"hush" of the white crowd, followed by the chaos and disorder that the "thundering" black rebel causes among both
the guests and the luxuriously appointed dining room. Bontemps's reconfiguration of this scene subverts the tradition
embodied in Behn's and Cable's novels. For not only does
Bontemps refuse to romanticize the "big-boned and belligerent" (121), "gorilla-like" black (119), he also refuses to
make Baissou into a tragic figure. More important, the revolution that Baissou helps launch in *Drums* is fundamentally
different from that of Oroonoko or Bras-Coupé because this
revolution is both organized and successful while the others are strictly personal, unplanned, and ineffective. For all
the romance of Bontemps's apparently white-centered narrative, he openly refuses to allow that or any other kind of
romance to undercut his depiction of black rebellion.

  Drums at Dusk also revises other conventions of the historical plantation romance, which has been a major com-
ponent of the literature of the U.S. South since at least the
1820s. Many plantation novels portray the hero as a kind of

cavalier knight who adheres to the chivalric codes of the southern aristocracy and fights to preserve the supposed order and stability of the entire plantation system. In Bontemps's time, novels like Young's *So Red the Rose,* Mitchell's *Gone with the Wind,* T. S. Stribling's *The Forge* (1931), Andrew Lytle's *The Long Night* (1936), Clifford Dowdey's *Bugles Blow No More* (1937), and Caroline Gordon's *None Shall Look Back* (1937) predictably stage this struggle as part of the U.S. Civil War (where the fight to preserve the old order usually becomes an act of noble sacrifice or tragic loss), but other works, such as James Boyd's popular novel *Drums* (1925), go back farther, to the Revolutionary War.[32] William Faulkner complicated this model of the planter hero in *Absalom, Absalom!* (1936), which also considers the importance of Haiti for the South. Depicting the rise and fall of Thomas Sutpen, *Absalom* expresses keen awareness that slavery was ultimately an untenable institution; yet the novel is also infused with a lingering sense of nostalgia and melancholy akin to that found (at that time) in many other works by white southerners. In *Drums at Dusk,* Diron is also modeled on the figure of the cavalier, but his heroism is tied to his willingness to stand up for the rights of the enslaved and oppressed, not a desire to preserve (or return to) the ways of the slavocracy. Moreover, where other plantation novels affirm the hero's bravery and nobility with scenes of combat (or duels, which were also common), Diron's heroism arguably stems from his ultimate decision *not* to fight. Instead of pushing the blacks into the background and appropriating their insurrection as his own, Diron steps back from the battle to let them fight for their

xxxiv   *Introduction*

own freedom as autonomous agents. Ultimately, Diron works for change without directly fighting the status quo, and in this way he becomes a uniquely nonthreatening liberal hero. Showing how passively accepting progress can become its own form of progressive activism, Diron stands as the model whereby Bontemps's white readers could ideally become "friends of the blacks" in their own right.

Bontemps further adapts elements of the plantation romance in his use of the marriage plot. As Michael Kreyling argues, the hero of the typical plantation novel must marry someone from a basically equal status, a "woman ideally suited to become the mother of a heroic culture." "By securing this match," Kreyling writes, "the hero ensures cultural uniformity and reinforces the possibility of perfect repetition over time. Crossbreeding introduces change. Change is the motif of history. Southern heroic narrative . . . aims ultimately at the abolition of history."[33] But, in *Drums at Dusk,* the upper-class hero Diron makes a more liberal, democratic marriage choice with Céleste, a woman who is below him in the social hierarchy. Politically, Diron rejects racial inequalities, and in his inevitable marriage to Céleste, he also rejects *class* inequalities.[34] Furthermore, although Céleste has been raped by de Sacy and is thus no longer sexually "pure," Diron's willingness to marry her is also a rejection, or at least a relaxation, of patriarchal strictures regarding the virginity of the bride. Thus, as Diron makes his way to a safer part of the island with his uncle and his future bride, with Toussaint there to protect them, the novel's conclusion enacts a radical revision of the conventional plantation romance: Where most novels make the

continuity of the white family dependent on the continuity
of the whole plantation order (or at least the ability to sal-
vage as much of the old way of life as possible), *Drums at
Dusk* posits that the continuity of the white family is wholly
compatible with emancipation, racial equality, and the total
destruction of the plantation system. Bontemps obviously
wanted his novel to be a popular success, which meant
finding an audience with both white and black readers.
And reworking the genre of the plantation romance in this
way helped him explore both the history of the revolution
and the larger idea of black liberation without becoming
inflammatory. Within the novel, Bontemps's Toussaint
reaches out to both races, reflecting the actions of the historical leader, who saw a practical advantage in promoting
white *and* black investment in an independent Haiti. Apparently following this model, Bontemps himself tries to
provoke a mixed audience to imagine a society in which
whites and people of color might join together in the common cause of liberty and equality—a notion that was truly
revolutionary in 1939, and remains so today.[35]

Where Bontemps allows Baissou to call for the revolt to
begin, the historical Biassou would become a general in
the emerging revolutionary army. And in 1793, both he and
Toussaint would align themselves and the troops they commanded with the Spanish, who were trying to wrest control
of the island from the French. Historian David Geggus writes
that Biassou's forces eventually "gave up campaigning for
quarreling among themselves and for living it up outrageously

at the expense of the king of Spain. The Spaniards soon realized that they had bitten off far more than they could chew. Such successes as they had they owed almost entirely to Toussaint." Eventually, the exuberant, outrageous Biassou was forced into exile. Unwelcome in Cuba, where the slave system remained strong, in 1796 he and twenty-six of his group arrived in the Spanish settlement of St. Augustine, Florida. Apparently Biassou remained a hot-tempered heavy drinker who lived large among St. Augustine's three thousand blacks and whites. (He had finally married in 1794, relinquishing the household of concubines that had scandalized the archbishop of Santo Domingo.) In Florida, Biassou maintained his rank of general and joined the local, respected black militia who fought against the Creek Indians in 1800–1801.[36] He died in St. Augustine in 1801 and was buried there with full military honors.

Meanwhile, Toussaint had become recognized as the leader of all Saint Domingue. The year Biassou died, Toussaint generated a new constitution for Saint Domingue, "summon[ing] an assembly of six men, one from each province, consisting of rich whites and Mulattoes—there was not one black," as C. L. R. James writes. "He was thinking of the effect in France," James argues, "and not of the effect on his own masses, feeling too sure of them." This new constitution abolished slavery but permitted the slave trade in order to bolster the labor force, asserting that once Africans arrived in Saint Domingue, they would be free.[37] Toussaint's political stature had grown immensely since those early days of the revolution, when Bontemps describes him as a "reliable coachman" (14). Almost fifty

years old in 1791, "le vieux" Toussaint is a calm and un-
assuming, even reassuring, presence on the plantation in
Drums at Dusk. He is an accomplished doctor in the region
and trusted implicitly by Bréda's manager, Bayou de Libertas (actually Bayon). As Bontemps's narrative reflects,
the extent of Toussaint's participation in the early stages of
the revolution is somewhat shrouded in mystery, though
we can describe his personal history and demeanor. Like
Boukman and Biassou, he had been born in the colonies.
His father was a member of a royal family in Africa, and
Toussaint was said to have spoken his father's language
fluently—the language of the Arada or Ewe-Fon people,
from the place now called Benin. Toussaint was, according to contemporary descriptions, "a small, wiry man, very
black, with mobile, penetrating eyes." He wore gold earrings so heavy that they disfigured his ears, a headscarf, and
outsized watch chains. His presence "suggested enormous
self-control."[38]

Despite what the novel implies, Toussaint was not in
fact a slave at the time of the revolution; he had gained
his freedom roughly twenty years before. And while he
maintained a presence on the Bréda plantation, he had
been not only a property owner but also a small slaveholder
himself after gaining his liberty.[39] Although historians dis-
agree as to whether or not Toussaint was involved in the
original uprising in August, within three months he had
joined forces with the insurgents and begun his political
ascent.[40] Toussaint was by no means an apologist for the
brutal nature of the plantation regime. But, a consummate
politician, he maintained cordial relations with some white

planters, viewed the colony's ongoing ties to France as ne-
gotiable, and encouraged exiled whites to return to Saint
Domingue in hopes of preserving at least some part of its
economy. By the middle of 1793 it was clear that he was
committed to the abolition of slavery, but the practicalities
of leading the new political entity developing out of the
revolution caused him to advocate repressive measures for
maintaining labor on the plantations. According to James,
Toussaint's belief that "he could handle" the planter class,
as well as his hesitation to realize that the French government would never endorse a free Saint Domingue, led to
his downfall—and to the rise of Jean-Jacques Dessalines,
his second-in-command. "As he ranged from one part of
the island to another," James writes of Dessalines, "wearing
out these inhuman persecutors of his people, this old slave,
the marks of the whip below his general's uniform, was fast
coming to the conclusion at which Toussaint still boggled.
He would declare the island independent and finish with
France. The old slave-owners were everywhere grinning
with joy at the French expedition; he would finish with
everything white for ever." In 1802, as battles raged between the revolutionary forces and the French army under
Leclerc, which was being decimated by yellow fever, Toussaint was arrested by the French. He was taken aboard the
French frigate *Créole* at Gonaïves and transported around
the island's northwestern peninsula to Cap Français, where
he was transferred to the French battleship *Héros,* bound
for Brest—the ships' names inadvertently inscribing upon
these waters the revolutionary leader's status as "Creole
hero." Toussaint was finally jailed in the stone fortress of

Fort-de-Joux in the Jura Mountains, and his health deliberately broken by his captors in a damp and frigid cell. He "was found dead in his chair," as James writes, on April 7, 1803.[41] But the French failed to halt the progress of the revolution by causing Toussaint to wither. On January 1, 1804, Dessalines proclaimed the colony's independence and its renewed identity as Haiti, the old Arawak word for the island meaning "mountainous land." Boisrond-Tonnerre, secretary of the revolutionary army under Dessalines, declared that to write the official decree, "We need the skin of a white man for parchment, his skull to bear down upon, and his blood for ink, into which we will dip a bayonet."[42]

———•—•———

The complicated events that finally led to Haiti's independence remain unstated in *Drums at Dusk,* Bontemps depending instead on the reader's knowledge that freedom, independence, and Toussaint's canonization as a hero will all become the inevitable results of the initial rebellion depicted in the text. But the history of the revolution is not the only history that Bontemps addresses here. He is also responding to the mainstream portrayals of Haiti—many of them rather lurid—that had been circulating in the United States, especially during the 1920s and 1930s, when the U.S. military occupied the island nation. Indeed, sensationalist images of Haiti extend even to early narratives of Haitian history. Thomas Madiou, born in Haiti in 1814 and educated in France, now considered the first "major historian"[43] of Haiti—his work was published in the 1840s—depicted Biassou as a man faithful to Vodou who had a tent set up at revolutionary encampments that "was filled with kittens of all shades, with snakes, with dead men's bones, and other African fetiches. At night, huge campfires were lit with naked women dancing horrible dances around them, chanting words understood only on the shores of Africa. When the excitement reached its climax, Biassou would appear among his *bocors* to proclaim in the name of God that every slave killed in battle would re-awaken in the homeland of Africa."[44] From this passage one gets a sense of the exaggerated images of Haiti that continued to shape the popular view, which Bontemps was writing against. In Haitian Creole, the term *bocor* refers to a magician, someone not associated with Vodou and certainly not a *houngan* or respected Vodou priest. This fascination with Haiti's perceived history of dark, mysterious, even shocking cultural traditions endured into the twentieth century, and indeed escalated with the U.S. occupation of 1915–1934.

The occupation was by no means the first instance of U.S. involvement in Haitian affairs. Connections between Saint Domingue and the United States stretch back before a nation called the United States existed, when the two colonies' economic interests were intertwined and the Saint Domingue plantation system "operated to the profit of Boston merchants as well as Creole masters."[45] The profits from their ties to this system underwrote the Americans' claims to independence from Britain.[46] And by the time revolution sparked in Saint Domingue, that island, "with a population of little more than half a million, stood second to Great Britain alone in the foreign commerce of the United States." Napoleon's troubles with Saint Domingue contributed to his decision to sell the Louisiana Territory to the United States in 1803—bringing yet more wealth to the United States even as the emancipatory revolution and the flood of Haitian émigrés stoked the fears of white Americans. Because of these racist fears of the new black nation in the Caribbean, the United States refused to officially recognize the Haitian government until 1862, under Lincoln. And subsequent relations between the two countries up until and including the Marine invasion of 1915 consisted largely of U.S. attempts to profit from Haiti's geographic location and quell any unrest there that might threaten U.S. access.[47] Ultimately, by the beginning of the twentieth century, the Haitian people had been effectively marginalized in their own country by foreign interests. As Sténio Vincent (president of Haiti between 1930 and 1941) remarked:

> The bank is German, the school system is French and *congré-ganiste,* import-export commerce is German, French, English, American, and Syrian. The Catholic clergy is French. The Protestant clergy is Anglo-Saxon. The personnel who control marine shipping, and our modest transportation infrastructure, are German, American, and French. The shoemakers are Cuban and Italian. The watchmakers and jewelers are Italian. The men's tailors are almost all Cuban. The carriage-makers are Jamaican. The few factories we have here and there for the processing of coffee and cacao, the two or three badly organized plantations, all this is in the hands of foreigners.[48]

In 1915, the United States invaded Haiti after the assassination of President Guillaume Sam by members of the Haitian (mulatto) elite. Following an attempted coup, Sam's prison guards had bludgeoned to death the hostages from elite fam-

ilies whom he was holding in an attempt to secure power.
The families of these hostages sought their bloody revenge.
At this point the U.S. ambassador in Haiti asked the U.S.
Navy, which maintained a presence nearby, to intercede.
Naval personnel disembarked the same day, partly because
the United States was also interested in establishing a naval
base in the Caribbean from which to fend off Germany at the
start of World War I and to oversee traffic through the Panama
Canal, which had opened the previous year. The consequences
of the occupation were disastrous for the people of Haiti.
Over the next nearly two decades, the United States "installed
a puppet president," Philippe Dartiguenave, who "dissolved
the legislature at gunpoint, denied freedom of speech, and
forced a new constitution on the Caribbean nation—one
more favorable to foreign investment," as historian Mary
Renda writes. The U.S. Marines also reinstated and enforced
a system of compulsory labor for all Haitians, rich and poor
alike, which was based on an 1863 Haitian law regarding
corvée, and which Haitians viewed as a new form of slavery.
When the native Caco uprising, a peasant revolt led by Charle-
magne Péralte, challenged U.S. control, two marines who
could speak some Haitian Creole blacked up with cork,
penetrated Péralte's camp, and killed him.[49] Together, these
events inspired the Haitian poet, novelist, and playwright
Jean Métellus to write of the occupation, "the Americans
tried to destroy the very soul of Haiti, the Haitian's very
being, after having denied him his independence, his right
to determine his own destiny."[50]
     Another (related) effect of the U.S. presence in Haiti was
to open that nation to travel and leisure. In 1936, the Co-

lombian Steamship Company, based in New York, invited tourists to experience Haiti's unique history: "the Colombian Line alone presents San Souci and the Citadel . . . palace and fortress of Haiti's King Henri Christophe. . . . Two added attractions at no extra cost."[51] In 1939, Bontemps's *Drums at Dusk* followed an outpouring of images of Haiti, from wallpaper to popular films—including the 1932 Bela Lugosi vehicle *White Zombie,* which incited a genre that eventually became unmoored from its Haitian origins. Literary works about Haiti were of varying quality, from Eugene O'Neill's *The Emperor Jones* (1920) to John Vandercook's *Black Majesty* (1928). Such works as William Seabrook's *The Magic Island* (1929) and the U.S. Marine John Houston Craige's *Black Bagdad* (1933) and *Cannibal Cousins* (1934) also had a wide popular impact. Despite the differences among these representations of Haiti, their emphasis and their influence were, by and large, remarkably similar. According to the anthropologist Melville Herskovits, writing in 1937, "Haiti has fared badly at the hands of its literary interpreters. Condescension and caricature have been called upon, especially in recent years, to provide a short cut to an understanding of the people and their institutions." As Herskovits pointed out, much of the fascination with Haiti revolved around the practice of Vodou.[52] And even the final title of Bontemps's novel, *Drums at Dusk,* suggests that either he or his publisher may have sought to capitalize on this trend (Bontemps's original title was "Troubled Island," and then "Purple Island"). Nevertheless, the text of *Drums* reveals that its author clearly wanted to find a way of writing about Haiti without exploiting it. Even with the romantic plot surrounding Diron Desautels, Bontemps succeeded.

The occupation that had revealed Haiti to people in the United States during the early twentieth century made it an object of complex fascination not only in Hollywood and for some Anglo-American writers, but also among a number of African American writers in addition to Bontemps. In Langston Hughes's *The Emperor of Haiti* and Zora Neale Hurston's *Tell My Horse,* for example, both published in 1938, Haiti functioned as a powerful symbol of the social and cultural value of blackness.[53] As J. Michael Dash writes, "Haiti would provide for black writers not a shudder of fear but a 'frisson' of recognition."[54] The children's book that Bontemps co-wrote with Hughes, *Popo and Fifina,* is another example of African Americans' desire to reframe perceptions of Haiti in the United States. It does not shirk the reality of poverty even as it idealizes the family connections that it shows as shaping the lives of poor Haitians. Although the book is set during the occupation, "American Marines" are mentioned only peripherally, as "owning" one of the beautiful beaches outside the Haitian capital. Their presence does not affect the family's life and work, but the story seems to look ahead to the eventual end of the occupation. The children's father has made them a kite that looks like a star; in one scene, as Popo flies the kite, another kite in the shape of a hawk attempts to cut its string. Popo's kite survives, however: his "big red star climbed the sky proudly, a true conquerer," having overcome the "evil bird with a broken wing."[55]

As with Hughes, Bontemps's close relationship with James Weldon Johnson no doubt influenced his interest in

and understanding of Haiti. Johnson had been one of the
first African Americans to criticize what the U.S. government
was doing in Haiti. Already known as a writer, Johnson had
also been U.S. consul in Puerto Cabello, Venezuela, and
Corinto, Nicaragua; in 1916, he became NAACP field
secretary. In this capacity, he visited Haiti in 1920 and
talked with peasants and politicians. He also met with
U.S. Marines, "who spoke casually of rape, killing, and
torture." Returning to the United States, Johnson became
an "indefatigable champion of Haitian independence,"[56] or,
rather, of renewed independence. Bontemps knew Johnson from his life in Harlem, and later listed Johnson as a
reference in his application for the Rosenwald Fellowship,
with which he planned to search out materials for new
children's books, as well as for the novel that would become *Drums at Dusk.*[57] Bontemps's attention to present-day
Haiti in *Drums,* however, is anything but direct. After the
withdrawal of U.S. forces, the nation's new constitution
enabled President Sténio Vincent to become, effectively, an
authoritarian dictator with a repressive regime. Thompson
argues that as Bontemps takes up questions of black rebellion
and Haitian nationalism in the novel, he "tacitly links Vincent to a heroic history of Haitian dictators and military
rulers, including Toussaint, Dessalines, and Christophe."
In this way, he adds, Bontemps "narrates revolution not
in terms of its event," but in terms of "ideological under-
pinnings" rooted in fascism: "an aestheticized masculinist
principle displayed in violence and guided by a radical,
religious belief in the Volk."[58] Given Bontemps's socially
progressive politics, however, as well as the fact that there is

no record of his ever having said or written anything about
Vincent, this reading of an even partially fascist ideology
in the novel is deeply problematic. Moreover, Bontemps
does not linger on any one leader of the revolution in the
novel, instead focusing on Baissou and Boukman, as well
as Toussaint, to show the presence and importance of mul-
tiple actors. And finally, his ambivalence about the violence
of the slave mobs could be read as a critique of the kind of
fascist militarization that was springing up in Haiti (under Vincent), in Europe, and around the globe at the end
of the 1930s. Like his engagement with Haiti's past and
with the dynamics of multiracialism and multiculturalism,
Bontemps's politics and his attitude toward contemporary
Haiti resist easy classification.

Later in the twentieth century, the Haitian Revolution
became the focus of renewed interest on the part of Caribbean writers, particularly between the late 1940s and the
early 1960s. Literary interpretations of the revolution include Cuban novelist Alejo Carpentier's *El reino de este
mundo* (*The Kingdom of This World*), published a decade
after *Drums at Dusk;* St. Lucian Derek Walcott's plays *Henri
Christophe* (1950), *Drums and Colours* (1958), and *The Haitian Earth* (first produced in 1984); and plays by two Marti-
nican writers: Édouard Glissant's *Monsieur Toussaint* (1961)
and Aimé Césaire's *La tragédie du roi Christophe* (*The Tragedy of King Christophe*) (1963). This interest corresponded
in part with the Algerian war and decolonization efforts
taking place across the Caribbean. *Monsieur Toussaint,* for
example, was published after Glissant was forced out of
Guadeloupe as a result of his work (with the anticolonial

Front antillo-guyanais) for the independence of French
overseas departments and his connections to militant Algerian intellectuals.[59] Commenting on the process that led
him to write *La tragédie du roi Christophe,* Césaire noted
that "Haiti . . . is a kind of magnifying glass for the Antil-
les as a whole, as well as for Africa; in studying the history
of Haiti, one can begin to grasp all the problems of the
Third World."[60] Thus Bontemps was one of the first writers
of the twentieth century to interpret connections between
the revolution and contemporary political struggles, and
to develop an inter-American literary consciousness. And,
as we can see with *Drums at Dusk,* Haiti offers insights
not only into "Third World" struggles, but also into the
machinations of imperialism. There is much room for rich
comparison between *Drums at Dusk* and these later literary
interpretations of the revolution. Readers might also ask
how the themes and issues addressed by Bontemps have
been reworked again by U.S. novelist Madison Smartt
Bell in his Haitian trilogy *All Souls' Rising, Master of the
Crossroads,* and *The Stone That the Builder Refused,* written
between 1995 and 2004. As Haiti continues to inspire and
intrigue writers across the Americas, the unique vision of
Bontemps's 1939 novel is an important touchstone for understanding both these later literary imaginings and the
historical contexts in which they were produced.

Ultimately, *Drums at Dusk* is a rare novel that entertains
even as its complexities reward close reading and careful
analysis. It asks us to consider Haiti's legacies within the
African diaspora and highlights the powerful role played by
Haiti in the New World as a whole. It directs our attention

toward the nuances of intra- and interracial relationships in colonial situations, as well as the effects of these relationships in "postcolonial" contexts. It insists that we examine the forms and networks of multiracial identities, kinships, and social relations in the Americas, where the political and the genealogical are profoundly linked. And it leads us to contemplate connections between romance, race, and politics in modern literature. Did Bontemps appropriate the form of a historical romance in order to reimagine the place of individual agency within the broader forces of "history"? Was he offering this novel as a comment and a warning on the state of race relations within the United States as its tensions with Europe continued to escalate in the months prior (as we know now) to the start of World War II? Was he trying to attract the political sympathies of white readers who might want to identify with Diron? After writing about Virginia in *Black Thunder,* did he turn to the complicated racial and social hierarchies of Haiti so that he could make an even stronger critique of the color line dividing "black" from "white"? Does the purple of his "Purple Island" thus have some kind of racial meaning? These questions and many others spring up from the margins of *Drums at Dusk.* They allow us to reevaluate our assumptions about revolution, race, and nationalism in this inter-American context. And in doing so, they prove that by capturing the moment just prior to the start of the Haitian Revolution, Bontemps succeeds in making us confront the ongoing impact of the revolution—perhaps better than if he had depicted the events of the revolution itself.

NOTES

1. In the *Journal of Negro History,* for example, J. D. Jerome called the novel "an achievement," while Rayford Logan's review in *Opportunity* claimed that the novel depended too much on the "romantic imagination" of its readers. Robert Bone saw the novel as "in every respect a retreat from the standards of [Bontemps's earlier novel] *Black Thunder.*" See J. D. Jerome, review of *Drums at Dusk* by Arna Bontemps, *Journal of Negro History* 24 (July 1939): 355; Rayford Logan, review of *Drums at Dusk* by Arna Bontemps, *Opportunity* (June 1939): 218 (quoted in Kirkland C. Jones, *Renaissance Man from Louisiana: A Biography of Arna Wendell Bontemps* [Westport, Conn.: Greenwood Press, 1992], 92); Robert Bone, *The Negro Novel in America* (1958; rpr. New Haven: Yale University Press, 1965), 122.

2. See, for example, Alfred N. Hunt, *Haiti's Influence on Antebellum America: Slumbering Volcano in the Caribbean* (Baton Rouge: Louisiana State University Press, 1988), especially chap. 2, "St. Dominguan Refugees in the Lower South," 37–83.

3. Jones, *Renaissance Man from Louisiana,* 2.

4. Although the Code Noir mandated punishments for any free, married man who took a slave woman as a "concubine" and had children with her, an important distinction was drawn if the slaveholder was not married. In that case, the man was directed to marry his slave mistress "according to the accepted rites of the church," and "in this way she shall then be freed, the children becoming free and legitimate." See also Doris Garraway, *The Libertine Colony: Creolization in the Early French Caribbean* (Durham, N.C.: Duke University Press, 2005), 214.

5. Many thanks to Arna Alexander Bontemps for these additional details about his father and the family as a whole.

6. Although his reading is problematic for what it implies about Bontemps's own political beliefs, Mark Christian Thompson offers an interesting assessment of the way Bontemps writes about revolution in *Drums at Dusk* by omitting it from the narrative. See "Voodoo Fascism: Fascist Ideology in Arna Bontemps's *Drums at Dusk,*" *MELUS* 30 (Fall 2005): 155–77.

7. Quoted in Jones, *Renaissance Man from Louisiana,* 76.

8. Arnold Rampersad, introduction to *Black Thunder,* by Arna Bontemps (1936, 1968; rpr. Boston: Beacon Press, 1992), ix–x; Jones, *Renaissance Man from Louisiana,* 80–81. For a detailed account of the Scottsboro incident and its repercussions, see Dan T. Carter, *Scottsboro: A Tragedy of the American South,* rev. ed. (Baton Rouge: Louisiana State University Press, 1979).

9. Jones, *Renaissance Man from Louisiana,* 80–81.

10. For a discussion of Bontemps's use of historical sources, see Mary Kemp Davis, "The Historical Slave Revolt and the Literary Imagination" (Ph.D. dissertation, UNC–Chapel Hill, 1984), 204–52.

11. Mary Kemp Davis, "Arna Bontemps' *Black Thunder:* The Creation of an Authoritative Text of 'Gabriel's Defeat,'" *Black American Literature Forum* 23 (Spring 1989): 34; Thompson, "Voodoo Fascism," 162–64.

12. David Patrick Geggus, *Haitian Revolutionary Studies* (Bloomington: Indiana University Press, 2002), 10.

13. Ibid., 21.

14. Patrick Bellegarde-Smith, *Haiti: The Breached Citadel* (Boulder, Colo.: Westview Press, 1990), 39.

15. Carolyn E. Fick, *The Making of Haiti: The Saint Domingue Revolution from Below* (Knoxville: University of Tennessee Press, 1990), 17.

16. Geggus, *Haitian Revolutionary Studies,* 10.

17. See Bone, *The Negro Novel in America,* 122–23.

18. Arna Bontemps, *Story of the Negro* (New York: A. A. Knopf, 1948), 67–68.

19. According to Robert Debs Heinl Jr. and Nancy Gordon Heinl, "The element in Saint Domingue most hostile to the *hommes de couleur* was not the high-born *grands blancs* but the lower-class *petits blancs.* It mattered not what the Assembly decreed; the *petits blancs* would never concede that *gens de couleur* were persons and equals because, if they were, so were the slaves. This was the reason why Ogé's object—to secure promulgation and implementation of the Assembly's March decree—however just and lawful, was doomed to fail." See *Written in Blood: The Story of the Haitian People, 1492–1971* (Boston: Houghton Mifflin, 1978), 40.

20. Ibid., 41.

21. Geggus, *Haitian Revolutionary Studies,* 11.

22. See, for example, Fick, *The Making of Haiti,* 92–93.

23. Thompson, "Voodoo Fascism," 168.

24. James writes, "Those who wished to believe and to convince the world that the slaves were half-human brutes, fit for nothing else but slavery, could find ample evidence for their faith." See *The Black Jacobins: Toussaint L'Ouverture and the San Domingo Revolution* (1938; rpr. London: Allison & Busby, 1980), 16. But when slaves killed themselves, he writes, it was often "to spite their owner" (15).

25. By the 1780s, the "most prestigious posts" on the plantations were held by slaves who had been born in the colonies. "Almost all the major leaders of the slave revolution were also locally born Creoles—this includes figures sometimes identified as Africans, such as Biassou . . . and (very probably) Boukman" (Geggus, *Haitian Revolutionary Studies,* 35). According to Bellegarde-Smith, Boukman was born in Jamaica (*Haiti,* 40).

26. See Fick, *The Making of Haiti,* 92.

27. See, for example, ibid., 93.

28. Max Beauvoir, "Slavery, Boukman, and Independence," in Cécile Accilien, Jessica Adams, and Elmide Méléance, eds., *Revolutionary Freedoms: A History of Survival, Strength and Imagination in Haiti* (Coconut Creek, Fla.: Caribbean Studies Press, 2006), 102.

29. Bellegarde-Smith, *Haiti,* 41.

30. Fick, *The Making of Haiti*, 113.

31. George Washington Cable, *The Grandissimes* (1880; rpr. New York: Penguin, 1988), 180.

32. For discussions of the figure of the hero and other conventions of historical plantation romances written during the antebellum period, see Michael Kreyling, *Figures of the Hero in Southern Narrative* (Baton Rouge: Louisiana State University Press, 1987); Susan J. Tracy, *In the Master's Eye: Representations of Women, Blacks, and Poor Whites in Antebellum Southern Literature* (Amherst: University of Massachusetts Press, 1995); and Paul Christian Jones, *Unwelcome Voices: Subversive Fiction in the Antebellum South* (Knoxville: University of Tennessee Press, 2005). For discussions of the conventions of plantation fiction in the late nineteenth and early twentieth centuries, see Lucinda H. MacKethan, *The Dream of Arcady: Place and Time in Southern Literature* (Baton Rouge: Louisiana State University Press, 1980); Anne Goodwyn Jones, "*Gone with the Wind* and Others: Popular Fiction, 1920–1950," in *The History of Southern Literature,* ed. Louis D. Rubin, Jr. (Baton Rouge: Louisiana State University Press, 1985), 363–74; John Pilkington, "The Memory of the War," in *The History of Southern Literature,* ed. Louis D. Rubin, Jr. (Baton Rouge: Louisiana State University Press, 1985), 356–62; Richard H. King, *A Southern Renaissance: The Cultural Awakening of the American South, 1930–1955* (New York: Oxford University Press, 1980); and Kathryn Lee Seidel, *The Southern Belle in the American Novel* (Tampa: University of South Florida Press, 1985).

33. Kreyling, *Figures of the Hero,* 16.

34. This democratic marriage is similar to what Anne Goodwyn Jones discusses in James Boyd's "very successful" novel of 1925, *Drums.* Here Johnny Fraser, the hero, comes of age during the American Revolution, goes to England to become a gentleman, but eventually returns to join the ranks of a different kind of hero, represented in the novel by "John Paul Jones, Daniel Boone, and the ragged revolutionaries." He also drops his aristocratic English lover, Eve, for his "strong country neighbor Sally"; and the novel thus "celebrate[s] the democratic ideal and the plain folk by working through a version of the Old South fantasy so that the protagonist rejoins his own family." There is no way of knowing whether Bontemps ever read *Drums,* and the original titles for *Drums at Dusk* (discussed later in this essay) suggest that he did not intend to reference Boyd's text directly. Nevertheless, the similarities between these plots are striking, for as Jones might describe it, Diron, like Johnny Fraser, "chooses another class, not of society or money or even blood, but of the heart." See Jones, "*Gone with the Wind* and Others," 365.

35. To this end, *Drums at Dusk* should also be read as part of the small tradition—if it can be called that—of novels written by African Americans with white protagonists, including Charles W. Chesnutt's *The Colonel's Dream* (1905), Zora Neale Hurston's *Seraph on the Suwanee* (1948), and James Baldwin's *Giovanni's Room* (1956).

36. Geggus, *Haitian Revolutionary Studies,* 18, 185. See also Jane Landers, *Black Society in Spanish Florida* (Urbana: Univ. of Illinois Press, 1999), and "Jorge Biassou: Black Chieftain," *El Escribano* 25 (1988): 87–100.

37. James, *The Black Jacobins*, 263, 265.

38. Geggus, *Haitian Revolutionary Studies*, 16, 22.

39. Ibid., 16.

40. See, for example, Fick, *The Making of Haiti*, 92; Geggus, *Haitian Revolutionary Studies*, 16–17.

41. James, *The Black Jacobins*, 290, 301, 365.

42. See Accilien et al., *Revolutionary Freedoms*, 54, for the original French. Adams's translation.

43. Geggus, *Haitian Revolutionary Studies*, 35.

44. Quoted in Heinl and Heinl, *Written in Blood*, 45.

45. Ludwell Lee Montague, *Haiti and the United States, 1714–1938* (Durham, N.C.: Duke University Press, 1940), 32.

46. See Ronald Bailey, "The Slave(ry) Trade and the Development of Capitalism in the United States: The Textile Industry in New England," in *The Atlantic Slave Trade: Effects on Economies, Societies, and Peoples in Africa, the Americas, and Europe*, ed. Joseph E. Inikori and Stanley L. Engerman (Durham, N.C.: Duke University Press, 1992), 212.

47. Montague, *Haiti and the United States*, 30, 32, 92, 102, 147–149, 164.

48. Quoted in Jean Métellus, *Haiti, une nation pathétique* (Paris: Editions Denoël, 1987), 43–44. Adams's translation.

49. Mary A. Renda, *Taking Haiti: Military Occupation and the Culture of U.S. Imperialism, 1915–1940* (Chapel Hill: University of North Carolina Press, 2001), 10, 172–73. See also Philippe R. Girard, *Paradise Lost: Haiti's Tumultuous Journey from Pearl of the Caribbean to Third World Hot Spot* (New York: Palgrave Macmillan, 2005), 81.

50. Métellus, *Haiti,* 43. Adams's translation.

51. Colombian Steamship Co. promotional poster included in Renda, *Taking Haiti,* 219.

52. Melville J. Herskovits, *Life in a Haitian Valley* (New York: Alfred A. Knopf, 1937), vii.

53. Hughes also wrote a "singing play" about the fall of Dessalines entitled *Troubled Island*; it premiered in Cleveland in 1936. For more information, see, for example, Edward J. Mullen, ed., *Langston Hughes in the Hispanic World and Haiti* (Hamden, Conn.: Archon Books, 1977).

54. See J. Michael Dash, *Haiti and the United States: National Stereotypes and the Literary Imagination* (Basingstoke: Macmillan, 1988), 56.

55. Arna Bontemps and Langston Hughes, *Popo and Fifina, Children of Haiti* (New York: Macmillan, 1932), 59.

56. Renda, *Taking Haiti,* 188, 190, 191.

57. Jones, *Renaissance Man from Louisiana,* 89.

58. Thompson, "Voodoo Fascism," 157, 169–70.

59. See, for example, www.lehman.cuny.edu/ile.en.ile/paroles/glissant.html.

60. See interview with Khalid Chraibi at www.la-tragedie-du-roi-christophe .blogspot.com/. Adams's translation.

DRUMS AT DUSK

CHAPTER ONE

1. Only ghosts walked on that pathway now. Ghosts—
and people so old they were about to become ghosts. Captain Frounier sometimes came that way when paying his
weekly respects to M. Bayou de Libertas in the other's
counting house behind the magnificent colonial mansion
at Bréda, for the captain was ninety-one, as toothless as a
sparrow, as wobbly in the joints as the spars of his own
sailing vessels and as violently profane of tongue as any
man this side of torment. Mme Jacques Juvet, once indentured as a house servant at this same Bréda, was also
attached to the path. In her case too the reason was simple. Mme Juvet was eighty if she was a day. Her teeth had
become fangs. Snuff left a nasty smudge around her old
mouth. She walked with a cane that resembled a corkscrew, and the slaves had already begun to shun her as a
witch. Mars Plasair liked the path not because he was
old but because he was coughing his lungs out and
was perhaps as near his ghosthood as the others who
walked there. Moreover he was a slave and had been
badly used.

Partly, it may have been the trees that gave the path its character. Elsewhere on the vast acres of Bréda there was the lofty murmur of long-necked coconut palms and the refined swish of banana leaves. Here a row of naked cottonwoods, blighted long since by a mysterious plague, stood like giant skeletons along the path.

Others than the ghosts found the path as unsatisfactory as it was unattractive. The footing was exceedingly bad. Some broken rocks had been scattered there once and covered with gravel. Subsequent rains had taken the gravel. This was not a circumstance to dismay a ghost, but it was the last straw where young Diron Desautels was concerned. And now, having beguiled himself into trying it, he cursed every foot of the way.

Yet, thank heaven, he was not obliged to continue as he had started. He might cut across the slope behind the slave quarters, come out on the carriage road and follow it till he reached the wooded sections of the hills. On second thought, that was precisely what he would do. As well as Diron loved to hunt, he was not willing to crack his shins in the pursuit of a few game birds while there was another way. It was still night, of course, the dark land still sleeping in lemon moonlight, but Diron knew that his seedy old falcon was alert only at daybreak, and he was determined to reach the hillside before the sun appeared. Furthermore he had promised to meet his uncle at the edge of the wood, and he did not propose to keep the older man waiting.

The clear slope was in reality a reaped grain field. It was bounded by a black hedge; and beyond that the level acres, dim miles of them, supported a remarkably heavy crop of sugar cane. Diron walked briskly now, the fowler sitting placidly on his left wrist. In his right hand he carried a stick, his only weapon aside from the pistol worn inside his sash-like belt. He was dressed in apple-green breeches and jacket, and his heavy mane, neatly gathered at the neck and tied with a silver cord, gave back to the moon a lacquered shine.

The sound of horses halted his steps before he reached the coach road, however, and Diron found a friendly shadow and waited. A coach at that hour? A slave-driven ox cart would have been nothing unusual. Neither would a carriage have surprised him had it been headed for Cap Français before daybreak. Plantation masters in the northern department of Saint Domingue were in the habit of making early business errands to the seat of their colonial government. But this present affair was not the same. Here was a coach drawn by fast horses coming out from the city at an hour when planters were generally expected to be asleep. Diron saw it come into view dimly and then flash by in a maze of dust and shadows. The clatter was enormous.

He came out upon the road and tried to imagine what fresh unrest this thing heralded. Of course, a peaceful mission was conceivable, but it was much easier to account for the presence of the coach in other ways. There was little enough of harmony between the Paris-appointed officials in Cap Français and their landed constituents, not to mention the turmoil among local classes and the tendency of sparks from the Revolution in faraway

France to land unexpectedly now and again on this island possession in the Caribbean Sea. So Diron Desautels, a young man who had taken a very decided stand on more than one of the questions that helped to cause the bloody confusion, felt a shiver of excitement.

Before the carriage vanished completely, he assured himself that it was headed for Bréda, which meant that if anything unusual brewed, he would—as a neighbor and friend of the overseer—hear more about it. Satisfied of this, he turned again toward the wooded hillside half a mile beyond. A smile twisted the corners of his mouth suddenly, distorted the thin, neatly trimmed but immature mustache on his lip. There was also another source of information available to him, if his curiosity demanded it, another means of finding out some of the things that went on at Bréda. But he refrained from calling her name at the moment, even silently to himself. He was not always as bold as he might have been.

The son of a naturalist who had made the Caribbean islands his field, Diron had spent most of his life in Saint Domingue, the French half of the island which Spanish explorers had at first been in the habit of calling *Haiti* or high land. At the moment both the young man's parents were in Paris again while the father, patient old scholar, was dutifully seeing a large volume of his observations of tropical flora through the press. But this serious occupation, if the whole truth must be known, did not completely explain the son's separation from his parents.

Neither did Diron's attachment to his uncle, M. Phi-

lippe Desautels, tell the real motive. While his affection
for that elderly gentleman was genuine, as his haste to
join him this morning on a fowling jaunt indicated, it
was definitely secondary. M. Philippe Desautels, lately relieved of his post as naval commissioner of the colony and
still in political disfavor in Cap Français as well as in
Paris, remained an aristocrat. He hadn't yet gone over to
the other side as had his nephew. Still his own adversities
had rendered him tolerant of the opposition. He knew
perfectly well what dangerous considerations had helped
to speed the rash boy's return from France after a short
stay during the previous year.

Diron had joined *Les Amis des Noirs*. This exuberant
society of violent anti-slavery partisans, counting among
its members such gaudy lights as La Rochefoucauld, Lafayette, Danton and Robespierre, had fascinated him from
the start. Brissot, its founder, was an old acquaintance of
the family. The writings of Abbé Grégoire stirred the
young Diron like lyric poetry. Beside these he had placed
Abbé Raynal's *Histoire Philosophique des deux Indes,*
and his destiny had been sealed. Two or three ringing,
eloquent phrases, the touchstones of their movement,
echoed in his mind continually. . . . *No part of the French
nation shall demand its rights at the hands of the Assembly in vain. . . . All men are born and continue free and
equal as to their rights. . . .*

Even now hastening to overtake the soft-voiced uncle
who had preceded him on horseback to the hillside, Diron
was sure that his tingling excitement owed as much to
these slogans as to the danger of his position in the local

scheme. His friend Sylvestre Viard had paid a price for holding just such views. Would that be a lesson to Diron? The boy stretched his legs in the open road and began to feel as tall as two men. Never. Never would he turn from his convictions. No matter what the consequences he intended to stand his ground. Fear and the shadow of fear both left him promptly. Hearing the dim tock-tock of a horse in the distance, he filled his lungs with air and whistled loudly. A moment later there was an answer. He had overtaken his uncle.

"Did you see it?" he asked when he was near enough to speak.

"I recognized the coachmen of M. de Libertas," the other answered. "Guests, perhaps."

"Guests, at this hour? After all, *Oncle* Philippe, Bréda is not an inn."

They had paused, but now they were walking again, the boy at the left and a step in advance of the horse. The uncle, wearing long gloves and an orange scarf, sat slim and erect on his saddle.

"No, Bréda is certainly not an inn, but I dare say it entertains as many guests as an inn during the course of a year. Shall we turn off the road here?"

"This is as good a place as any. We can tie the horse in the clump there."

On the ground, the older man adjusted his jacket, inspected his well-oiled fowling piece.

"A few more men at Bréda wouldn't hurt," he reflected. "It's overrun with women."

Diron laughed.

"In that I agree heartily."

"And I accept your agreement with salt. You might not be so ready to agree if the women at Bréda were as beautiful, say, as the dark-haired wife of your young friend."

"Mme Sylvestre Viard?"

M. Philippe Desautels clearly had not meant to have that name spoken in just that way. He was in a pleasant mood, and he certainly had not hoped to call up morbid associations.

"I refer to her type," he added quickly. "Not necessarily herself."

"It's hard for me to think of Paulette as a type," Diron said slowly.

"Of course, there aren't many as beautiful as Paulette Viard."

"And few as unreliable," the boy added.

"I once knew one as unreliable," M. Philippe Desautels insisted. "Oh, quite as unreliable. Consequently I've never married."

"And I know one as beautiful," Diron said, repeating his uncle's tone. "Quite as beautiful. Consequently—"

"I know. Consequently you're between two fires."

"It's not as bad as you think. But about that coach. I have a feeling it wasn't bringing guests. No ordinary guests, at least."

"If our curiosity holds up," the uncle smiled, "we'll eventually know all that is to be known about their affairs at Bréda. I suggest we get on with the *houchiba.*"

Their object being the hunting of birds, Diron was as willing as the uncle to get on with the business. They

separated, walking several yards apart, and became silent
as they climbed a dewy slope covered with *tchia-tchia*
trees and thickets. Almost immediately a gray paleness
came to the eastern sky. The place was alive with twit-
tering. Long dry pods rattled on the lacy trees. Doves
drummed sadly. Striding alone now, a stone's throw from
his uncle, Diron unhooded his falcon.

But even as the bird sprang from his wrist, he assured
himself that his interest in the Bréda household and its
guests was not the sort of curiosity his uncle playfully
imagined it to be. Perhaps if *Oncle* Philippe had not
been away from Paris so long he would not feel so far
removed from the terrible business that was still drench-
ing her streets with blood. In that case, perhaps, the
arrival of strangers might tend to suggest things to his
mind. But then, unfortunately, he'd have to suffer the
same restless discomfort that troubled Diron at this very
moment.

2. Céleste Juvet, sleeping in a maid-servant's room overlooking the driveway, was awakened by the first blast
from the coachman's horn. Her presence did not mean
that she was connected with this household. She was there
because for days there had been great expectancy at the
Bréda plantation; and Céleste, who at fifteen was not to
be left at home alone in that wanton paradise called Saint
Domingue, had come along when her gnarled old grand-

mother was summoned to help with the preparations. Now, aroused suddenly, the girl sat erect beneath a canopy of mosquito netting. A hushed silence followed the shrill announcement below, but in the next instant there was a scurrying in the yard and busy activity at the ovens and cook stoves behind the great French mansion. Then something that suggested a gust of wind flung the door open, and two shadowy, near-nude women rushed through the room to get a view of the driveway from Céleste's window. Both of them wore negligible, weblike night dresses and night caps, and neither had bothered to find slippers or dressing gown. Neither paid the slightest attention to the girl in the bed.

Céleste flushed momentarily with embarrassment. Prematurely ripened in a warm tropical climate, she seemed at times a trifle more than her age; but as she watched the women, childishness was written clearly on her face.

"Yes, it's the count," the older one chuckled.

"Curse his old bones."

They had about them, as they snickered together, the air of two who shared a secret that was almost too rich to keep. Yet their merriment was clearly tinged with a certain dark resentment. There was malice in every tone they uttered. The first one bent forward, resting her hand on the window frame.

"The triumphal return," she said sarcastically.

She was a statuesque old person, far above average height, but her teeth were bad, and her large bones showed unpleasantly at the elbows, the wrists, and the ankles.

"I'm dying to see who he's brought this time," the other giggled.

"Mind what you say," the older woman cautioned, pointing her thumb at Céleste's bed without turning. "Big ears, you know."

The second woman, apparently a dozen years younger than her companion, was broad of hip and shoulder and had the muscles of a man. She was perhaps forty, but she had been overfed and already her eyes were becoming beady. It was impossible to distinguish her smile from her frown, her lips making an identical pattern for each. Heeding the other woman's caution, she lowered her voice and commenced to whisper.

Céleste didn't mind. She had heard enough. Mme Juvet had already told her what this perfectly irrelevant old couple was doing at Bréda, and knowing that, Céleste could well understand why they scampered through her room to get a first view of the Count Armand de Sacy on this latest of his very infrequent visits from Paris to his cousin's colonial estate in the new world. Céleste had at first regarded the two females, whose names were Claire and Annette, as simply a part of Bréda like the hundreds of slaves or perhaps her friend Mme Bayou de Libertas, the overseer's wife. But Mme Juvet would have her know they didn't really belong. The slaves had their place. M. Bayou de Libertas was employed. But these two—no, they didn't belong.

The Count de Sacy, it seemed, was a man of means who could afford to indulge a taste for variety and change in his mistresses. He had found it convenient (and stimu-

lating) when his ardor flagged, to personally escort his
former favorites across the sea for a vacation at this magnificent island plantation in the northern department of
Saint Domingue. He had tried it first with Claire, the
statuesque one, some twenty years earlier. Surrounding
her with ebony servants, locating her in an elegantly
appointed room, just down the hall from the one Céleste
now occupied, he had assured her that she would be
divinely happy till he returned—at the moment he was
compelled to make a most urgent business call at Jamaica
—and that they could later return to Paris together. Of
course, "circumstances" delayed his return, so he wrote
two or three soothing and reassuring letters, then took
ship directly to France and forgot about her entirely.

Ten years later, with much the same guile, he brought
Annette to Bréda. Much younger than the woman she
had supplanted in his affections, plump where the other
was gaunt, richly dressed, wildly perfumed, she had at
first shown only scorn for the strange, pale Claire. But
time put the boot on the other foot. When the count left
Bréda and returned to his respectable family in Paris,
Claire ridiculed the other woman openly. Mme Juvet recalled that the two fading courtesans had called each other
vile names, hurling *bitch* and *strumpet* back and forth
till the words lost their mordant and satisfactory flavor;
then they had entered upon actual hostilities. Claire spat
in Annette's face; the latter retaliated with a smart open
palm across the older woman's mouth. But Claire got
along tolerably well without the front tooth she lost in
the encounter, and Annette eventually forgave the slimy

insult. By the time Céleste began noticing things at Bréda in her occasional visits there, the two were as intimate as sisters. Every day they put on brilliant afternoon dresses and lunched together on the leaf-fringed terrace. In the mornings they donned riding habits and rode horses through the banana grove. In the afternoons they drank a bottle of wine each, smoked black cigars, then slept till the supper hour.

Ten years having elapsed since the arrival of Annette, the two had become bitterly philosophical about the whole business. They giggled a great deal as they stood at the window of Céleste's room and tried to speculate whether the newest arrival would be fair like Claire or dark like Annette. Would she be good company after the count had left her, or would there be unpleasantness before she became resigned to her lot?

Céleste, unnoticed in the excitement, slipped out of her bed and took her place at another window as the tumult increased downstairs. A half-dozen blacks were prancing around the gaudy coach, swinging traveling boxes and bags to the ground, hustling them around to a side entrance. The dreamy-eyed Toussaint, down from the driver's seat, stood at rigid attention beside the coach door, his head tied in a madras handkerchief, a wiry pigtail hanging out, while a half-grown black boy held the bits of the team. At length the count emerged, a man as tiny as a woman, his immense curls only partly hidden by his hat, and began scratching himself like an aged dog, now stroking his sea-legs, now digging at his crotch. He spent a moment finding his snuff box and filling his lip. During the pause a spot of light, the first of the morning, revealed a wine-colored coat with wide skirt and white lapels, gray silk stockings and shoes with large paste buckles. Presently he turned and extended a diffident hand to the woman inside the coach.

"There," Claire said. "She's going to get out now."

"He probably won't even bother to lie to her as he did to us," Annette said.

"She's a neat little trick, though. You wouldn't think ... so soon. Nice walk, too."

"She may have bad breath."

"*He* seems to have piles."

"But he still looks fit—considering everything."

"Fit? Yes, but he's lost a lot."

A moment later both of them left the room, disregarding its young occupant to the last. Céleste did not mind. At no time had she ever been made to feel too utterly at home at Bréda, and never before had she been more pleased to regard herself as a stranger on that rich estate. The aristocracy, such as she had seen of it, did not entice her, even at fifteen.

Whether or not she had anything to fear at the hands of the élite she had never considered. She was pretty, uncommonly pretty, despite an early hint of plumpness, and men already noticed her—a few men, at any rate. If at Bréda she was out of her depth, she did not mind. Mme Bayou de Libertas was a sweet character, plumper than Céleste would ever be, and thoughtfully kind whenever the girl was on the place. Gratitude for this was the only tenderness Céleste felt for the gaudy, feudal Bréda and its patrician elegance.

When the newcomers passed out of sight below, she left the window and commenced dressing.

3. M. Bayou de Libertas whistled in his kettle of warm suds as three grinning blacks in loin cloths doused and splashed and mauled him gleefully in what he regarded as his special-occasion bath. In the deep wooden vessel that served the quality at Bréda for ablutions he squatted wretchedly, his knees propped higher than his chin. A fourth slave stood near by with additional pots of hot and cold water. M. Bayou de Libertas was a fool about bathing and he didn't care who knew it. Why, if it had been left to his own discretion—and if it had not been a shame to take up so much of the slaves' time, considering all the really urgent work—he might have taken a complete scrubbing every day of his life. He just naturally liked it, and he didn't mind how much other people laughed at him.

Today, alas, he was compelled to cut short the pleasant operations. The coachman's horn, blown a moment or two earlier by the reliable Toussaint, had indicated the arrival of the count; and M. de Libertas certainly did not hope to have that high-born gentleman find him wedged in a wooden kettle, covered with snowy suds.

"There now, we'll have to leave off with that," he said loudly, one eye shut fast, the other perfectly round and blinking like a pigeon's eye. "You'll have to get me out of here now."

The African beside the door put down his pots. At a nod from one of the other three he joined them in the complicated chore of extricating M. de Libertas, one leg at a time, from his bath. With feet on the floor, arms resting on the sides of the kettle, aided by the expert and painstaking help of the four blacks, M. de Libertas gradually rose. Through it all he fairly shrieked with pleasure.

But there would be no more whistling at present where he was concerned, he told himself soberly as he gained his feet. As overseer at Bréda and master of that estate in the absence of its true owner, he had much to think about even at this hour of the morning. There were always a few important considerations—apart from the social rites so cherished by the tiny nobleman—when the Count de Noé's cousin and representative returned for one of his rare visits, just as there were when M. de Libertas made his yearly trip to Paris. And this year problems were multiplied due to the bloody business in Paris and all the local complications that grew out of it. The overseer's mind at this hour, however, was chiefly perplexed over a batch of half-sick slaves, drooping, vomiting, and fainting at their work.

The morning clothes of M. de Libertas were neatly arranged on a sofa and chair in his bedroom, a slim black valet waiting ceremoniously beside them. But first there was the somewhat hurried business of shaving.

Then when the barber had retired with his razors and mug and towels, the hair-dresser, tall and mincing, a willowy African with a woman's hands and a woman's puckered mouth, came in for his session. An hour had elapsed since M. de Libertas had roused from sleep in his net-canopied bed in the adjoining room, but the overseer was still in his underdrawers and Madame had not yet blinked an eye. Presently, however, the inquisition of hot curling irons, stiff brushes and jerking combs over, the slim, ghost-like Mars stepped from his place between the chair and the sofa and began dusting his master's neck and shoulders with powder, preparatory to slipping a freshly ruffled shirt over the gentleman's head.

"Well, Mars, today's another day. How are you doing?"

M. de Libertas was genuinely kindly, and nowhere did his good humor show itself more than in his dealings with the slaves of Bréda. His smile was always ready, despite a mouth which could show some of the worst dental work in the French colonies.

"I can still get around," the valet said.

"But you're not well."

"I *have* felt better, monsieur."

"Yes, I can see that you have. How about the others?"

"Toussaint looked at us this morning while the boys were hitching the carriage. Felt our foreheads. Said he took it to be some kind of fever."

"How many of you are complaining now?"

"Eight, monsieur. Three down and out—five of us dragging our tails around."

"With the four that died, that makes twelve who've had it."

"Yes, monsieur."

"When you finish with me, Mars, get the other four and bring them with you to the counting house."

"Yes, monsieur."

"I'm going to have the count look you over before breakfast and see what he makes of it."

Supporting himself by placing one hand on the back of a chair, Mars finished his work, brushed a speck of lint from M. de Libertas's shoulder. The gentleman overseer stepped to a mirror and inspected himself. He had a comedian's face, a pock-marked nose, no eyebrows, absurd wrinkles; but he was, as ever, well got up in his clothes. That is, well got up above the waist. M. de Libertas never looked at his own legs. They were travesties on the fashion of knee breeches, and he knew it. They were no more than broomsticks with gross knots for knees. But this circumstance notwithstanding, they were this morning encased in silk. And now, in silver breeches and flowered waistcoat, sky blue coat and dark hat, M. de Libertas felt that he was ready to greet the rising sun as well as a nobleman from Paris.

"Mars—my stick and snuff box.

"H'm."

Sniffing gingerly as he went, M. de Libertas started down the hall. At the head of the stair he discovered that he had developed a little hiccough—curse the luck. After all his care here he was hiccoughing like a bumpkin as he went to meet the cousin and personal representative of the Count de Noé, owner of Bréda. He was startled presently, however, by women's voices and the abrupt opening of a door; suddenly, thanks to Claire and Annette, his hiccough vanished. There in the door frame stood the two half-dressed women, their long stockings pinned to their corsets, their cheeks spotted with round dabs of rouge.

"Was that a neigh I heard?" the overseer asked soberly.

Claire showed her teeth.

"Just a little misguided whinny," she said. "Annette heard your footsteps and thought you were the count."

Two ebony slave women stood behind the pair, clinging to the strings of their half-laced corsets. A third black woman left the room carrying a chamber pot and passed down the hall toward a rear stair. The door closed; the overseer continued down the steps, one hand sliding on the carved rail.

4. When she had emptied her long-necked sprinkling tin, Mme Jacques Juvet turned from the flower beds and began stamping her feet on the stones of the terrace. She had been there since the count's arrival; and now that the ornamental plants had all been given due attention, she felt free to leave. Wearing a pair of man's boots, she had caught up her skirts almost to her knees, leaving a pair of wretched old shanks hideously exposed in the gray morning. But Mme Juvet was not a pretentious person; she dealt in small exotic plants, and that, rather than putting on airs, was her business at Bréda. She was not afraid of work either, for she was by no means one who could enjoy the luxury of a slave. She and Céleste had their own living to make, now as when her unfortunate son was living, and they were accustomed to making it with their own hands.

She had not asked her old friend Bayou de Libertas to furnish her with help for setting out the new plants he had ordered for the beds bordering the terrace. She and Céleste had done the job alone, though it kept them till after dark and prevented their returning home the night before; but now that she had given the plants a final watering, she did not mind stamping a little wholesome mud on the stones of the terrace or the boards of the veranda. In Mme Juvet's opinion the place was too gaudy anyway. Why, who ever heard of alternating dark and light stones in such a way as to make a terrace resemble a chess board under foot? It could well stand the mud from her boots; if not, there were slaves enough at Bréda to lick the stones clean, if need be. One small item she would spare those vivid stones, however, just for good old Bayou's sake. She went to the banister, leaned over fastidiously and sent a robust spout of tobacco juice into the hedge beyond. It was the only thing to do under the circumstances. She simply couldn't bring herself to spit on the immaculate stones at this hour of the morning.

She tightened the strings of her bonnet, retrieved an old corkscrew walking stick she had left in a clump of young shrubs, started around to the rear doors of the great house. Barefoot blacks, male and female, were shuffling back and forth under the covered passageway that led to the outdoor kitchen. Stopping abruptly to avoid a collision with the young wench who carried the chamber pot, old Mme Juvet found herself in the direct path of a calf-eyed boy loaded to his chin with soiled bed linen.

"Hell and tarnation," she muttered. "Let me get away from this place before I have to crown one of these pot-bellied black sons for stepping on me."

The old woman was waiting for Céleste, standing in a shaft of bright morning sunshine inside the back door, when she saw the tiny de Sacy and Bayou de Libertas regarding her from the large rooms beyond, laughing behind their hands. They had scarcely turned their backs when the bright-haired Céleste came downstairs, and advanced to the spot where her grandmother stood. Smooth and shiny despite drab clothes, the girl seemed remarkably fresh beside the untidy old person whose side she approached. Her arms were round, the curves of her bosom trim.

"Grandma Jacques!" she said, outraged.

"Stare at me if it does you good—what ails you now?"

"Look at yourself—you're a fright. Your skirt pinned up past your knees."

The woman lowered her eyes, examining her feet and legs. A moment later she exploded with laughter, a high-pitched cackle that echoed through the paneled and mirrored rooms beyond.

"I saw those two old dogs wagging their tails and grinning." Again she paused to laugh. "Laughing at me, were they? Well, they've seen worse legs, I'm sure."

She turned, allowing Céleste to unfasten the pin.

"If *you* don't mind it, I do. Let's hurry, please."

"Where you got that stupid shamefaced way of yours is more than I can understand. It didn't come from any of your kin that I ever knew. I'm not a heifer, you know."

"Never mind, grandma. I understand."

"Well, I'll explain anyway. I'm an old cow—and a dry one, too. Now if it had been you they were ogling—"

Céleste's color came swiftly.

"Please," she said.

"You don't like to hear that, hunh?" She pinched the girl's cheek with a hand that felt like a turkey's foot. "Ah, somebody besides your grandmother has been pinching those peaches, if I guess right."

"Grandma Jacques!"

"All right, I'm coming."

In former days Mme Juvet had lived from hand to mouth on her small plot of land. That was before the idea of cultivating ornamental plants, exotic ferns and flowers had occurred to the old woman and her afflicted second-son. Céleste pictured her grandmother in those times as a linty creature with a cow. Her uncle, now dead, she remembered as a blind man with narrow shoulders, a rude stick and a bad temper. Happier living conditions had changed both of these unpleasant characters remarkably. The wretched grandmother had discontinued her habit of bringing smoked meats or young fowls or garden greens home under her apron. During his last years the uncle learned to dig in the earth, and his temper mollified. Both of them began to have a care for the child Céleste.

Céleste's own parents, long sundered, had been less fortunate. Both of these had fallen in the wake of tragic and cyclonic passions—passions of a type long associated with Europeans living in the tropics. Which is not precisely equivalent to saying that both were dead. Hugo Juvet still lived, so to speak, but the havoc within him had been so great he seemed another person. And while he now preferred cities like Dondon, Gonaïves and Port-au-Prince to Le Cap and the company of strangers to the friendship of old acquaintances, he had not abandoned his native city completely. Twice a year, sometimes perhaps as often as once in three months, he would return to the old haunts. Unless it slipped his mind, he would visit his mother and daughter on these occasions. But he was unwilling to face the city of his youth without first drinking excessively, and consequently his memory was never good while he was there. Hugo Juvet, a wreck ready to be grounded, had found such comfort as men may gain in the fellowship of other wrecks in the same condition.

The feeling Céleste had for the man was hard to describe. Neither she nor her grandmother liked to discuss him. In this, if in few other matters, they were in perfect agreement. Some things the older woman had been constrained to tell, however. She was responsible for the girl's knowledge that once, quite briefly to be sure, Hugo had been loved by two beautiful women, both far above him in family and rank. And having told that much, she had been virtually forced to add a few details. For example, the first woman, to whom he was married, had been older than himself, frail, soft-voiced and quietly resentful. The second had been a girl in her teens, a tempestuous girl with raven hair. After the inevitable clash Hugo had found himself guarding an empty cage from which both his birds had escaped. He was alone, broken and old. His resentful wife commenced to move in a set of profligate aristocrats, thereby launching a career that led to a scandalous death by poisoning. Her rival, the disturbing dark-haired girl, became the wife of young Sylvestre Viard, but not before she had first been the mistress of a high commissioner celebrated for his hatred of Jacobins.

But the coarse old woman, whose arm Céleste held affectionately as they walked, denied responsibility for the report that in his present daze Hugo Juvet enjoyed hiding behind a door, in an alleyway, in a rose hedge, beyond a stone fence—anywhere he might, without being observed, catch a glimpse of the young woman's carriage as it passed in the road. Whether or not he was still fascinated by Paulette she could not say. Moreover, it sounded insane to link those two names now. There was too much distance between them. Paulette's experiences, whatever they had been, had lifted her, it seemed, by the same means that such experiences had torn down and destroyed others. Love affairs, scandals, suspicions in connection with the tragedies that had befallen her former rival as well as her well-to-do young husband—these things somehow failed to crush Paulette. She was too young, too gay, too high-spirited. Perhaps, too, she was made of a different fiber. But it no longer mattered to Mme Juvet.

The two reached the road and paused while the grandmother filled her lip with snuff. Presently and without warning, Mme Juvet weakened in the warm sunlight, tottered dizzily.

"Tired?" Céleste asked, taking her arm more firmly.

The old woman shook her head.

"Sick," she said. "Funny how it came so sudden. I'll be right in a minute."

A moment later, Céleste still lending support, they began walking again.

5. Five of the blacks came to the counting house as directed. Led by the barking, consumptive Mars, they filed into the little chapel-like building facing the main driveway behind the great house. Their spent, hangdog faces did not alter, even when they flopped on the stools and benches in the back room. Mars, looking clean and fastidious beside the grimy field slaves who accompanied him, turned his over-bright eyes from one to another of his companions. Two of the fellows were giants for size; it was hard to imagine their being ill, burning with fever. One was a woman, coarse-featured and hard-eyed. Her naked breasts, hanging against her belly, were wrinkled

and drawn like the udders of a beast. The last was a child, a frail, sad-faced boy of about twelve. For some reason he looked curiously like a girl. It may have been the result of sickness; he had been crying. All five of them jerked their heads up abruptly when they heard footsteps in the adjoining room.

The count, following the overseer, groaned aloud as he entered the small dark compartment.

"God, what a stench!"

"Except Mars there, the rest are all field workers," M. de Libertas explained.

A third man, standing somewhat behind the others, burst into a wretched old bird-like cackle. Captain Frounier, having joined the other two at breakfast, took the count's squeamishness about body odors for a laughing matter.

"Bless me," he said, still laughing, "you should bring a cargo of them across the middle passage in one of my vessels—just *one* cargo. That would fix that parlor smeller of yours, Count. They say that one reason why God Almighty is against us slavers is because he can't stomach the reek of our ships when they get about sixty days out in mid-summer. You know they're pretty crowded down in those holds sometimes, and of course we don't provide chamber pots." He laughed again, quite alone in his merriment. "God's pains, my lord, these niggers of yours don't smell so bad. They're downright fragrant beside some I've handled."

"We may lose this batch if we aren't careful," the overseer remarked quietly. He turned to Mars. "I suppose the other three were too far gone to make it up here?"

Mars nodded.

"Out of their heads," he added after a pause.

"What have you been doing for them?" de Sacy asked M. de Libertas.

"Toussaint's been looking after them," the overseer answered. "When it comes to roots and medicines and that sort of thing, we haven't got anybody better than Toussaint."

"The coachman?"

"H'm. You'd think he was a doctor from Paris the way they send for him on the other plantations around here and in Cap Français."

"He scares them," the count smiled, snapping his snuff box. "He's so old and dried up, they probably take him for some kind of devil man."

M. de Libertas gave his visitor a queer little stare. Most of the other's observation he was willing to pass over with a shrug, but he was definitely not in agreement.

"He isn't as old as he looks, my lord," he said. "Not more than fifty, perhaps. He takes things seriously, and he really knows his herbs. I've taken his medicine myself."

"These were too much for him, though?"

"I'm afraid he hasn't done these much good," M. de Libertas admitted.

Captain Frounier caught himself tottering and steadied his old legs by leaning against the door frame.

"That's because there's no help for them, if you ask me," he said. "It may just be pining that's killing them.

When a slave starts to pine away, there's no cure for him in this world or the next."

"Oh, I can cure pining, if that's what it is," the count laughed. He drew an embroidered handkerchief from his pocket, blew his nose ceremoniously. A mischievous twinkle came to his eye. His face had been freshly shaved and powdered; his skin was fine, unblemished. Only on his neck was there a suggestion of age and wrinkles. M. Bayou de Libertas had a fleeting impression of a marble face on a tiny, decaying body. At the moment, however, the nose was brilliantly red as a result of the blowing it had received. "Bring them out into the light where I may have a better look."

"Yes, monsieur."

M. de Libertas looked at Mars sympathetically. The lean, trim black turned his eyes without speaking, rose and walked slowly through the counting room and out onto the veranda. He was followed directly by the four other slaves. A moment later the three Frenchmen walked into the sunshine that filled the entrance to the small building.

"I prescribe an emetic," the Count de Sacy said, twinkling, as he looked Captain Frounier in the eye.

Again the tottering old captain chirped with merriment.

The slaves, wan and baffled, looked at one another anxiously.

"It may not be just pining," M. de Libertas suggested. "The fainting, the vomiting and the fever, you know—it might actually be something they've caught."

"Nobody pines at Bréda," Mars ventured recklessly.
"We get good treatment here all the time."

The men ignored him.

"A good strong emetic won't hurt anyhow," the count
said, answering his cousin's overseer. "Discontent, unrest, longing for home—among slaves these constitute a
disease, a very contagious disease."

"M. de Libertas has come off as well, if not better than
anybody in this half of the island when it comes to keeping the blacks healthy. They like him, too—damned if
they don't."

"What do you think of my prescription, Captain?"

"Oh, a good emetic is always good," the old man
laughed. "You can't be too careful."

Suddenly the count's literal intention dawned on
M. de Libertas.

"Not Mars," he protested earnestly. "Don't try it on
Mars, please. Mars is in decline already; he's consumptive.
It won't do him any good—it can't."

The other two laughed, as Bayou de Libertas thought,
a trifle drunkenly.

"It won't hurt him too much," the count insisted, slapping the overseer's shoulder. "I'll lighten up on him for
your sake, M. de Libertas. I'll make him be last. Stand up
here facing the sun, all of you."

The blacks took their positions obediently, hands
clasped behind their backs, eyes blinking in the fierce
light of the early morning sun.

"The wench there, that female," Captain Frounier said
to M. de Libertas as the count arranged the slaves, set-

ting each head at the proper angle. "That big wench—
is she played out yet?"

"I'm not sure."

"Ought to be breeding, if she's not. Look at the muscles
on those arms. Maybe she fights the studs."

M. de Libertas shook his head.

"Not likely," he said.

"You can't tell," the captain insisted. "You come across
all kinds."

The count seemed to be satisfied with his preparations.
The five sick-dog slaves held their heads back with grim
effort, their locked hands twitching nervously behind
their backs, their foreheads wrinkled with pain and puzzlement.

"Now," de Sacy directed, "open your mouths wide."

One by one, more confounded than ever, they let their
lower jaws drop. The two huge fellows stood first in the
line. After them stood the woman, then the child and
finally Mars. The count turned to Captain Frounier with
a wink. A moment later he stepped in front of the first
big black, rose high on his toes, peering deep into the
sick slave's mouth, then with studied aim and unruffled
deliberation, the diminutive nobleman puckered his own
lips and spat heavily into the wretch's mouth.

The stocky black wrenched his face into a mask of
horror. His eyes closed, he made at first as if to scream,
but the cry did not come forth, only contortions of unspeakable indignity and revulsion. The child flinched
painfully at the sight. Mars groaned and caught his breath.

"*Mon Dieu!*" M. de Libertas exclaimed in anguish.

Captain Frounier squinted. Either he had missed the sight or, amazed to see the count actually going through with the foul prank, he was unable to believe his eyes. There was still the shadow of a grin on his old countenance, but the mirth was gone. He had surprisingly missed the joke, but his eyes were peeled to see the act repeated.

The overseer turned his back to the scene as the count, one hand pressed against the ruffles of his shirt bosom, the other held apart in a gesture of exquisite scorn, rose on his toes the second time, puckered, spat. The second African behaved a trifle more steadily than did the first, but a gleam of hatred came to his eyes.

"This'll get next to *you*," the count laughed, coming to the woman. "You'll feel new-made. M. de Libertas," he turned to the overseer, "you might bear this in mind. It's a real aphrodisiac to the females. This wench will be throwing her petticoat by night. Mark it."

"Well, it's a new wrinkle, at least."

M. de Libertas was visibly sickened and outraged. He kept his face averted, and there was shame and humiliation on his countenance. He had the sudden and unaccountable feeling that it would be hard to look Mars directly in the eyes again. And Toussaint—God, how could he face Toussaint again after this got around?

The woman stiffened, gulped, showed no more feeling than a beast might have shown. Slowly she raised her shoulders, tossed her head. Her pride was untouched. The child, when his turn came, moved his head, caught some of the spittle on the side of his face and threw himself upon the ground screaming. Presently he was gagging and vomiting, his entrails wrenched within his body. The count ignored him and turned to Mars.

The frail consumptive swayed like a shadow in the sunlight. Just as the count puckered his lips, Mars closed his mouth, set his jaw.

"Open your mouth."

Mars stood as if in a trance; he neither heard nor saw.

"He isn't himself," M. de Libertas protested. "He's been working sick. I can say that for Mars. He isn't really a disobedient slave."

"I'm not in a sweet humor myself," the count said, his lips tightening. "I've missed a share of sleep. Open your mouth."

When Mars refused the second time, the tiny nobleman lost his temper. In the next moment he was stamping and kicking his feet with game-cock fury. Finally a thrust from one of his short legs caught the slave sharply in the groin. The willowy black went to his knees, clasping his groin.

The count, his work finished, led Captain Frounier into the counting room. M. de Libertas remained outside, absently slapping a closed fist into an open palm. A moment later he leaned against the door frame. He was weak with shame and a feeling of depression. Having hesitated to look Mars in the face a moment earlier, he now ached to see what expression the faithful black, his valet, would have on his face when he rose. But Mars limped away without showing his face.

6. When the sun disappeared, the fortress-like hills of the northern department grew massive and dark against the sky. A buccaneer wind arose beyond Le Cap, reeking with the smell of the sea, gave the lacy *tchia-tchia* trees a ruffian swish, turned up the pale green petticoats of the cottonwoods. Life began at nightfall where the Creole élite was concerned, began with the zooming insects, after the burning day and the golden tropical languor. Even Diron, wellborn but admittedly without sympathy for the élite, felt his heart pound as the breeze swept the road on which he was riding.

He was tired, of course; he had been in the woods with his hawk before daybreak; and now that night was practically in sight, he was still on the move. There had been no rest, not by a pretty sight, but the afternoon had been tolerable where he was concerned. M. Pierre Sylvain's printing establishment, where the boy had spent the time reading, had enjoyed a fair current of air. Diron hadn't minded the heat, hadn't even noticed it as long as he read. M. Sylvain's was the most satisfactory collection of books to which Diron had access. If the printer was pleased with an occasional mess of doves—well, Diron was more than delighted with the exchange of courtesies.

The ride from Le Cap out to Diron's home was always interesting. Much of the intervening land was under cultivation, but there were still many places in which the thickets grew boldly down to the roadside. For some reason Diron never found these dull. Sometimes he imagined this fondness to be derived from his father's fanatical love; more often, though, he felt that the country itself was responsible. There was a softness about the tropical verdure that was positively seductive. The waxy green banana leaves, the giant ostrich necks of coconut palms and their top-knot tufts, the absence of brambles and thorny bushes, the fantastic worm-like pods dangling everywhere—of these, without doubt, a spell was blended. Sometimes fearful and repellent, sometimes enticing, the Haitian thicket was never dull.

When finally he turned his little mare off the public carriage road, the horse and rider entered a cocobola grove, emerged a few moments later directly in front of a small house, cloaked to the gables in leafy shadows and built in the usual French colonial style. It sat high above the ground and was approached by swirling stairs banistered with wrought iron as delicate as lace. Like all other houses of its type this one was built of stucco, pastel tinted. A stone's throw away, rising above the red tile roof of the dwelling, a lofty miniature, a pigeon house, could be seen on the top of a pole. A small stable, an out-door kitchen and a cluster of thatched out-buildings huddled in the shadows beyond. The air here was scented with verbena and honeysuckle. A cottonwood bough swept the grass roof of the stable. As Diron approached a door closed audibly; that sound was followed immediately by footsteps near the stable entrance.

Dismounting quickly, Diron led his mare around to

the out-buildings. There a small, white-clad figure stood among the shadows on the drive.

"Tucking my birds in again, Céleste?"

"Sometimes I think you don't care for them," she said, indicating his game cocks, hawks, pigeons and the like. "It's not safe to leave cages open as late as this."

"I'm afraid I become careless, depending on you."

"Of course, I don't deserve thanks. I don't know why I do it."

"But I do thank you. You know I'm grateful. Come, let me stroke your hair."

"Never mind, thanks. I'll run home now; it's dark."

She found the path and started toward some small bright windows beyond a field. But she had gone only a few steps when he called her back.

"Yes?" she said, returning.

She carried a bonnet on her arm. She had worked during the afternoon; her hair was damp where it clung to her face. She had not removed the black, fingerless gloves she used in digging around the small nursery plants.

"You spent the night at Bréda?" She nodded. "There was a coach this morning?"

"The count is there again—Armand de Sacy."

Diron hesitated, reluctant to make an indelicate observation to her. Then—

"Another lady?"

She hadn't aimed to twitter, but there was no denying there was a lady with the count. Having admitted as much, she turned again and ran across the intervening field. Diron unsaddled his mare in the drive, removed the bridle from the animal's head. He stood holding these till the door opened beyond the ridge. Then he went inside and hung the harness against the wall, threw the saddle across its peg.

So the count was at Bréda again. Well, so much the better. He would be sure to see and hear things not aimed to flatter or please a nobleman who was perhaps finding it hard to escape the fire in Paris. Indeed, things had been rapidly going from bad to worse in the colony since the upheaval in France. The fact of the Revolution had never been accepted by the Colonial Assembly or by the Creole aristocracy.

Two years had passed since the rabble of Paris stormed the Bastille. That news had struck the aristocratic government of Saint Domingue, the most wealthy and profitable overseas colony of the day, like a thunder stone. A period of hushed amazement had followed, then suddenly excitement broke. Enthusiasm became frenzy. Every class translated the fall of the Bastille into an opportunity for itself. The planters took it to mean that the independence of the colony would follow, with their own stars ascending. Low-class whites, *petits blancs,* saw in the incident an example of what they might accomplish against the autocratic rulers of Saint Domingue. While the free mulattos, an equally numerous class, offspring of *grands blancs* masters and their savage mistresses, watched eagerly for an opportunity to gain the political rights that had been denied them. Tricolor cockades blossomed overnight. Everyone was pleased with the prospect until—until the truth was learned. None of the results they had so sanguinely imagined were in prospect. In fact, it was scarcely clear yet, in the summer of 'ninety-one, just what would happen. That was the reason, as Diron puzzled the thing through, that the colonists were all bumping about like men in a daze.

Meanwhile, there was no doubt that local conditions, public and private relations, had become worse in the wake of the trouble in Paris. The three classes were more bitter than ever in their mutual hostility. The *petits blancs,* thirty thousand in number, composed largely of the wastrels, the unwanted, the outcasts of France, filled the streets of Le Cap, crowded the waterfronts, lolled in the taverns and brothels, brooded, waited. The medieval luxury and power of the ruling planters was their bitter cup. The callous indifference of these landed gentlemen to the want and cruelty suffered by the rabble of the streets galled the others beyond words. They became no more cheerful when they considered the mulattos. Many of these had inherited vast wealth from the profligate noblemen who sired them. In fact, about one-tenth of the plantations were in the hands of these mulattos. They owned slaves. Their children were educated in France. A year earlier, when they had offered a petition to the National Assembly in Paris, they had been able to accompany their request with a token of $1,200,000. They were well-to-do as compared with the *petits blancs.* Thus the three groups sat apart, mused, meditated, munched. And hatred was their bread.

Diron was not sure just where his allegiance belonged, and he cared much less. For how unimportant was the quarrel between ten thousand aristocrats, thirty thousand low-class whites, and forty thousand mulattos in Saint Domingue when there were five hundred thousand— half a million—slaves on the island still in the chains of unspeakable bondage! Nature was being thwarted and opposed by perverse and corrupt man. The whole creation cried against the infamy of man's vile institutions. All the woes of the human family were easily traceable to the same point: denial of the natural, elemental rights of man.

There were others who shared these views with Diron —others right there in the northern department. M. Pierre Sylvain, for example. Brieux, Gratien, Augière. Probably, too, M. Bayou de Libertas, though his employment as overseer at Bréda created certain difficulties. A number of others, too. Diron could not afford to talk wildly, considering the delicate conditions in the island. Yet there was work to be done, and he was here to do it. He would not be silenced utterly. The dozen or two actual members of the society now residing in Saint Domingue could not safely disclose their connections yet, but they were not asleep. They were the mustard seed.

Drums had commenced to rumble dimly among the hills, a dark legendary throb against a wall of night. One gust of wind brought them as near as the carriage road beyond the little grove of hardwood trees. The next carried the sounds as far away as Africa. Yes, admittedly, one could steal the black man from the jungle, but one couldn't steal the jungle from the black man. It was a popular bromide, but true. Those voodoo drums awakened as regularly as the moon rose. Somehow they never became commonplace. Even when one had heard them every night for most of a lifetime, as Diron had, there was always that strangeness, that suggestion of ghostliness, weird masks in the haunted darkness, witchery. He fastened the stable door, went around to the front entrance of the house.

M. Philippe Desautels had come out on the steps when he heard the drums.

"The blacks get together oftener than they used to," the older man said, indicating the direction of the throbs.

"Maybe we pay more attention to them since we moved out of town," Diron suggested.

"I presume they can afford to kick up their heels. They have so much less to worry about than the rest of us."

Diron reached the door and paused.

"Did you get some sleep this afternoon?" he asked his uncle.

"I certainly did. And I'm not rested yet."

"Oh, you just like to pretend you're feeble," Diron laughed. "We didn't walk enough to tire you that much."

"We didn't? Well, it's pleasant of you to remind me of it, but I think I'm a better authority on that than you."

"I haven't felt sleepy at all, nor hungry either. And I haven't eaten since morning."

"Unfortunately I'm unable to live on discontent, as you do. I must have some rest occasionally. Even food is hard for me to dispense with. And philosophical books intended to make people unhappy about the present state of affairs do not make me forget these needs."

"Don't worry," the boy assured him. "I'm probably hungrier than you at this very moment. Any news to-day?"

"A note on your writing table."

"Important?"

The uncle shrugged.

"I take it to be social."

Diron showed disappointment.

"Oh."

M. Desautels followed his nephew into the living room, stood apart as Diron tore the note open and read its contents by the light of a candle.

"One of these days," the older man observed without ill-humor, "one of these fine days, young man, there will be a summons for you if you continue your meddling with colonial affairs."

"A summons," the boy laughed. "Yes, that's just what this one amounts to."

"I happen to know better this time."

"A summons to dine and dance. Mme Bayou de Libertas. I'm afraid I'll have to disappoint her."

Diron handed the letter to his uncle who also read it deliberately.

"Well, I can't see your objection."

"My disapproval of the people who'll be there is so complete—" Diron began.

"But you'll only be young once," M. Desautels protested.

"There's also the problem of a lady."

"Why, take whom you like."

"That would be impossible. I'd be expected to bring Mme Sylvestre Viard."

"I'm afraid I can't help you a great deal there. But I'd still say bring whom you please. This isn't Paris. Besides, there has been a revolution. There are never enough ladies at these things. Almost anyone you fancy, if her clothes are correct, will be quite welcome."

Diron was not convinced, but he finally confessed that, things being as they were, he hadn't the will to stay away.

"There'll be cock fights," he added. "That's some compensation."

"Besides, you and Paulette will make a good pair for the occasion. Her hair is as black as yours."

"*Oncle* Philippe—please."

"They tell me you dance a shade too well, Diron."

"That's a libel," the boy smiled. After a pause he added quite seriously, "There'll be a time to dance when there's freedom in Saint Domingue, *Oncle* Philippe."

CHAPTER TWO

I. Her top sails down as if from faint and exhaustion, her stench rising to high heaven, the *Hottentot* rocked at anchor in the harbor of Le Cap. Owned by Captain Frounier, though no longer sailing under his personal command, the vessel had weighed anchor in the early afternoon to await further orders with regard to her cargo of slaves from the Gold Coast.

At her side a tiny hand-propelled craft from the shore waited, three naked boatmen holding the oars rigidly like black metal figures. On the deck Captain Frounier and his two companions prepared to descend the ladder.

"What's a good way to deal with bad slaves, Count?"

"Burn a little powder in their hindquarters."

"Blow them up?"

"Make examples of them."

The old man cackled.

"Want to take another look at those females before we leave?"

Count Armand de Sacy paused, giving M. Bayou de Libertas an inquiring glance. The other shook his head slowly. The overseer's round-eyed, lashless blink suggested a rabbit.

"No? I thought as much," the count said, facing Captain Frounier. "I've had about as much as my belly will stand. I'm not squeamish. I like a stable and that sort of thing. But, *mon Dieu,* don't open those hatches again till I get ashore."

The ninety-year-old commander cackled loudly.

"Now you get an idea of a first-class stench, monsieur."

"I could have done without it."

"But the cargo—you'll agree it's a fine load of black flesh."

M. de Libertas, taking the remark to himself, immediately showed reserve.

"If packing them in there spoon-fashion hasn't hurt them," he suggested, "they ought to be all right. I should think, though, they'd be worth more if your officers didn't pack them so tight for the crossing."

"Crowding weakens them," the captain admitted. "You lose more, too, if you try to overload. But you wouldn't call this a tight cargo, surely. Some traders bring them two deep."

The overseer hiccoughed, turned his face toward the sea.

"Of course, it's not my business."

"It's cheating in a way," Captain Frounier hastened to confess. "But lots of slavers are not above it."

"Messieurs," the count said, looking sick again, as if a pale green shadow passed over his face, "messieurs, let's go ashore. I shall vomit if we don't."

A sailor wearing earrings and a curled mustache led a string of tall, emaciated black boys around the deck. The legs of the latter reminded M. de Libertas of sugar-cane stalks. The average age appeared to be about fifteen, but not one of the slaves was less than six feet tall. They were chained together. This was the customary afternoon period of exercise on deck.

"Well, this means that the hold is open," the captain said. "There will be another whiff coming this way if the wind turns. This might really be the time to leave, Count."

M. de Libertas was first down the ladder. He was followed by the count. Then came Captain Frounier, as doughty as a cockroach, despite his years. The boatmen wriggled their little craft away from the large vessel, pointed it toward the shore. Presently the sun dropped out of sight.

Mountains rose about the harbor in the gathering dusk like purple battlements. They seemed to come down to the water's edge. That, of course, was a sun-down illusion. There was some distance between the long white beach and the encircling range. Within this space the city of Le Cap was built. From mid-harbor its unbroken stretch of colonial roofs appeared to curl around the sea-line like a twisted serpent.

The bay itself was a solid, deep-toned jewel, except at the edge where the surf broke mysteriously and without evident reason, sending a wash of white suds up the beach. Through this surf the small boat skimmed finally, and the boatmen drew the tiny craft ashore. Ashore, the count stretched his legs, adjusted his wig, took two hearty sniffs from his snuff box. He was wearing a buff coat with a wide skirt and breeches of the same material. A gay, quilted waistcoat stood out vividly against these sedate garments. The tiny man's fingers were as heavily ringed as a pirate captain's.

"M. de Libertas," he said when the other two had joined him on the beach, "name your favorite tavern."

The overseer awakened from his reverie, blinking as usual and scratching his chin.

"Monsieur," he said. "Le Cap is a jungle of taverns. There is one for every palm tree."

Captain Frounier laughed, tottering as unsteadily as if he had already had his stimulant.

"But not one too many, Count," he protested. "There's not an empty one in the lot."

"Which do you suggest?"

"That depends on what you like."

"I like a gay place." The little man chuckled deeply. "But, of course, good food and proper drinks are not to be scorned."

They crossed the sandy beach. Toussaint was waiting beside the scarlet, gold-trimmed coach. He swung the door open as the men approached, revealing upholstery of pumpkin-colored beige.

"The *Hôtel de la Couronne*," M. de Libertas told him.

Inside the coach Captain Frounier put his chin on his bosom and dropped off immediately into a little cat nap. Doubting his sleep, perhaps, the other men said nothing more about the business in hand till they reached the tavern.

Even at their table the three mused quietly over their drinks. They had little in common, beyond the purchase of some new slaves. The night had not yet begun at the public house. In a distant corner one table was on top of another, legs up, and a servant was finishing the mopping. The empty spaces of the room gave a certain sadness, but the place was not really deserted. A small group of government officials had preceded the count's company into the tavern and occupied the six seats of a near-by table. Among them M. de Libertas recognized the military commandant of the garrison, a second gentleman who held the position of intendant of the island under the governor general, a third who served as aide of the navy commissioner and at least one president of a provincial council, all of them members of the Colonial Assembly at Cap Français. Meeting the eye of the commandant, M. de Libertas nodded vaguely.

A bevy of young entertainers, rose-tinted mulatto girls, came through a rear door, took seats provided for them along the edge of a dancing platform. They had lovely tired eyes and a grace that suggested languishing flowers.

The Count de Sacy brightened instantly. His eyes peeled, he began to scratch and twitch in his chair.

"Ah!" he exclaimed. *"Chocolat au lait."*

M. de Libertas nodded.

Captain Frounier chirped happily, now wide awake again.

"Some of these may be mine, for all I know," he boasted. "We tried to get all the wenches in the family

way when we were bringing them across. The females
bring more in the open market when they're that way,
you know."

M. de Libertas promptly excused himself, went outside for a breath of air.

Tables had been drawn out there, following a custom
imported from Europe and particularly suited to warm
tropical afternoons and mauve tropical evenings. Above
the door of another tavern across the way a tiny balcony
protruded. It had a wrought iron fence; and a waiter,
his towel still on his forearm, was leaning over the little banister, gaunt wrists and hands stretching far out
of his coat sleeves, lighting a row of fairy lamps in the
dusk.

M. de Libertas knew as well as anyone that politically
Saint Domingue was in a sad state. Personal virtues,
humanitarian sentiments, local patriotism—all were in a
regrettable plight. The streets of Le Cap were alive with
sinister men, outcasts, adventurers and downright crim-
inals. They infested the alleys and back streets, creeping
along the walls like vermin, darting into dark holes, ef-
facing themselves against shadows. The trouble with the
ruling class, the Creoles born in the island, was that they
simply didn't care what happened to Saint Domingue
so long as they made enough money to return to Paris
in splendor and live out their days in that city. And the
horror of the situation was that most of them seemed in
a fair way to achieve their wish. The income of the
island was by far the largest of any colony in the world.
Only God or the devil could change its destiny now and

save the delightful place for those who loved it for its own sake. Men like M. de Libertas had little indeed to anticipate in the island to which they were genuinely attached.

At bottom, perhaps, selfishness, meanness and personal vice explained everything. The *élite,* entrenched behind a slave population that outnumbered all whites and mulattos by nearly ten to one, had resisted the Revolution when news of the event reached Cap Français a couple of years earlier. Furthermore, by playing the *petits blancs* against the free men of color, they had easily kept themselves in the ascendency. Such monstrous and cruel outbreaks as the affair of the Dondon road had hurt them, in their own opinion, scarcely at all.

Vincent Ogé, a young Paris-educated mulatto, son of a noble father and his coffee-brown mistress, had returned to his home, inspired by his friends among *Les Amis des Noirs,* to attempt to secure for his group the political rights granted them recently by the General Assembly but nullified by the local authorities. With his friend J. B. Chavannes and a large number of mulattos he had attempted to win by force their legal rights. When the encounter with a detachment of soldiers was lost, the two leaders had fled across the border to Spanish Santo Domingo. Returned to the authorities at Le Cap, both the young men were broken on the wheel in the public square before a large part of the townsfolk. The incident was closed, but the tension remained. The muddle grew more involved. Yet nothing seemed to ruffle the *élite.*

The Count Armand de Sacy and his noticeably soiled companion broke into M. de Libertas's meditation. Night had completely enveloped Le Cap, an indigo sky bearing down upon the city with here and there small round holes hollowed out of the darkness by flickering orange lights. On their own coach Toussaint had lit a carriage lamp. The horses stood in an accumulation of dung on the cobblestones.

"Did you finish your drinks?" M. de Libertas asked perfunctorily.

"We're quite prime, thanks," the count replied.

"I got more of that last one on these blasted ruffles than I got in my belly," Captain Frounier observed, mopping his shirt-front with a wet hand. "That idiot filled my tumbler too full."

They were snugly tucked in when Toussaint climbed to his seat. The immaculate tock-tock of well-shod hooves on the fine road was reassuring. A sense of luxury, if not of well-being, pervaded the coach. M. de Libertas decided to put by his dark thoughts. The drive was too pleasant for sad reflections.

"Gentlemen, I like this air," he said seriously.

"That's what I guessed when you left us," the count said.

The captain's eyes were foggy, his lips hung apart.

"Air?" he inquired sloppily. "You really like air?"

"It makes me feel fine."

"Properly aged rum will do as much, perhaps more." The old commander's tongue grew thicker and thicker.

M. de Libertas could understand how it was that the old fellow had got more of his last drink on his shirtfront than in his belly. He had exceeded capacity and perhaps sloshed some over. There would be no trouble getting him home, however. Though his place was a full two miles beyond Bréda by the carriage road, he could safely be dispatched in Toussaint's care. To simplify matters even further sleep was visibly weighing down on the old man's lids. If he dropped off now, he'd never know when the other two left him.

They followed a twisting road, up a considerable hill, down a lesser one, and discovered presently that the city had vanished. The road became a gravel way crossed frequently by cart paths. Tall and odorous thickets came down to the road's edge from the hillsides. Toussaint allowed the horses to walk.

Suddenly whistling sounds awakened in a mango grove. The coachman reined his horses a bit tighter, himself intent on the curious sounds. It might have been a flight of strange night birds, but this seemed less likely to M. de Libertas after he had listened a few seconds. There were birds that whistled among the mangoes at night— well, perhaps there were—but certainly they did not fly with a sound of galloping feet, thrashing the leaves as they went. The fact was that the whistling was farther away than at first it had seemed. It circled through the vast grove like a chorus of merry witches, and M. de Libertas for his own part was convinced that the flock was mounted, whatever its description.

Toussaint brought the horses to a full stop.

"What do you make of it?" The overseer leaned out from the door as he spoke.

The coachman bent low and blew the carriage lamp.

"Bandits, monsieur," Toussaint answered calmly.

"Did we have to take a risk, M. de Libertas?" the count asked angrily, clearly imputing blame to his cousin's overseer.

"There have always been bands of runaways, Count de Sacy. With wooded hills so near, there have always been some slaves who couldn't resist the temptation."

The clatter of galloping hooves was unmistakable now. A horde seemed to approach the road head-on. The whistling grew louder and louder. Certainly there was something eery about the wild birdlike music. The thought of tight-lipped savages clinging to the mane of their unsaddled beasts, riding hard, whistling because they could not conceive of silence under such circumstances, because they were at the same time far too prudent to raise their voices, was not easily shut out of the mind.

"I'd say this was more recklessness than anything else on our part," the count repeated, visibly disturbed.

"None of us knows what to expect, monsieur. None of us, ever," M. de Libertas answered wearily. "This sort of thing has increased since the affair on the Dondon road. Violence and the threat of violence are both common. We do not postpone our errands or go into hiding just because trouble is lurking for us."

The count leveled his eyes angrily. Captain Frounier was happily oblivious.

"Lax government explains a great deal," the little man said, setting his jaw ominously.

"Yes, no doubt." M. de Libertas's voice had shriveled to a whisper. "But blind and greedy owners are not to be excused either."

Meanwhile, Toussaint had quietly pulled his horses into a roadside clump. He may have caught the recriminations passing, scarcely veiled, between the men inside the coach. Choking back their fears now, both of these became silent. A moment later, following a vague cart path, their horses leaping a rail fence at the road's edge, the band swept across the road a few lengths ahead of the coach, plunged into the darkness and shadow of another grove to the left.

"They didn't see us," the coachman whispered.

"Then for heaven's sake," the count cried, "get us back to Le Cap."

M. de Libertas knew that the danger was past but he did not feel disposed to differ further with the count. He had nothing to urge anyway.

2. Coming out of a thicket, the dark riders rushed down a slope, plowed through a field of sugar cane. After the leafy grove and the shadows of the thickets, the stars seemed like lamps in the Caribbean sky. Many of their horses, it developed, were not horses at all, but mules.

Some of the black savages were neither savage nor black. A few moments later all of them came panting into a pocket created by folded hills.

A rumble of voodoo drums filled the shaded retreat. No attempt was made to muffle the sound. No one tried to trace drums in Saint Domingue. In fact, if one had secret reasons for gathering a number of blacks together in the mountains at night, there was no safer way to divert attention than by beating voodoo drums.

A haunted light flickered strangely on the clearing where nearly a dozen drummers were pounding their hollow-bellied instruments in a frenzy. Some squatted with tiny drums between their naked knees. Some stood on tip-toe, beating giant affairs almost as tall as themselves. Others adjusted themselves to every size of instrument between. Their faces were painfully distorted.

Into the throbbing blue light a troop of naked dancers shuffled. They were masked and painted. One carried game cocks under each arm. Another had a hen for a headdress—a live hen that nested placidly on the dancer's round skull.

One by one the slower riders of the band broke through the bush, leaped from their mounts and joined the circle around the dancers. A wastrel gendarme deserter, wearing the scarlet breeches of his regiment with a makeshift jacket, came down to the front. The former member of a privateer's crew stood beside him, a toothless wreck with huge earrings, a turban and a tight sash into which he had slipped his knife and pistol. Several other leather-brown Latin faces dotted the predominantly black circle when it was complete, most of them the faces of desperate men abnormally hardened. But one that was neither desperate nor hard came down to the center of the circle after the dance ended.

Diron Desautels, still breathing hard as a result of his strenuous ride, paused before speaking.

"I want to say this," he told them simply. "It's been a great thrill—different from anything else I can imagine— but I won't be riding with you again. After all, the aim is not sport. We wish to see slavery abolished. That is our will, and I believe our will is stronger than the will of those who wish to retain the practice. We shall triumph. Our enemies have divided minds. Every man who denies the Revolution, who denies to the humblest subject of the empire the blessings of *liberté, égalité et fraternité,* wars against his own better nature.

"I have told you about *Les Amis des Noirs.* There are thousands in Paris who abhor slavery. We have pledged ourselves to see it abolished. But we are not getting on fast in Saint Domingue. There are too many other class controversies. Things are so muddled in the government that there is no chance of introducing another problem in any place where it will do good. I, personally, intend to try other means. Meanwhile, I scarcely need to repeat that if ever you blacks feel strong enough to help yourselves, you will have the active sympathy of many *blancs,* including myself."

A menacing black called Boukman, as squat as the stump of a tree and as motionless, narrowed his tiny eyes, frowned.

"You helped, monsieur. I don't think you will betray us now," he said bluntly.

"There are reasons why I shouldn't ride with you."

"Yes," Boukman grunted. "I know. We're stupid. Slavery has made us stupid—like oxen."

"Slavery is vile. It insults the Creator as well as the Creation."

"Two of us will go with you as far as the hill that overlooks Le Cap."

On the road, half a mile from the hilltop, Diron whispered to his companions:

"I'm still for you—I hope you understand. But it doesn't do any good for me to stay. Some of your men—they seem afraid of me. It's all right, of course. I understand. God knows they have reason to distrust white faces."

"Yes," Boukman said, his voice gruff as usual. "That's it. Stupid. Some of us don't know one from another."

"You might as well go back now."

Without answering, the two blacks turned their mules and plunged into the wild hedges.

Diron began to think that Boukman was about the ugliest, the bluntest, the most unpleasant creature he had ever seen. The fellow seemed, furthermore, to impart a measure of his sour unpleasantness to his companions. There was no sweet disposition among them—nobody like Toussaint the coachman, for example. No smile to compare with the lovely smile of Choucoune, the little mulatto modiste who occasionally sewed at Bréda. All told, Boukman's was a fairly repulsive bunch. Diron could, with a little effort, dislike them strongly. But he could not forget that the rabble who stormed the Bastille were mostly a tough and sinister lot. It took their kind to do the dirty jobs. Boukman had called the slaves stupid.

Yes, slavery was to blame. It was responsible for such creatures as Boukman and his associates. Liberty, equality and fraternity would make even a cutthroat and a slave beautiful.

From the top of the last hill Diron looked down upon the lights of Le Cap. The gay Creole night was still young.

A small, strikingly assorted company of guests was enjoying a morning meal in the pale-tinted breakfast room of the *Hôtel de la Couronne* when Diron entered. Sunshine streamed through tall, continental windows. A thin stir of air rippled yellow hangings.

In one corner a near-sighted old scholar squinted at an open book between sips of coffee. At another table a solitary guest lay face downward across the breakfast things, his hair in disorder, saucers scattered, the young man's white satin coat badly mussed. He was ignored by the waiters. Diron recognized him as a minor poet of the aristocracy. Still praised by certain elements of the Latin Quarter, scene of his early excesses, he had come to Saint Domingue during the Revolution, made a successful fight to regain his broken health in that tropical climate and remained to squander the same physical resources in the rum shops and bordellos of the Caribbees. Once he had been considered a political refugee, but now that seemed less credible, and Diron knew privately that the man was a recent convert of *Les Amis des Noirs*. This morning, as usual, having not yet seen his own bed, he had passed out ungracefully across the platters of bacon and preserves, his coffee upsetting.

Diron accepted a chair that faced the open windows, giving his back to these guests, the bookish one as well as the solitary. Two brightly rouged young actresses sat at the table to his left, breakfasting with an officer of the grenadiers. Members of a stock company playing in the Cap Français Théâtre that season, they had already established themselves among the guests of the *Hôtel de la Couronne* and its dapper host, M. Coidevic. Aggressively pretty, they wore dark riding skirts this morning with tiny black hats, and they appeared to Diron to have robust appetites. Twice he saw the ebony waiter refill their cups of coffee, lacing each with a peg of rum.

The small stir of morning air filled the room with a brackish suggestion of the sea. Other guests were chatting in the doorway and the hall outside. Presently Diron received the attention of a waiter, drew his chair into place. Wearing gray stockings, a coat of pale blue, and a white waistcoat, he fancied that perhaps he was not the same person who had been escorted to the edge of the city by a pair of the runaways and brigands with whom he had consorted. He smiled deeply, passed an approving hand over his glossy mane, felt the silver cord that held the hair at the back of his neck. His curls were in order; life was good.

His first intimation that someone was approaching his chair came with a whiff of gay scent. A young woman approached his table. She wore a Creole turban, an India silk bandanna becomingly turned at the corners. Her dress was short waisted and of a thin stuff that revealed a broadly striped muslin petticoat beneath. She was tall, and she had a dark lingering gaze that pleased or annoyed a man depending on his state of mind.

"Early bird," she said lightly.

"Hardly," he answered.

"No, don't stand," she urged. "I'll sit here a minute."

"I'm not early, Paulette. I spent the night in Le Cap."

She laughed softly.

"I guessed as much—darling."

He looked at her strangely.

"Occasionally one has other things in his mind than just women."

"Then you needn't have squirmed."

"Did I?"

"Who is it now, Diron?"

"I'm free," he asserted with some emphasis. "I serve no man—no woman."

He couldn't help feeling a little pleased with a certain unintentional loftiness in his manner.

"Not even lip service?"

"You jest, Paulette," he said embarrassed. "It isn't becoming."

"I'm abandoned," she said, her eyes changing their color swiftly. "Please don't mind. But twice this week you've come to Le Cap. Neither time have you thought of me. Is there someone else now?"

"I'm not in love, Paulette. On my oath."

"Then why?"

"You wouldn't understand."

"Perhaps I would," she insisted. "Why don't you admit you belong to *Les Amis des Noirs?*"

"Why don't *you* confess that you're an informer?"

"But you're joking, Diron. I'm serious."

His expression darkened.

"Sooner or later," he said with almost childish seriousness, "sooner or later we'll have to settle on who's joking."

She laughed it off.

"Do you hate me?"

"These are dreadful times," he said, warming. "Terrific things have happened in France. There is danger in the place where we stand. One must not be unstable or frivolous—not now."

"You give me the shudders. Positively. Isn't love proper in bad times?"

"Necessary—always," he said.

"But you're not getting on with your breakfast. I'll leave you."

"You needn't."

"Yes." She was standing again. "You seem prophetic today. Why don't you come read my palm after you've eaten? Hold my hand and tell me what's going to happen to me in the holocaust."

"I'll come," he said.

She smiled, turning her head sweetly.

Diron knew well that he couldn't quench her gaiety, no matter what disasters he predicted. He wouldn't try again. He stood beside his chair and watched her till she had passed through the door. Then he resumed his meal. A moment later the count entered the breakfast room with M. de Libertas and Captain Frounier. Diron nodded.

A little later, when he was through with his coffee, he passed near their table.

"We are expecting you at Bréda," M. de Libertas smiled.

"Thank you. I intend to come, monsieur."

"Be sure to feed your cocks gunpowder," Captain Frounier remarked.

The count's face was averted, as if he failed to hear the remarks of the other men. It was evident that he had been putting up a certain resistance to Captain Frounier's attempt to place a portion of his new cargo at Bréda. Just as evident, too, was the fact that he had prepared for breakfast without the aid of hairdresser or valet. The count looked—if not definitely frowsy—ten years older than he had appeared the day before. He was not an exceptionally tidy eater, and his mouth was already greased by his bacon. He crunched noisily and now and again opened his mouth while he chewed. There were crumbs on his bosom.

M. de Libertas noticed that the count had not recognized the young man.

"You perhaps do not remember M. Diron Desautels," he said.

De Sacy touched his lips with the serviette, acknowledged Diron's bow with a slight nod.

Almost immediately he seemed again lost in his abstraction, crunching, looking out the window, allowing his lips to part as he chewed.

Diron passed through the hall and out into the yard.
Several stable boys were in the drive, holding two horses
each. One of the dusky youngsters held Diron's mare.
Coaches stood on the opposite side of the way. One of
them was the familiar red and gold affair driven by the
dreamy, sweet-voiced Toussaint. Riding through the
arched entrance, Diron observed that the yardman had
failed to blow the gate lamp. The tiny, faint light reminded him of his own glowing enterprises. Like that
flame they seemed dim and ineffectual at this hour of
the morning. At night—well, things did not seem the
same at night.

3. Meanwhile, the morning hours were busy ones in
the sewing room at Bréda. Apricot-colored Choucoune,
her mouth bristling with pins, knelt on the floor, check-
ing the length of statuesque Mlle Claire's skirt. Two of
her younger sisters were at the cutting table. A third, her
work across her knee, was basting a long pink sash on
a dress of rose organdy. All of them wore zebra-striped
muslin skirts and colorful Creole turbans. Clusters of
lacquered curls hung against their faces.

Choucoune had gained her skill in Paris. She and her
assistants were in demand at scores of great houses in
the parish, but there was none at which they would
rather sew than at Bréda. The sheer amount of work re-

quired here was a delight to Choucoune's business-like modiste's heart—what with Claire, Annette and Angélique, their newly arrived companion, plus Mme Bayou de Libertas, the overseer's wife. Mme de Libertas had mentioned another. Yes, distinctly, there would be five of them to fit this time, she had said.

Claire's thin straw-colored hair was tied in a loose knot. Her lips were pursed about a small black cigar.

"Mon Dieu! I could scream," she said, glancing over her shoulder at the figure in the mirror.

The small, kneeling Choucoune looked up bewildered, almost frightened.

"Is Mademoiselle displeased?"

"Displeased? Look at that hump. I look like a camel. All hump and nothing up here." She patted her flat breast. She had begun chewing on her cigar; Choucoune was obliged to suspend work a moment while Claire went to the spittoon in the corner.

"Oh, don't look at your bosom," the pretty modiste said. "That will come out fine—a row of silk ruffles in the lining of your basque. You will have the proper curves and fullness, mademoiselle."

"Well, I hope so."

"Does the skirt please?"

Craning her neck to see the mirror was a disadvantage to Claire; it caused her to grimace and expose her bad teeth.

"I suppose it's the best you could do with a hump like mine. Black is my color, but pretty chance I have to wear anything black down here in this frying pan."

Choucoune sucked her tongue against her teeth sympathetically.

"Yes, Saint Domingue is too warm for dark clothes," she said.

The dress she was making for Claire was a plaid taffeta. It fairly bubbled with flounces, and it represented a compromise shade between Claire's taste for black and the need for cool, gaily colored clothes.

Satisfied with the fitting, Choucoune summoned one of her sisters to help her slip the unfinished garment over Claire's head. Another of the rosy girls went to notify Mlle Annette that she might come now. In her knee-length slip, Claire slid into a big chair near the window. Standing for Choucoune had wearied her; besides, she had half a cigar to finish before she could even consider getting back into her dress. There were no servants at hand, and Claire was herself too utterly spent with the exertion of a fitting to even raise her own arms.

Annette seemed more muscular than ever when the girls removed her blowsy morning dress preparatory to trying on her new garment. She stepped up on the eight-inch pedestal for the skirt measurement first. After she had been there a few moments, Claire pulled herself out of her chair, allowed one of the young dressmakers to help her into her dress.

"I can't get used to making so much over a chicken fight," Annette said when the other woman was gone.

"Perhaps it's not so much the cock fight as what follows," Choucoune suggested.

Annette had been standing for perhaps quarter of an

hour when she requested a stimulant. A house servant, responding to the bell, brought rum presently. Annette smacked her lips and braced herself as if to endure an hour of pins and chalk.

Her dress was made of lavender barred muslin with huge insets of lace and net about the hem.

"A fitting is purgatory with the sun in those windows," she complained.

"Still the early morning is better than later," Choucoune assured.

"Perhaps so. But what's it all for? A chicken fight. And what follows?"

"No fête is unimportant at Bréda, mademoiselle. The clothes of the ladies make the event, not the entertainment," Choucoune told her.

"This sort of thing only makes me long for Paris."

"I know that feeling. There now—look in the mirror. How do you like yourself?"

Annette went to the glass. For a few minutes she said nothing though she seemed fairly well pleased. Finally, a trickle of sweat running down her neck, she raised her arms and allowed the girls to remove the new dress.

Annette was laced into a punishing corset. There was less than a hand's breadth between it and the tops of her stockings. The staves murmured audibly when she twitched. Ten years younger than the gaunt Claire, Annette was at the same time ten years beyond her own bloom. Her two spots of rouge had been badly smeared by perspiration.

"How do I like myself?" she repeated, pouring more

rum and water into a tumbler on the small round table beside the window. "Well, I have my hopes. You are doing a good job on the dress, but I'll need something different for the morning."

"Oh, indeed," the modiste said with stress. "And a diaphanous dancing dress for the evening, too."

When she left the room a few moments later, Choucoune and her sisters settled down to a period of intensive work. They wore tiny white aprons with sashes encircling their waists, tied into large bows behind. Each wore a silver thimble with a solid gold band. They carried spools in the pockets of their spotless aprons and needles stuck in the bosom of their blouses.

"Is the green sprigged muslin ready?" Choucoune asked, gingerly picking basting threads out of Annette's lavender-barred creation.

The youngest girl indicated that the garment to which the older sister referred was not being worked on because they could go no further until after Mlle Angélique came for her session on the pedestal. Fortunately, and unlike the two women who had preceded her, Mlle Angélique was young and shapely. That look of sour disappointment that came over each of the others as they stood humbled before the mirror need not come to her. It was a pleasure to sew for a young woman like Mlle Angélique.

"You didn't ask either of them whether they wanted vanilla pods sewn into their dresses," one of the sisters reminded Choucoune.

"Mlle Claire left two pink sachet bags. They are under those cuttings on the table," Choucoune said. "That will take care of her dancing dress. In the others, and in Mlle Annette's you'd better sew pods. They'll need all the pleasant scents they can get in this weather."

Angélique came into the room. She seemed tired and bewildered. Her eyes were sad, deeply shadowed. There was a spot of color on each of her cheeks, but it was not a healthy flush. She was sallow. She had, moreover, an odd, courtesan-like diffidence of manner and movement. She had a way of resting one hand on her hip, of swaying more than seemed necessary when she walked.

She looked the room over deliberately, paid brief attention to colorful dresses lying on the table and across the laps of the seamstresses.

"This one is yours, mademoiselle," Choucoune said smiling.

"You have your hands full," Angélique observed. "So many of them to make at one time."

"We love it, though."

"I used to sew," Angélique said remotely. "I liked it—but I wasn't satisfied."

"Ah, that's the trouble. Always thinking about fêtes and balls and carnivals—thinking and wishing."

Angélique stood where the girls could unsnap her hooks and remove her dress. The sprigged muslin had tiny puffed sleeves and a neck low enough for evening wear. It was unusually becoming. Angélique made a circle of her arms, touching them above her head. Her back to the mirror, she glanced over one shoulder and then over the other. She was not deeply interested. The dress would be satisfactory, no doubt, when finished. But even when she turned for a full view of the front, she seemed to care very little.

"I like your sewing," she said after great length. "This is really a lovely dress. If I hadn't already so many more than I can wear, I might be really excited."

Choucoune pouted her little claret mouth professionally. She rounded her large eyes, wrinkled her forehead, showed as much distress as seemed appropriate. Surely Mademoiselle was unhappy. And what a pity, indeed—especially since she looked so well in her clothes. Perhaps the trip was to blame. Often it required weeks to recover from the forty-five-day passage from Paris to Cap Français.

Angélique did not answer. She hadn't heard the little mulattress at all.

"I should be in sackcloth," she said dismally. For an instant she broke strangely, emitting a single, painful sob. "I'm in a trap, Choucoune. You know, don't you? Everyone knows. I've seen the slaves snicker. He means to leave me here. I could die."

Choucoune looked about the room and saw that each of her sisters had turned pale with embarrassment. Pretending not to hear, each was sewing feverishly with averted face.

"Let me get Mademoiselle a drink," the modiste said, darting toward the small round table.

"Thanks." A moment later, her glass half empty, she added, "You girls seem happy."

"Yes, terribly," Choucoune assured her.

"Lovers?"

One of the girls, the youngest, giggled. Choucoune blushed. The other two looked up, their faces pleasant but otherwise expressionless.

"Occasionally we're noticed," one ventured cautiously. "The men of our class, you know."

"That reminds me. There has been a revolution in Paris. Maybe you've heard about 'The Rights of Man,' *Les Amis des Noirs*—things like that?"

"We've heard the words. We often wonder just how they're meant."

"I'm wretched," Angélique said, faltering again. "I'm tired of dancing. Tired of men. I'd like to fight."

When the girls got her into her house dress again, Choucoune led her to the door, visibly pleased to be rid of one who disturbed them.

"A little rest, some spirits—you'll feel better, mademoiselle."

"There's no one else to whom I can talk," Angélique said tragically. "Please don't be impatient with me."

"Oh, we're used to unhappiness."

"What are the names of your sisters, Choucoune?"

"Clothilde, the plump one, is older than me; Marie and Anna, the other two, are younger. And there are more of us at home."

Choucoune said the last words for a smile, but Angélique, beyond the door, was far too miserable to laugh. Twice since she entered the room there had come from the young woman the suggestion of a sob breaking, yet her eyes were hard and dry as she left.

Late in the afternoon Mme Bayou de Libertas came to
try on the rose organdy with the pink sash. About herself she was little concerned. She had never been pretty,
even as a girl; and now with her hair sparse and half
gray, her chins more numerous than she cared to count,
her crumbling teeth a streaky grey, she had no illusions
whatever.

There might have been some question about organdy
for a woman of her age, but that did not trouble Mme
de Libertas. It looked as well on her as anything, and if
people imagined she was trying to appear coquettish at
her age—well, that was their own stupidity, not hers.
Mme de Libertas was unworried. She had a surprise up
her sleeve for the guests whom she had invited to Bréda
—a surprise that would furnish them with something
really worth their chatter.

Her husband would hold forth in the cock pit for the
pleasure and entertainment of the count and the guests,
but the rest of the occasion would be hers, and she felt
that she could manage it well enough.

There were many things in Saint Domingue to distress an honest heart. The government was in a turmoil,
the moral state of affairs was bad, very bad, crime was a
problem; but Mme de Libertas, whose heart was certainly gold itself, had remained unbowed in the face of
these deplorable conditions which she abhorred. She
laughed quickly. She ate well. She fairly quivered when
she was amused. She belched without embarrassment
when she chose. She pampered the slaves shamelessly,
plying them with good left-overs from her table. Years

ago she had had a lover. Now a tight corset was her only vice.

"Don't try to make me too grand," she cautioned Choucoune. Then, pointing to the young Céleste, who had slipped inconspicuously into the big chair near the window, she added, "There's the belle. I want you to out-do yourself on her."

"Ah," Choucoune exclaimed, her eyes brightening.

"Mlle Céleste has never been out before."

"I get more and more frightened as the time nears," Céleste suggested from her chair.

"You'll be more confident when Choucoune finishes with you."

"Perhaps—if the cat doesn't get my tongue."

"Forget it, darling," Mme de Libertas said with feeling. "Cleverness is not necessary. It's against you, if anything. Creole men do not expect a belle to be witty."

Satisfied that Mme de Libertas's rose organdy hung properly, Choucoune asked the girls to remove the garment while she attended Céleste. The young Céleste slipped out of her Creole blouse and high-waisted skirt as nimbly as a child.

"Your turban too," Choucoune advised. "It won't match the dress."

The girl's hair fell down her back when she removed the silk bandanna, but the modiste promptly fixed it for her, coiling the rope on top of her head and fastening it with a single pin. It was not meant for a coiffeur, but only a means of getting the hair where it could not interfere with the dress. Yet Céleste was struck with surprise as she glanced sidewise into the mirror and saw the change it worked in her appearance. She looked definitely grown up. She began to feel assured of a point that had annoyed her for months. Even a stranger could now see, she felt, that she was a woman and not a child.

Choucoune, still working deftly, slipped a striking India muslin, deep bordered with gold, over the girl's head.

All the sisters stopped to watch. That Céleste was a dazzling contrast to the other women they had fitted, even without a proper head dress, was only too apparent. The dress they had made her was gaudy, to be sure, and might have raised the question of modest taste in a European city. Here, however, on an island of palm trees, poinsettias and cock fights, it was eminently in key. The change it wrought in Céleste was a miracle.

Here indeed was a subject to delight the modiste. Choucoune was tempted to rhapsodize. The little colored woman's heart beat fast. But she decided to forbear. Perhaps the child did not know her own beauty. It might upset her to stress the point too much at the present.

4. In Mme Bayou de Libertas's sleeping room a fluffy, canopied bed suggested a great, lavender-sweet hen, the clean white chamber pot an egg under her wing. Returning after the fitting, Céleste began to notice how cozy and cool the silky quarters were after a session in the sewing room on the east side of the enormous colonial

mansion. But that too was in keeping with the character of the one who slept in that fluffy bed. Mme de Libertas had always shown a generous and kind interest in Céleste. Even in early childhood the girl had been gratefully aware of it.

In those days the girl had been allowed to romp as freely as the backyard chickens. She went to bed with dirty feet, tied her braids with rags, made playmates with the black youngsters in the slave quarters, became as brown as a savage in the tropical sun. But even as far back as that Mme de Libertas had seen something striking in the child. Céleste had dim memories of this same room with its rich bed and canopy associated with those days.

"I can't forget a trunk you had in here when I was small," she said as Mme de Libertas entered.

"That's the same trunk," Mme de Libertas said, pointing. "Under that peach cover."

"Nothing could have been more enchanting."

"Those old-fashioned clothes?"

"Yes, and the smell of camphor. Scraps of silk. Trinkets."

"There are some in there, perhaps. Sachet bags. A few perfume bottles. A jewel box."

"Until then I hadn't imagined so much jewelry existed."

The strings already dangling, Mme de Libertas kicked off her shoes and rested her feet in a pair of straw slippers.

"None of the stuff could be worn now—almost none. Still it shows I was once smaller than I am now. And there may be something in the box that you can wear in your hair."

Céleste finished tying her turban, giving more time than usual to turning the corners of the thing becomingly before the mirror.

"I'm terribly nervous," she said.

"Forget it." The woman smiled. "Cock fights are nothing. This coming affair would be as depressing as the rest if I didn't have you."

"I'm sure you're teasing."

"Not at all. The men are always glad to see a new belle."

"I'd hate to see you disappointed," Céleste said.

"I couldn't possibly be. Why, just think of these envious, jealous females. They'll have cat conniptions. I expect to laugh myself sick."

"But they may have reason to be offended."

"Because you are not of the *élite?* That's silly. A pretty face and bright petticoats will get you over that fence, my dear. These mincing, high-toned courtesans colic me."

"You forget about the count."

Mme de Libertas blew through her puckered lips to show her derision.

"The count," she scoffed. "His kind usually prefers 'chocolate' when they come out here. They lay their titles down when it comes to wenches."

Ready to leave, Céleste felt another moment of awkwardness. How was she to thank Mme de Libertas? How could she ever be properly grateful for the interest the woman had taken in her? The older woman quickly hushed the attempt.

"But all the clothes," the girl protested.

Mme de Libertas sucked against her teeth.

"I needed you for my party," she said. "I was in a pickle. So please don't insist on thanking me."

They parted, the woman patting Céleste's hand maternally. The girl went directly to the terrace. She had left her grandmother piddling with plants, and on her return the old woman was still digging her corkscrew cane in the dirt around some hedge sprigs of her own growing.

"These have come along fine," Mme Juvet said, half to herself. "Maybe we can sell M. de Libertas sprigs to plant that other walk leading yonder."

"Are you ready to go home, Grandma?"

"Well, I should smile. Waiting here half the afternoon, and you ask me if I'm ready to go home."

After walking a few moments they turned into the ghost-ridden cart path that ran between the rows of dead sycamores. In the bright afternoon when one could see the rough spots it was a less perilous way than at night. But Mme Juvet knew it so well she could have as easily walked it with her eyes closed and never stumped a toe. Presently there were sounds of lumbering wheels behind them. The two paused, stepped out of the wheel lanes and waited for a line of ox carts to pass. The procession was not moving fast, and by brisk walking the two might easily have kept ahead, but Mme Juvet was beyond the age for fast walking. She was subject to sudden sick spells. Besides, she could never be comfortable walking with teams coming along behind her. There was always that outlandish feeling, knowing her own lack of nimbleness, that the beasts would suddenly break into a gallop, perhaps tread her old bones down in the road.

Holding the old woman's arm, Céleste waited with her grandmother for the lazy, bumping carts to move out of the way. There were three of them. In each there rode eight emaciated Africans, newly arrived and sick from the abysmal passage. They were not the common variety of blacks most frequently seen on the plantations of Saint Domingue. Their high foreheads and long, narrow faces suggested the northern tribes, less often handled by the experienced dealers in black flesh. Moreover, these had a curious hue. There seemed to be a touch of purple in their pigment. Their faces wore crushed, humiliated expressions. Passing the vivid girl and her incongruous old companion, some of them averted their faces as if embarrassed. The women, there were nine of them, bore the indignity better than the men in most cases. Two or three of the former were so young they were scarcely distinguishable from boys, even with their firm, small breasts uncovered.

"More slaves," Céleste observed.

"Humph," the old woman grunted. "There's ten of them now to every white in the colony, and still they come by the cart load. It's the ruination of us that aren't possessed of property and have a living to beg or steal."

"We shouldn't complain, should we, Grandma?"

"I'll wait to see what kind of match you'll make before I answer that."

"Grandma! Sometimes you have no shame."

"No, I'm too old. I suppose I've had to do too many evil things to still have shame." She snorted hoarsely as a cloud of dust from the cart wheels covered them. "Curse that dust," she mumbled.

"Well, please try to find something pleasanter to say to me than that," Céleste told her sharply. "What kind of match do you expect me to make?"

Mme Juvet chuckled.

"A planter. A nobleman in exile. I don't know. Somebody grand. Perhaps someone with a good business. A tavern, slave pens, a bordel—I don't know."

Céleste lost her breath, horrified.

"Grandma!"

"It's too late to expect pretty talk from me, child. But my ideas are sound. Mme de Libertas seems to think so, too. She's taken quite a fancy to you."

"Your ideas are ridiculous and scandalous. Why, I don't believe an aristocrat would even notice me. Even Diron pays no attention, and he's just a neighbor."

They were in the cart-wheel ruts again, walking slowly. Presently they left this way for another that crossed a field and obliged them both to climb through the rails of a crude fence. In time this one crossed a coach road and brought the pair to the summit of a knoll from which a back view of their own small house was possible. Some distance further along they came to a spot where an ancient and bony cow stood chewing her cud and fight-

ing a swarm of large tropical flies that plagued her. Mme
Juvet stopped, drew the peg to which the wretched old
creature was tethered, led the beast behind her the rest
of the way to the house. Céleste, lost in her own thoughts,
had walked a stone's throw ahead while her grandmother
paused. When she noticed that she was alone, the old
woman was already coming along with the cow.

5. Mars Plasair, the barking house-servant whose body
was already racked with consumption, saw the new
slaves arrive and recognized them immediately for members of a sulking tribe not easily enslaved. Some of their
tribesmen had the habit of leaping from the decks of
the ships and drowning themselves when not closely
guarded. At best their dispositions did not make them
attractive to most planters. Mars was a little surprised
to see that M. Bayou de Libertas had not himself dis-
couraged such a large purchase of these doubtful workers.
But of course M. de Libertas was an unusual overseer.
He had the good will of the blacks that he worked, almost without exception. Perhaps he had concluded that
he could make peace with the worst of them.

Toussaint had driven the coach just ahead of the ma-
nure carts in which the slaves were loaded. Having seen
the gentlemen enter the house, the old coachman had
given his reins to the stable boys and continued across

the back fields towards the quarters on foot. Now Mars
was following him. The sun was intense. Mars was convinced, however, that it was not the sun that made his
head throb. He was feverish. He could scarcely drag his
feet. His energy was gone.

Old Toussaint was lucky. There he was on the path
where he had been met by his enormously fat wife. Toussaint was not really old, not more than fifty, at any rate,
still every one called him *vieux* Toussaint. And what a
tough-fibered creature he was! Mars could remember
when all the other blacks called him *fatras bâton* because
Toussaint had been so skinny in childhood. Now only
Suzanne used the nickname for him; and that was because she was his wife. Toussaint had weathered as much
torment as any of them. Still he kept his sweet old ways.
He seldom laughed, but his smile was always ready. He
seemed to live in another world, like a prophet in vision.
Mars put that down as a consequence of the other's reading. Toussaint had been taught to read; and being doctor
to practically all the blacks in the parish, he got around
a great deal and managed to keep himself in books.
Toussaint didn't seem like a fellow slave. Even M. de
Libertas did not regard him as an ordinary black.

Of course, Mars stood well himself. He had no com-
plaint. He never put himself on a level with old Toussaint, though they were both near the same age. The
ability to read struck a difference through the ranks of
men. But over and above that gift Toussaint was not
to be considered run of the mill black flesh. He had a
spark. Mars always thought of the coachman somewhat

as he might think of a man with eyes living in a country of blind beings.

At the moment it did Mars no good to see the quiet good humor of the other. The madras handkerchief with which Toussaint tied his stiff, pig-tail braided hair was covered with dust as was his coat. Now he had taken the fat, moon-faced black woman by the hand and started across a plowed field. The woman's voice was loud, her teeth white and prominent. She laughed at the top of her voice as her bare feet plopped in the soft dust. Toussaint was amazingly devoted to her.

But Mars could not stop to muse. He had been told to attend the new slaves and see that they got their stint of fish and rice and peas and that they did not lack a place to flop on the ground and stretch their legs when night fell. He could see them now from the distance huddling together in consternation. Poor devils, they didn't know how lucky they were to become a part of Bréda. If they kept their eyes open, they would find out, however. The expression "as lucky as a Bréda slave," current throughout the northern department was not entirely without meaning, Mars thought. Even that foul, show-off stunt by the Count de Sacy—he called it an "emetic"—did not utterly counteract the years of considerate treatment the blacks had received at the hands of M. Bayou de Libertas in a colony where barbarous cruelty was the rule.

Mars paused to blow, taking little tentative breaths in rapid succession. But though he drew a half dozen where a single full inhalation would have sufficed, he was never revived. He aroused himself once more, doggedly shuffling his feet along with the same inadequate strength. It was a misery to have to keep stirring when one wasn't fit. Still it was better to be alive under any conditions than to be dead. Toussaint himself was authority for that conclusion. Even as recently as the day of the counting-house experience he had repeated the same thought. Mars had been lying on the floor of his hut, faint from vomiting and crying after his return from the ordeal. He had felt as if he wouldn't live to see another morning. He couldn't even remember seeing Toussaint enter the dark stall-like quarters, but the old coachman's words had touched him strangely.

"Don't die yet, Mars. You may get a better death if you can wait a little while. That spit—why, that only hurt your pride. You needn't let it kill you. The point is not to let insults bow you down. There's sure to be a reckoning."

CHAPTER THREE

1. Count Armand de Sacy kicked the sheets aside and rolled out of his bed in a stomping fury. It was not yet morning. The tall windows, flung open to admit a breath of ocean air, framed a square of purple sky and stars. No better sleeping weather could have been asked. Moreover, de Sacy was dead tired. Yet he found it impossible to sleep beside a sniffling woman.

"How long do you intend to keep it up, for God's sake?"

Angélique pulled the sheet over head and said nothing.

"What do you expect, wench?"

A moment later, brooking tears, she rose on her elbow.

"Nothing," she said. "I expect nothing from you—naturally."

"How am I to sleep with that sniffling?"

"You might provide another room for me," she said.

He adjusted his sleeping bonnet, found a dressing robe and slipped into it. Pawing uncertainly along the side of the bed with his toes, he located a pair of slippers. A moment later, discovering that they were not his, he kicked them aside and continued to search in the dark till he found a pair that would accommodate his feet.

At the window he could hear through the darkness the haunting pat of bare feet on the soft earth. A moment of shock followed in which he tried to account quickly for the activity of the blacks at such an hour. Presently he recalled with mounting indignation that this was the day—the day on which guests were expected for cock fights and related entertainment. It was like Angélique to impinge upon his rest and good humor at a time when he needed both so urgently. Not only did he object to the loss of valuable sleep but also to the overpowering distaste which a slobbering, clinging woman invariably aroused in him.

"Confounded baggage," he grunted, pacing. "You have no gratitude. You want the moon."

The next moment he was at a small table pouring rum into a tumbler.

"I feel like garbage," Angélique said. "You're a swine. You sicken me. I'd rather be a slave in a hovel."

The count gulped, choking momentarily. He replaced the tumbler with a bang.

"We sicken each other, my pretty dove." He forced the words through firmly clinched teeth. "But I would not liken *you* to a filthy swine. I was just thinking of an average milk cow."

Angélique drew herself to a sitting position beneath the canopy. A hint of daylight had come to the blue window. The bed, the furnishings and the shadowy woman were now visible in outline to the heated de Sacy.

"You're a reckless man," she told him with a level voice.

"I'd be the last to deny it," de Sacy replied.

"You're a blind old lecher."

"A lecher, perhaps—thanks to you and others. But blind? I wonder."

She took a deep breath, paused to calculate.

"You may find you have overshot the mark this time."

The count rested his hand on the bedpost, tried to digest her threat.

"You have no cause to be bitter," he said. "You should thank me for benefits too numerous to recall. Claire and Annette must have poisoned your mind."

"I despise you," she cried, "I despise you. I wish I were dead."

"That, sweet wench, bores me intolerably."

"But I'm not so unattractive as the other two. I won't be so easily contented, either. Why, I'd rather share a slave's pallet."

He yawned, gave her his back and lapsed into silence. The activity on the grounds was increasing. De Sacy could now see the hurrying shadows. The roar of ovens in the cooking shed, some yards removed from the great house, reminded him of activities ahead. Suddenly he decided to dress and go out of doors. He went into a small adjoining room and closed the door. A few moments later, responding to de Sacy's bell, a slave appeared at the door, a thin tall male with the features and hands of a woman.

"Monsieur," the black whispered tentatively and with a questioning tone.

"Dress me," the count told him.

Half an hour later the ebony valet flecked the powder from the shoulders of the count's coat, removed the net sack that held the nobleman's freshly made curls. The room was no longer dark enough to excuse the use of candles, and the African quietly snuffed the two he had earlier placed on the dressing table. De Sacy remarked with surprise that the savage himself was wearing satin and that the fellow's queue was freshly larded to give it a gaudy shine. But the slave assured him that Mme de Libertas was to be thanked for the costume. It was her opinion that the presence of a count at Bréda, particularly a relative of the Count de Noé, owner of the estate, should create a festive atmosphere. Besides, there would be other guests today. And cock fights.

"*Monsieur*," the black said again, indicating that he was finished.

De Sacy twitched his shoulders, waiting for his hat and stick, went into the bed chamber without speaking to the slave.

Dry-eyed now, Angélique tossed for a moment on the soft mattress, then seemed to sleep. The count opened a drawer that had been scented with a quince. Some place in its recesses he found a jewelry box. Then for a moment he gave attention to a selection of rings for the morning. Later, the drawer locked, he snapped his snuff box open, took two dips and left the room. On the stair he was passed by Mars. The wasting old house-servant panted horribly, endeavoring to speed his steps. Agitation and distress were written vividly on the black face. But de Sacy had his own woes this morning. He paused only long enough to see that Mars was headed for the rooms of M. Bayou de Libertas, then continued down the steps.

On the grounds of Bréda he found an elaborate preparation in progress, a preparation greatly in excess of what he took to be the off-handed nature of the occasion they were expecting. In the clump of trees west of the house almost an acre of picnic tables had been laid. Behind the cooking shed fires already smoldered in the barbecue pits. Half a dozen gleaming blacks, perspiring before the flames, squatted to avoid smoke. Enormous porks, suspended on spits, dripped their juices on the rosy coals, began to give the morning air an enchantment of odors. The tawdry scarlet and gold coach was in the carriage yard a short distance away getting a thorough polishing.

The cock pit, also removed from the solitary mansion, was surrounded by shade trees. Benches and rustic seats had been arranged to accommodate a gallery of fastidious spectators. Without venturing far beyond the immediate out-buildings of Bréda, de Sacy could see slaves scattering a fresh layer of gravel to surface the battleground of game birds. The sun pushed upwards with tropical urgency. A day of diamond brightness had dawned.

Suddenly it occurred to the count that he had allowed his controversy with Angélique to slip completely from mind. Feeling very much like one of the game cocks he had just been contemplating, he stamped his small heels in the path with fierce hauteur, snorted, chewed his lips grimly. A moment later he had circled the stables and was returning to the walk that led to the side entrance of the house. He did not reach the door, however; for presently, in a flurry of excitement, M. Bayou de Libertas rushed out of doors. He was stockingless; the buckles of his shoes were not fastened, and he had hastily stuffed his long night-shirt into the handiest pair of breeches he could locate. His humorous, lashless eyes were blinking with despair when he reached the count.

"Mars just told me what happened," he said, whispering tragically.

"He didn't say anything to me," de Sacy said.

M. de Libertas added nothing but indicated with his finger the ghost-ridden path used by the ox carts in driving from the big road to the Quarters. Irritated rather than excited, de Sacy walked beside the overseer, matching the other's long strides with short ones in a proportion of about five to three.

Finally, snatched from his abstraction, M. de Libertas seemed to realize that he had annoyed the count.

"I beg your pardon, Count," he said, still walking hard. "It's about that new batch of slaves you got from Captain Frounier."

"Sick?"

"Worse. It was homesickness, I suppose."

"Oh, homesickness can be cured," de Sacy assured him.

"Yes," M. de Libertas said. "No doubt."

"But if the brutes are not sound," the count said, "Captain Frounier will have to take them back or replace them. They're not paid for yet."

"The captain has your note, monsieur."

"So he has. Still we might require him to make good any of the stock that proved sickly before we made payment in full."

"Monsieur, that will never be," M. de Libertas told him, growing a trifle impatient on his own part.

With that remark both of them lapsed into silence for a short space. Still fairly trotting to keep up, the count pursued the half-dressed overseer along the wretched cart path. Suddenly, coming into sight of the ruined sycamores, M. de Libertas halted with military abruptness. Beside him the count showed more amazement than his face had formerly seemed capable of registering. Presently, however, his countenance lengthened; a horror greeted him so unexpectedly and with such force that he seemed momentarily on the verge of screaming.

"*Mon Dieu,*" he gasped. "It's not so. It can't be."

"There they are," M. de Libertas said frigidly. "Every one of them. Twenty-four in all. They took it hard."

Before the men stretched a line of swinging corpses, one to a tree. Ghastly, shocking, terrible, they seemed to have organized a sort of demonstration in protest. It was mass suicide.

Chastened by his own thoughts, the count began to speak in a whisper.

"It doesn't seem real, monsieur."

"I've seen it happen before."

"But wasn't this rather extreme on their part?"

"Some Africans are strange. They'd rather die than be enslaved. They wouldn't have made good workers in that state."

"A pretty sight to show guests! You wouldn't take it for an omen, would you?"

"I don't believe in signs and omens, Count. Still almost nothing is without its causes and consequences. This may have meaning of a sort." M. de Libertas turned his head as he spoke, looked across the fields through misty eyes. "I'd rather not think about it, however."

2. The diamond-bright morning held dismal prospects for Diron Desautels, too. Removed a number of miles from the shadows of Bréda's ghost-haunted cart path, he had his own wretchedness for company. In a moment of stupidity he had submitted to Mme Viard's urging and promised to meet her carriage on the coach road, ride his horse alongside the remainder of the distance. She simply couldn't abide the thought, she professed, of arriving at Bréda unescorted. It would be just too—too humiliating.

This way, Diron now told himself, the humiliation was his. With no one else to claim his attention, he might—had it been his will—have afforded himself a certain abandon. She was—why deny the obvious?—she was indeed a richly luxurious creature. But Diron had a queer distrust of the sleek, dark-eyed young woman. Moreover, her attitude toward the glamour of revolution annoyed and angered him by turn. If it was true—but it was vain to enumerate his suspicions of her again. These were not the things which repelled him. If anything, they gave her a sinister charm. She depressed him only because she saw no beauty in the ideals of the Revolution. With him the poetry of liberty, of the brotherhood and equality of men, was positively basic. Even the perfume and flattery of a woman, when it did not take this into account, was incomplete and unsatisfactory to his present mood.

Cock fights were another matter. At the moment he sat on his own steps holding the string to a trap he had set in the yard, fifty feet away. An old Negro peeped around the corner of the stable. One of Diron's favorite fighting cocks had escaped the coop. Now with grain sprinkled under a box-like cage and the cage itself propped up by means of the stick to which Diron's cord was tied, both Diron and the black waited for the bird to come into the trap. The slave had been sent from Bréda, an accommodation to the expected guest, to fetch Diron's birds. The old fellow had probably not suspected that he should also have part in the sport of catching the fowls.

A moment later the cock was flapping wildly within the cage, and the old slave was jauntily coming from behind the stable to lay hands upon him. Diron stood on the step, stretched his arms above his head in the lazy sunshine. His boots gleamed. He had selected nankeen breeches; his hair had a raven shine, but he had not yet put on his shirt. Now he might go inside and finish dressing.

His changes of clothes dispatched with his fighting cocks, Diron mounted his beast an hour later, paused to adjust the reins as the little mare danced on the board floor, proceeded through hanging cobwebs to the stable door and out onto the red crushed-brick drive. The heat of the day was already intense. Diron continued unhurried, availing himself and his horse of every patch of shade he found along the roadside. Bréda was a full mile and a half by the difficult foot way that led from Mme Juvet's back gardens and joined the cart path near the plantation's slave quarters. By the coach road it was twice as far.

A cloud of dust moving steadily out from Le Cap heralded the approach of a carriage. Diron reined his mare boldly in midroad and waited for its arrival. He had been there only a few moments when the horses came into view, red nostrils distended, a vivid blaze on each face. And as Diron had suspected, their burden was a familiar green fiacre in which, muffled safely against dust, sat the sleek Mme Sylvestre Viard with her hunchback coachman. She ordered the horses stopped; and when Diron drove alongside, she took his hand in hers and pressed it warmly. She seemed ready to burst with gladness.

"The dust will choke you if you drop behind," she warned.

"I'll try to keep up," he assured her.

"Everything is terribly dry—dry enough to burn."

He nodded.

"Dry is the word. You haven't spared your horses."

"Don't reproach me, please. I adore the beasts. But *you* were waiting."

He smiled curiously, half pleased, half irritated.

"I hate to see them so drenched."

"They may take their time now, the darlings."

"Fine."

"You look marvelous today—smooth and shiny."

"And you're at your best, Paulette."

"You haven't seen me, really."

"No, I suppose I haven't—only your veil and dust cloak. Still I have some intuition."

"I wish you wouldn't trust it. I'd rather you looked at me occasionally."

Diron smiled.

"A whim, I suppose."

"Yes, and a very foolish one. I can't for the life of me imagine why it should seem important to me, Diron."

Discomforted again, he averted his eyes.

Diron's little mare, held sharply in check, bounded forward as the young man's grasp on the reins relaxed. An instant later Diron halted her and waited for the other horses to catch up. With conversation suspended, the luxurious whine of carriage springs and the immaculate tock-tock of properly shod beasts were the only sounds following the small equipage.

The pace was slow, but in time they reached the gate pillars at the entrance to Bréda. Coming from the opposite direction, a lumbering closed coach, an elegant tan affair that seemed somehow awkward and overweight in its tropical surroundings, turned into the drive just ahead of them. A fantastic black postillion, wearing yellow boots and yellow smallclothes with a green uniform, was mounted on one of the foremost horses, while his apparent twin sat in the coachman's seat popping his whip grandly. The green fiacre, now wearing a veil of dust, waited to follow the other vehicle into the private drive. Reining his mare once more, Diron entered last.

As he neared the pale stucco mansion with its clump of palms and peppers, Diron was pleased to drop further and further behind the bustling rigs. Here the drive was firm and well-kept. A rose hedge grew on either side the half-mile approach. Just in front of the colonial house the driveway broadened into a great curve. This sweep of gravel was filled with coaches and saddle horses and open carriages. Guests were alighting nimbly, calling greetings to friends and commands to their maids, coachmen and postillions. The closed vehicles belched rich perfumes when their doors swung open. Silks whispered. Gay colors fairly screamed in the brilliant sunlight. Scurrying black servants sweated beneath mountainous loads of dress and hat boxes. Others, having unhitched their beasts, led the animals around to the distant stables amid the confusion of trailing harness. Here and there, stepping leisurely from her carriage, a Creole belle managed to expose a handsome length of lace pantalet. Presently a lean young black was standing before Diron, his hand on the mare's bridle. Diron took in the whole scene with a sudden gasp of excitement.

His horse dispatched, he left the drive a few moments later and walked slowly toward the wide verandas. Surely a good half the parish had turned out, Diron thought. Dark-haired girls with golden, sun-touched complexions loitered on the broad stairs inside. Their dark, shaded eyes

lingering uncomfortably, they nudged one another as
Diron came into view. As bright as flamingos and perhaps
as numerous, they idled on the stairs, first one and then
another leaning over the handrail of the banister. Almost
without exception they wore silk bandanna turbans becomingly turned to suit their individual charms. And
despite the warmth of the day all seemed remarkably cool
and subtle.

There was a hubbub in the drawing room beyond the
French windows; and the west veranda, which still had
shade, was thronged by young males as poised and alert
as tomcats. All of these wore ruffled linen shirts; many
had ruffled cuffs that hung over their hands with a careless sort of elegance. At the moment the omnipresent
Mars was among them, bowing and scraping as silently
and inconspicuously as a shadow and offering the men
tall glasses from a silver tray. Diron joined the group,
nodded half a dozen brief greetings, accepted the drink
which Mars proffered and seated himself quietly.

"Some of the aims simply miscarried," a blunt-featured
dandy was saying without much caution. He had the air
of a local, would-be diplomat dipping into world affairs,
and Diron listened only because no one else was saying
anything whatsoever at the moment. "We supported the
Revolution at first, you know. We took the slogans to indicate that independence would be given to the colony
of Saint Domingue. Now this is what it turns out to be."

"It hasn't turned out to be anything at all—yet," a nervous, middle-aged aristocrat answered. "Independence is
what we insist it shall be, monsieur."

"You favor independence for the colony, don't you, M. Desautels?" the blunt-featured man asked suddenly.

Diron was as surprised as if he had suddenly been awakened from sleep.

"Well, I'm against tyranny," he said hesitantly.

"And what would that mean where we're concerned?"

Diron felt a flash of anger, but he didn't propose to argue at the moment.

"We must work out our own destiny, M. Solange," he said. "It is our right—and our obligation."

"I can't say I admire your tone. It smells of contact with Jacobins," the blunt-faced, foppish Solange added.

"He means it is our obligation to exercise our rights," the nervous-voiced one suggested a little uncertainly. "Is that not it, monsieur?"

Diron laughed.

"Gentlemen, this is my first," he said raising his glass. "My wits are not yet up to yours."

"Drink, monsieur," someone boomed. "If the Revolution is to keep a gentleman from his drink, I say let's resist it. Do you agree, M. Nadya?"

"You *do* sound like a Jacobin," the nervous M. Nadya smiled. "I had the notion that we were among those marked for extermination. Now you come up with this engaging new suggestion that perhaps we are in a position to carry on or suspend the Revolution at will. I'm confused."

"Properly so, monsieur. Soon I shall be in the same state. Another drink, Mars."

Arsenne Brieux, the deteriorating poet, was present as was also Alexandre Gratien and Victor Augière, the latter two near Diron's age and all secretly affiliated with *Les Amis des Noirs*. These four gravitated together, and into their midst came M. Bayou de Libertas with his human sympathies. But political matters were not in their minds, unless it could be said that the business of reducing the island's rum reserves was political. At any rate, they were together at one end of the veranda and making important headway on that ambitious design when the call to dinner was sounded.

None of these was among the first to reach the grove, however. They came after the first rush and formed another of those uncertain little masculine groups so hard to dissolve at festivities. But Diron stayed with them for a purpose. He had no mind to chain himself to young Mme Viard longer than was necessary, and until now he had discovered no other possible escape.

The tables had been spread with delicate linen and the most exquisite tableware. Overhead the leaves made a canopy against the sun. The serving had commenced. A swarm of slaves, under the supervising eye of Mme de Libertas, slipped in and out among the guests. Others, crossing the field in a sort of hippity-hop, communicated hurriedly between the smoldering meat pits and the tables. They couldn't always run, but neither could they slow down to a walk, so they had struck a gait that was half-way between.

The personal servants of guests, their coachmen, postillions and maids, had been provided for on the shady side of the Bréda stables where Toussaint was in command.

While Diron and his companions lingered at the edge of the grove, the tables gradually filled. As usual at this sort of gathering in Saint Domingue, there were more men than women. The Count Armand de Sacy was among them like a belligerent bantam among cockerels of the barnyard breeds. He wore a flame-bright orange coat over fluffy white small clothes and tight breeches of the same spotless whiteness. His coat was narrow, with a huge collar over which powdered hair fell in long locks. Diron noticed with amusement that the count's trunk seemed a trifle too large for his legs, his head a bit too heavy for his shoulders—an appearance perhaps emphasized as a consequence of his hair-dress.

While Diron eyed him, de Sacy was taking his place at the head of the first table. He was flanked by two women, both taller than himself, and Diron noted with considerable relief that one of them was Mme Viard. The other, the neat-figured Angélique, was as usual more striking from a distance than from a near view.

Some moments had passed and most of the guests had been served when, leaving the other four men, Diron came face to face with a larger group who were decidedly otherwise engaged. There were half a dozen of them, including the blunt-featured Solange and the nervous, middle-aged Nadya, and they all surrounded a particularly striking belle who had been served on a seat apart at the foot of a tree. His curiosity piqued, Diron drew near. A moment later he stood among the group, speechless with amazement. His arms fell weakly to his sides; his mouth sprang open foolishly. The girl, a miracle of freshness and beauty, reclined against the stem of the tree, munching indifferently from the plate in her hand. In a confusion of delight and wonder, Diron tried in vain to convince himself that it was really Céleste—Céleste who only a few weeks past had been a child—who had here become the cynosure of so many eyes.

"Surely Mademoiselle sets a high requirement," Solange was saying, rather foolishly, rising on his toes and twisting his ruffles to assert a sort of priority. "Why, of all these gentlemen ... certainly, certainly—"

"I lack judgment," she protested. "I can't make up my mind. Perhaps mid-day is a difficult hour."

She crossed her legs, exposing the toes of green morocco slippers. Her dress was pale green, laced smartly about the waist and billowing over hoops in the skirt. The neck was cut low after the manner of dancing dresses; and Céleste's small white breasts, pressed upwards by her staves, suggested young birds threatening every moment to escape. Vivid color rose to her cheeks as Diron joined the group of men.

Suddenly, and without conscious reason, Diron felt himself trembling with angry jealousy. He looked at her reproachfully, but quickly modified his tone.

"I don't know you, Céleste. You're another person."

"Sit down, Diron, and be served. You've been walking in the sun after those refreshments on the veranda."

"You're beautiful, honestly."

"Don't your principles forbid excess?" she asked.

"My principles forbid me to leave this spot, nothing else."

Giving up the party manner for a moment, she smiled a childish smile and indicated the grassy spot of ground beside her feet. The other men began to turn away politely.

"Sit down," she urged.

"How did it happen?" he asked, ignoring her command.

"My being here? Mme de Libertas is to blame."

Claire and Annette reached the grove, looking intolerably bored, slipped into conspicuous seats and began flapping palmetto fans.

"I must compliment Mme de Libertas. She saw your possibilities," Diron said.

"You're not laughing at me?"

He shook his head sadly.

"I mean it, earnestly."

The girl had a luminous, phosphorescent quality. Diron looked at her and then at Mme Viard, repeated the comparison several times before he realized that he had become mute at a moment when he was expected to say something.

"You heard about the twenty-four new slaves," Céleste said, apparently knowing the turn of his mind.

He shook his head, and she told him briefly what had happened. His face clouded with a puzzled look, but he showed no visible sign of emotion. She, too, became darkly serious as she spoke.

"We should beat our breasts," he said.

"Would that help?"

Diron accepted a plate from the tray that passed in front of him, seated himself on the ground at Céleste's feet. At the far end of the table the count laughed boisterously at one of his own remarks. Presently the tables became noisy again with small talk and rapid chatter. For several moments Diron sat without touching his food.

"I didn't know about the incident," he said finally. "But I seemed to feel a shadow on us here."

He pondered again. Then, quite abruptly, he came to himself and began eating with relish.

3. Mme. Bayou de Libertas was flat on her back, sniffling the salts and breathing hard. Her eyes had been closed since they brought her to her bedroom, but now the lids fluttered ever so slightly. She had fainted at the edge of the grove, immediately following the meal; and now, her wits returning, her first concern was to know what ill effect, if any, her misfortune had had on the gathering.

She was a lugubrious spectacle on the bed. Her dress had been unhooked all the way, her corsets unlaced, her shoes unstrung and her stockings rolled down. She had perspired, and her face was streaked, two crude spots of color remaining on her cheeks. A slave woman, standing at the head of the bed, kept a wet towel on her forehead. Another kept a palmetto fan in motion. The pillow had been removed from beneath Mme de Libertas's head, so that her chin was forced up and her neck seemed stretched beyond its normal length. In this state her girth seemed fully twice what it had been when her clothes were fastened.

She had felt it coming on early in the meal. In her concern for the guests she had eaten hurriedly. Between the effects of excitement, a stomach out of tune, a too tightly laced corset and an unusually bright sun, she had been overcome. She hadn't the slightest idea how she had reached her bedroom. But now her husband was standing sheepishly near the door. Céleste was sitting calmly on a rosewood ottoman beside the window. The room was brightening for Mme de Libertas as if dawn had been just breaking in the morning.

"I feel terrible," she said, almost in tears.

"Don't try to speak," her husband commanded tenderly. "You'll feel better when you've rested a few moments."

"I can talk," she insisted. "It's the embarrassment that troubles me most. Wasn't it awful?"

"Not at all," Céleste said brightly. "Scarcely anyone saw it happen. Only the slaves and two or three of us who were lingering behind. Most everyone had already returned to the house."

"Besides, you faint quite prettily for a woman of your age—and weight," M. de Libertas chuckled, blinking his round, lashless eyes.

"Don't laugh," she urged, wrenching her own face to keep from smiling. "I know it seems absurd. I'm not the languishing kind. Honestly, I wasn't pretending. I'm terribly ashamed. I'd rather anything else had happened."

"Some things would have been much worse," Céleste said seriously.

"Darling," Mme de Libertas said, her eyes brightening as her voice faded. "I'm pleased with you—enormously pleased."

"You're a perfect kitten," M. de Libertas said, coming to the bedside and tweaking his wife's chin. "We managed you beautifully—the six or eight of us. Compose yourself now. The other ladies are all in exactly the same position you're in, getting a little rest before the cock fights."

"Not all of them," she said. "I hear voices."

"Well, many of them."

Visibly satisfied with her condition, he smiled broadly and left the room.

"You must go too," Mme de Libertas said to Céleste, her half-closed eyes fixed fondly on the radiant girl. "I'm all right now. Let Zoune unfasten your hooks. Sleep a while if you can."

Céleste admitted innocently that she had done nothing all day that was in any wise tiring to her. What she thought, furthermore, but did not say, was that she was perhaps far too robust to ever be a perfect lady. Still she was ready to do what was expected of her, particularly if Mme de Libertas expected it. She rose from the ottoman, her billowing skirt swinging prettily, and stood before the mirror. She discovered for the first time that the new dress she was wearing made her look perhaps an inch shorter than she had imagined herself to look—this despite her morocco slippers and the length of the skirt. But she did not mind, everything considered; half

ashamed of the thought, she seriously suspected that she
had something that could not be measured in inches or
described in exact shades. Was it beauty? If she could
only be positively sure, she thought swiftly, life would
be greatly simplified. Removing the silk headpiece and
shaking her hair loose, she turned to obey Mme de Libertas's suggestion.

The slim, half-naked Zoune rested her fan, laid it on a
bed table. Her polished body glistened as she stepped into
the light that streamed through the window; her orange
turban blazed like a flower in the sun. She followed the
girl dutifully out of the room.

Left alone in the room with her savage-looking maid,
Mme de Libertas rose to a sitting position, pointed toward
the chamber pot under the edge of the bed. When the
slave woman brought it, the good-humored matron leaned
over, tickled her palate with her forefinger and quickly
lost her dinner. A few moments later, her eyes wet and
her lips puffed, Mme de Libertas looked up with final
satisfaction. She felt greatly relieved. Now that she had
her wits again, she knew exactly what had ailed her from
the first, and she had her own way of relieving the misery.

"I couldn't let them see me," she said to the woman. "I
ate too much. I ate till I fainted." She laughed a deep
abdominal laugh. "What other delight is there for *la
volupté*, when one is past the age?"

When the slave was unable to reply, the sturdy Mme
de Libertas slipped off the bed, instructing the woman
to undress her. Out of the dress and petticoats that had
been her undoing, she stood for a moment in a corset

so formidable that, hanging loose, it suggested dangling armor. Mme de Libertas accepted a purple bed gown from her maid and finally wriggled out of the whole fearful harness of staves and laces.

"Now," she said, pouring wine into a tumbler on the dressing table, "I can make a fresh start."

The black maid was already busy getting the room back in order.

A good many of the women who thronged the bedrooms were asleep when, half an hour later, Mme de Libertas passed down the hall, peeping here and there to assure herself that all guests were comfortable. A small crowd, overflowing into the sewing room, was still very much awake, however. A lively exchange of the best gossip was in progress.

"He's talkative," a brightly tinted young woman was saying tentatively, her knees propped, her arms locked around them where she sat on top of a cutting table, "but it's definite that he prefers chocolate."

"Well, here's one who won't shed tears," answered an almond-eyed companion with intensely black hair. "Nadya is certainly not to my taste."

Mme de Libertas stepped inside. At this hour of the afternoon the sewing room was by far the coolest upper room of the house. Moreover, a roistering breeze was billowing the curtains, dallying with the skirts of the women. A suggestion of the Caribbean Sea mingled with the reek of Persian perfumes. Mme de Libertas stood against the door frame and waited for a lull. Then, quite unexpectedly, she made an observation which immediately pricked the ears of the younger women.

"It's much too late to expect anything new from Creole gentlemen," she said generously. "The taste for 'chocolate,' as you call it, is still an aristocratic taste. Most of the mulattos stem from the *élite.*"

"So much the worse," said the voice from the window bench, the owner of which, suddenly rising, turned out to be the statuesque Claire.

She was instantly followed by the muscular Annette.

"Let me out," Annette remarked. "I smell politics coming up."

"Wait, I'll go," Mme de Libertas said quickly. Her voiced showed a certain hurt, and it was clear that she had not seen the pair when she joined the group.

The two ignored her protest, however, and continued into the hall. A moment of silence followed.

"What's that about the count and those two?" the almond-eyed girl asked.

No one seemed eager to give an explanation as long as an authority such as Mme de Libertas remained silent. Finally, however, the young woman on the table ventured a brief and particularly coarse summary of the facts. The older woman made no denial, and the question was allowed to die.

Someone wanted to know if a certain well-mannered guest, now napping in another room of Bréda, had actually ordered one of her female slaves maimed in protest against her husband's intimacy with the wench. Another wanted to know if a recent poisoning in the parish could not be traced to jealousy. Mme Viard, stretching her trim long legs into the part of the seat just vacated by Claire and Annette, showed a little uneasiness and promptly suggested that the count—to change the subject with their consent—had been guilty of some uncommonly low remarks while at table. Someone else wondered if that did not indicate that the diminutive nobleman had designs on Paulette herself—since he'd have little incentive to become risqué with Angélique, his present mistress. But Paulette would have none of it.

"He repels me," she urged. "His hands perspire. They feel clammy."

"What a pity," the almond-eyed girl sighed. "He has a cunning walk."

"If I were a belle," Mme de Libertas said with mischief, "my preference would run toward such a man as young Diron Desautels."

Her strategy failed. No one answered immediately. Paulette's features twisted. For a moment she seemed intent upon something outside the window. When she turned, finally, a flash of anger accompanied her words.

"It appears that you have primed your protégé with the same preference," she said.

"Oh, I'd take an oath," Mme de Libertas protested, cut by the charge. "God punish me if I've ever called his name to her in that way. I was speaking playfully, Mme Viard."

"There must be something," Paulette insisted more quietly but with her face averted again.

Mme de Libertas tried to explain away the wretched impression she had given so unintentionally. She had no malice toward Mme Viard, none whatsoever, and surely she had never previously thought of Diron in connection with Céleste. Moreover—but, no, she could not say this. She suspected, though it would have been murderous to hint it there, that that meditative young man, for all his glossy dark mane, for all his fastidious bearing and fine features, had a mistress from whom none of them was likely to woo him soon. She suspected that Diron was, like M. Sylvain, the printer, and some other bookish people she knew, like Robespierre, Danton and Lafayette in Paris, Augière, Gratien and Brieux in Saint Domingue, a Jacobin and a Friend of the Blacks. Why, if you talked about the Revolution, Diron would almost confess outright, despite the danger of maintaining such sympathies in the northern department.

"I meant," she stammered feebly, "I meant I'd admire a young man with an interest in great affairs, if I were a belle again. Nothing more."

The girl on the cutting table clasped her knees a bit tighter.

"His beauty is against him," she giggled. "Those shoulders, ah; those melancholy eyes—fatal. He's cut out for great affairs, but not in connection with the state."

The tension broke with this light-hearted remark, and Mme de Libertas found it possible to slip away without embarrassment. Her final impression was that before her arrival the group had exhausted her young neighbor as subject for their comments. The summary announced by the rosy girl on the table sounded like a repetition of one that had previously been reached.

Once outside the door Mme de Libertas hurried to her room.

4. The sun was definitely westward, and the men, with perhaps half the women, proceeded to the cock pits. Shadows from the grove now reached the circle with its surrounding benches and seats. To the east and across a field was the rear wall of a stone stable. With the sun against its orange lichens the old structure gave an enamel shine. A dozen plow oxen jostled one another in a near-by pen.

Joined on the path by the wavering Captain Frounier, Céleste walked without speaking in the shade of the trees. Evidently the cocks were already in action. Shouts rose periodically from the assembled men. Later this chorus was pierced by shrill darts of female laughter. Looking on the backs of the group who formed the excited circle, Céleste saw arms thrust into the air now and again.

"One of the cocks must have been spurred," the girl said after a particularly enthusiastic outburst.

"Yes, we're missing something," the old captain agreed.

"I don't like to see them bleed."

Captain Frounier laughed with ancient condescension.

"But it wouldn't be a fight without blood."

"It's a shame to let the prettiest birds get marred and torn."

"Oh, the pretty ones are the ones that win," the captain assured her. "You wouldn't call a cock pretty that got himself spurred in the head."

Céleste didn't attempt to follow his reasoning.

"Were you at dinner, Captain Frounier?" she asked.

"No. Just this minute arrived," he answered. "A short day is a long one at my age. Give me the cock fights, a hand of cards perhaps, and some drinks, and I'll call it a big day."

"No fireworks?" she laughed.

"Are they going to have fireworks, too?"

"I've heard they are."

"Well, I suppose I can stay awake for a few Roman candles."

They pressed through the crowd, and Céleste got separated immediately from the old man.

The men who formed the circle, perhaps thirty of them, were essentially the same ones that Diron had found on the veranda at the time of his morning arrival. The count, of course, had joined them, along with M. de Libertas and now Captain Frounier. Most of this group stood gallantly behind benches which had been provided for the dozen or so young women who had a taste for the sport. Not so the count. He sat with patrician elegance amid the colorful females and at this very moment made an autocratic demand on their attention.

Céleste found sitting space across the pit and promptly discovered Diron looking at her with woe in his eyes.

He had rested his foot on the edge of a seat and now leaned forward, his elbow on his knee, his chin in his hand. Half a dozen blacks, polished like ebony, lay on their bellies in the pit. Each of them clasped two eager game cocks, one in either arm. Other slaves, squatting a few paces beyond the circle and charged with the keeping of still other birds, gaped eagerly, though they saw nothing more than coat-tails and well-dressed hair.

"Those two are mine," Diron said, coming to the bench on which Céleste was seated.

"Which two?"

He pointed.

"The red one and the black."

"I should have recognized them."

"You've tucked them in occasionally."

"I don't know why I came. I despise fighting."

"I can't resist it," he confessed.

She absolved him, smiling lightly.

"But look—"

Another pair of cocks had been freed in the pit. They came together heatedly in a quick series of savage thrusts, then stood apart with extended bills and began picking spots. During the lull Diron recovered enough to see that Céleste was expecting him to say something.

"We must have grim amusement," he observed.

She didn't like him in that mood.

"You might be more cheerful," she said after a flurry of fighting in which one cock got some blood on his spur.

Presently the enamel feathers of the fighting birds were

smeared and dripping. The copper shine of one, the metal brightness of the other, both seemed a mockery to Céleste as the darker bird tottered. She saw that blood was running into its eye, causing the unlucky cock to blink wretchedly. His alert, copper opponent, sensing his advantage, was now flying at the bloody loser with mad venom. One of the thrusts went home. The dark bird spread his wings loosely, dropped his head, toppled. On the ground, given up for dead, he suddenly regained a flash of insane strength. He flapped his wings, hurled himself back and forth on the sand. By this time his eyes were fixed; his bill, thrust as far forward as his neck would reach, was locked open. Amid the shouts of the men, the screams of the women and the grunts of the slaves, a black stooped down and picked up the winning bird. Another took the dead one in hand.

"You don't like it," Diron said.

"I'll stay," Céleste told him meekly.

"One of mine fights now. The black one."

A moment later the enameled black bird was facing a lustrous silver opponent. Shadows, lengthening across the fighting place, failed to dim the shine of the vivid cocks. They leaped fiercely, as if demon-possessed, and hurled each other backwards with cruel thrusts. Each leap went higher than the preceding one, and presently the birds were coming together a half meter above the earth. After a dozen vicious flurries they were still unsoiled and fighting desperately.

"They might stop now, while each has all his parts, and make peace on equal terms," Céleste suggested.

"That would satisfy neither them nor us," Diron said. "And I'd disown such a bird."

Across the circle the count extended his hand, holding out a gold piece.

"I'll take the silver one," he offered.

"Very well," Diron said, accepting the wager. He ran his hand deep into a pocket and produced his own coin.

M. Nadya got a bet with Captain Frounier. Half dozen other bets were as quickly made. The birds eyed each other sharply and went into the air again.

Céleste waited till there was another lull in the contest. Gaining Diron'e eye, she said, "You're not what you seem to be—not really."

His eyes brightened.

"What do I seem to be that I'm not? Tell me."

"You seem gentle and sad. That's the way you've always looked to me."

"I'm not gentle," he assured her, laughing. "That's not me at all."

"And you shouldn't be melancholy either. It isn't reasonable."

The cocks were desperate again. The count rose from his bench to cheer. Some of the women were nearly hysterical. Among the men there was increasing tenseness. Captain Frounier, his mouth sprung wide, licked his toothless gums stupidly. A tiny trickle of slobber ran out of the corner of his lips. Tears of excitement streaked his cheeks.

Suddenly, with an inspired jump, Diron's dark bird over-leaped his silver adversary, raking the other bird with the needle point of his spur as he went over. The full effect was not instantaneous. The silver cock, upturned on the sand, quickly righted himself and rushed into another flurry of wild feet and wings and bills. A moment later, however, bright claret stains marked the light metal feathers.

Céleste watched with divided interest. Presently Diron, too, became less intent upon the birds.

"Mine will win," he said. "He has drawn the blood."

"Yes," she agreed.

Twilight came to the scene like blue smoke sifting through the trees. Unable to keep her seat, Céleste rose and stood behind the bench. Two or three women left the group. Each time the circle was broken to make way for one of them the men crowded together a little closer than before.

A moment or two later Diron's cock sank a spur flush into his antagonist's head. A little spurt of blood sprang up, and the contest promptly ended. Céleste saw Diron and the count settling their account on the far side of the pit. She turned and sniffed at the little perfumed handkerchief in her hand. She had commenced to walk away absently when Diron joined her.

"I'm afraid I can't stand any more," she said.

They walked toward the house. Céleste's morocco slippers pinched her feet on the uneven path. In the windows of Bréda orange lights blossomed.

"I'm miserable," Diron said. "I feel terrible. Do you think it could be love, Céleste?"

"Why, I wouldn't know love if I saw it," she laughed.
"Tragic, gay or otherwise—I wouldn't recognize it."

Diron's countenance fell. She allowed him to hold her
hand, and he inspected it strangely, turning it over in his
palm, feeling the texture of the skin, measuring its length
against the length of his own.

"Of course not. You're a child," he said.

"I wouldn't know love, no matter how it dressed."

"But in that case," Diron asserted, pressing her hand
and drawing her arm, "in that case you will have to
learn."

Suddenly she saw tiny lights springing up in the shrubs
and trees. Gleaming birds killed and were killed in the
blue light. Disaster threatened in a thousand ways, for
Diron clasped her savagely.

"But I'm still not sure. Not too sure."

"In that case," he said. "In that case—"

She made no comment when he took her hand and
started once more toward the colonial house in the
shadows. On the veranda they paused, and she pressed
his arm warmly before taking leave.

"Isn't it tragic?" she said, a gay twinkle in her eyes.

"Worse than you know," he told her. "Like doom."

She felt a momentary sadness but not enough to keep
her from running on the stairs. Diron, without moving
from his place on the veranda, saw her take her skirts like
an armful of sea foam, raise them above the danger of
being stepped on and, revealing legs plump and neat
under pantalets, race lightly up the stairs and vanish. She
did not know she was being watched.

CHAPTER FOUR

1. He stood motionless on the blue veranda. Twilight deepened as shadows altered their substance and shape. Céleste's footsteps faded on the stairs. Now, turning to one of the sturdy out-door seats, Diron withdrew from the light of the broad entrance, sprawled and threw out his feet with a sigh. Presently a breeze came up, bustling, heavily scented by the ocean, and rattled through the palms. Diron felt dust on his eyelashes. He could smell the dryness of the fields.

He had been alone nearly half an hour when the others returned from the cock fights. They shouted noisily on the foot walk, and came on the veranda tottering in each other's arms. Rum had been served at the pit. They distributed themselves on the seats and benches along the veranda. Several women from within, hearing voices, came out and sat on the steps, spreading their billowing, foam-like dresses demurely. A moment or two later Mars came and lit half a dozen ornamental lamps along the rail.

"I hope it won't disappoint you ladies too much if I leave you now," old Captain Frounier said, tickled by his own deviltry. "I despise fresh air, and besides I'd like to see what the chances are for a game of whist."

"You're cruel," Annette told him, following Claire to a bench near Diron. "I expect to pine away in just no time."

"I know you salt water men," Claire added in her coarse voice. "You're all fast and unreliable."

The captain nearly bent double with merriment.

"You've been around too much," he chirped.

He was followed by de Sacy who, without saying so, seemed to dislike the cooling breezes of the veranda as much as his older companion. The count, however, returned a moment later when a strange carriage raced into the wide sweeping driveway, made a complete turn and pointed its horses toward the gate again before coming to a full stop. It was plain that the individual, or individuals, making the call did not intend to remain at Bréda, and the curiosity of the guests on the veranda was instantly piqued.

M. Nadya, a few paces from Diron's seat, looked at his friend Solange mischievously.

"Complications?" he asked.

"Could be," M. Solange admitted. "Do you have permission to be away from home, M. Nadya?"

"Oh, emphatically. And you?"

"Mine is countersigned," M. Solange said with stress.

Diron's friends, Brieux, Gratien and Augière, joined the others in laughing at these two, but Arsenne Brieux was visibly disturbed.

"I may have neglected my pass," he confessed hazily.

"Is your conscience clear?" Diron asked.

"Perfectly—though my wits are not."

Diron observed that the almond-eyed belle had seated

herself on the arm of Arsenne's chair and allowed him to rest his head against her. She stroked his hair as he spoke.

"You men would be more entertaining," she said dryly, "if you didn't joke about your black mistresses in the presence of ladies."

"I'm a beast," Arsenne remarked sleepily. "You recognize that I'm a beast, don't you?"

The carriage door opened. Scarcely visible from the veranda, someone stepped to the ground and hurried directly toward the wide steps of Bréda. A moment later the figure became clear. A vivid, saffron girl, richly dressed and savagely beautiful, came swiftly to the center of the veranda. Her dark hair gave a polished enamel shine. Her dress, though made of crêpe, was without stiffening, without plaits in the skirt and without sleeves. Her back, her bosom and part of her waist were uncovered, and the rest of her form was visible through the scantiness of a sort of flower-petal white dress. Coming rapidly up the steps, her high red heels clicking sharply, she fairly snatched the breath from those who saw her.

"Monsieur Brieux?" she asked of the hostile eyes fixed upon her.

The poet pulled himself together calmly.

"Yes, Manoune," he answered without resentment.

She retreated timidly when her eyes fell upon the woman on the arm of his chair.

"I'm sorry, monsieur," she said. "I'm terribly sorry—but there's something that concerns you. I didn't know any other way—"

Her voice had commenced to quaver. Her excitement

was so real that there was no hiding it even for the space of a moment. Arsenne Brieux rose unsteadily, allowed the mulatto girl to lead him down the steps and into the shadows of the path.

Diron's heart skipped a beat.

"Pretty trick," the Count de Sacy observed, standing between the door lamps.

"I'll take a pure black one for mine," M. Nadya suggested. "Either one thing or the other. I don't like to confuse an issue."

Diron was convinced that the mulattos were upset in some way. He knew Arsenne and Manoune too well to take the girl's errand for an act of jealous concern as the others seemed to take it.

"Manoune doesn't usually follow him around," he said, unable to restrain himself from speaking.

"Come to think about it, she doesn't," Gratien agreed.

"Confuse the issue," de Sacy said, still chewing on Nadya's remark. "Humph! All women are complex. It's a part of their magic."

"All women are complex, but some are more so," Nadya argued. "It's a part of their magic and part of their peril, the more so in the case of one like Manoune."

"Don't be a pair of asses," Diron said, vastly irritated. "If the mulattos are cutting up again, some of you may have to fight your way into Le Cap tonight."

Arsenne was on the steps again, and the girl was hurrying down to the waiting carriage on the driveway.

"I must go," the poet announced. He turned to the count. His manner was tired; the effort to collect his thoughts and make sense with rum in his brain had exhausted him. "With your leave, monsieur. . . ."

"You must eat," de Sacy protested.

"It is impossible," Arsenne told him, visibly shaking. The last trace of levity vanished instantly. Nadya, more nervous than usual, looked at Diron with puzzled eyes. De Sacy was definitely angry. The word *ass* was not one he relished when applied to himself. Still no one spoke immediately. Arsenne Brieux went inside and returned a few moments later followed by one of the Bréda house servants. He proceeded directly to the road where his mistress was waiting for him in her carriage. He was out of sight when Mars, coming to the door, broke the tension by summoning the guests to supper.

De Sacy turned swiftly and went inside ahead of the others. A few guests followed immediately but a large number disregarded the summons. Eventually this latter group began rising also and drifting through the entrance doors. Angry enough to fight, Diron refused to leave his seat. Alone in the cool shadows, he knotted his brows and tried to think dispassionately. He was soon interrupted, however.

Yes, he was sure of it. Faint, wavering, almost legendary, a sound traveled along the edge of the hills, through a grove and across the big road. Diron was absolutely certain. He knew that chorus of whistling. Boukman, Baissou, Jean-François—their crowd was out racing their horses, leaping fences and working themselves into a frenzy. Of course, with the band he knew that there should be drums. Diron pricked his ears attentively. There they were, throbbing like the heart-beat of the earth.

There was devilment in the air, and Diron made no mistake about it. Still the business did perplex him. He could not think of a good reason why the fiery Manoune should call for her dissolute lover in such agitation and summon him so urgently.

Diron's brow was still knotted when Paulette came outside looking for him.

"What's behind it?" she asked him pointedly.

"I wish I knew," he answered.

"Brieux is spirited away by his mulattress and you—you remain out here when everyone else goes in to supper."

Diron refused to become interested, though he glanced at her momentarily and saw her eyes shift away.

"Yes," he said curtly. "That's true."

"You confess being a Friend of the Blacks."

"I confess? Why, I simply state it. It isn't much of a secret. I have my own thoughts about the Revolution, too. But I seem to remember hearing you say you didn't care about politics."

"I'm afraid, Diron. Now with you abandoning me, I feel terrified."

"Silly, Paulette."

She looked directly into his eyes.

"No, Diron, not half silly. If there's to be political strife here, I'd like to be near you. You seem to be in touch with things."

"You seemed to impress the count," Diron suggested.

"And you—you did right well by yourself, too."

Diron rose, facing the door.

"That reminds me—I'm hungry," he said.

In the hallway they were met by Céleste who, having changed her dress again, was brilliant in a costume that appeared in the lamplight to be made of silver tissue. Even with her hair bound to her head with a band she seemed fluffy beside the sleek, tall Paulette, whose syrupy black hair had that half sinister shine when seen under the light. Céleste stood near the foot of the stairs, puzzled and perhaps a little afraid.

"Now *I* am reminded," Paulette whispered tactfully. Then she added, loud enough to be heard by Céleste, "My seat, I was informed, is to be the same one I occupied at dinner—or relatively the same one."

"Which proves what I said. You were a success," Diron laughed.

Paulette ignored the girl at the foot of the stairs and walked ahead to the dining hall. Visibly pained, unable to say anything appropriate, Céleste dropped her eyes childishly.

"I loathe Madame Viard," she whispered when Diron offered her his arm.

2. The food had scarcely been touched when the clamor broke. Count Armand de Sacy, irritated from the first by the huge gorilla-like black who had been assigned to stand behind his chair and attend him with a more spe-

cial care than the waiters could give, kept glancing
around at the powerful slave. The table itself was a picture of Creole opulence and colonial taste. The linen, the
silver, the glass and china ware all reflected a new world
civilization that took its key from the aristocracy of Paris.
Only the Creole tendency to excess and the hovering
presence of a regiment of African slaves gave the scene a
character distinct from any number of its continental
prototypes.

Some of the slaves employed in the dining hall did not
belong to Bréda. They had been borrowed from neighboring estates for the occasion. This was not unusual. Of
field laborers there were more than enough at Bréda, but
these could not be transformed into immaculate house
servants at a moment's notice. It was necessary to aug-
ment the available number tonight by borrowing here
and there from neighbors. An exception, as everyone
knew, was Toussaint, assigned at the moment to the wine
cellar; but Toussaint was a coachman rather than a field
hand. Even Suzette, his wife, was considered unfitted
for the house work.

These observations only made the count more uneasy
in the presence of the blunt-fingered giant behind him,
and he purposed definitely to have M. de Libertas remove
the beast before the meal had proceeded much further.
A dark girl might be acceptable in that position, perhaps
even a long-legged chocolate boy, but this brute—the
count simply couldn't abide the bright beady eyes or the
fierce glances the fellow kept shooting across the broad
room.

Paulette took the chair at his left as the tiny nobleman, suddenly standing, bowed very low. There was a striking nimbleness about de Sacy when gallantry was an issue, and his stiff white collar, his freshly powdered hair, his tight pink breeches and flashing buckles did no harm to the impression.

The hour had come for petty jealousies to crop out in catty remarks. Arsenne Brieux's name came up here and there. The table buzzed with half a dozen little heads-together conversations. In the midst of this the noise broke. There must have been a regiment of drums. The tremendous impact stunned the ear. As alert as a sparrow, his mouth filled with food, de Sacy choked with consternation, grimaced, began looking at his companions as if to accuse them for his fright.

Diron had already scented treachery. There, wearing the garb of a waiter, big-boned and belligerent, stood Baissou, prominent member of the rebel band that haunted the hills. The others were at this very moment riding their horses, whistling. And there—good Lord, how near were they?—there were the drums. Baissou should have been with them. Not here.

Suddenly a hush swept the room, and in the silence shouts of distant voices could be heard between the throbs of demoniacal drums. The stunned gasp was not broken till a moment of utter panic followed in which the massive satin-clothed black behind the count's chair sprang to the top of the table with a single leap, his boots crashing glasses, scattering plates and bowls, and raced toward the window overlooking the drive.

"*Vive la liberté!*" he thundered.

Men guests leaped to their feet. The women screamed. Chairs toppled backwards. At the crest of the tumult a window shattered, and through it went the powerful black with a wild lunge that hung the frame around his shoulders. A moment later his feet were scuffing the driveway noisily.

De Sacy, as pale as a dead man, bit his lips, slobbered at the corners of his mouth, swore bitterly in a soft, unnatural voice.

The remaining African servants vanished through the nearest doors or retreated, purple with fright, till their backs touched the walls. They were all safely out of the way when guests began fleeing the wrecked dining room. The women beside de Sacy were in as wretched a state of despair as any present. Paulette had been splashed, to her great disgust, by a glass of wine. Her scarlet mouth showed intense hardness as she stood, one hand on the back of a chair, looking at the front of her dress. Angélique, her trim figure instantly losing its grace, bounded with the crowd toward the door. Presently the count was caught up by the tide and carried along.

He was through the door and the table had been all but abandoned when the tiny nobleman observed that Madame de Libertas, who continued unmoved at her place, did not remain seated because it was her will to linger. She had sunk limply into the chair, her chin falling helplessly on her bosom. She was in a faint. De Sacy pretended not to see her.

They might as well have remained in the dining room, except for the marred and soiled table. There was no better place to go. There was no visible reason for panic. De Sacy withdrew from the crowd when he reached the hall and began seeking the overseer, M. de Libertas. He found him cornered with Captain Frounier.

"Wasn't that a pretty time for the ape to crack up?" the old man was saying.

Light broke instantly for de Sacy. It hadn't occurred to him till this minute that the African's amazing behavior might have been the result of insanity.

"Yes," he said quickly, "that's it. The drums caused it. They're still animals, you know. The jungle stays in their blood, no matter how far you take them away."

"There are a lot of ways to look at it," M. de Libertas suggested. "Sometimes it's hard to understand the slaves."

"They hear a lot of talk about politics," the captain said. "You can't take them for fools all the time. It's a fool that talks about the trouble we've had in France before his blacks. They catch one word here, another there, and this is what happens. *Vive la liberté.* You heard him say it."

"Was he one of our people, M. de Libertas?"

The overseer shook his head, absent-mindedly.

"He was borrowed," he answered finally.

"Do we have responsibility?"

"Perhaps not, monsieur. I'm still wondering about what you say. He didn't seem out of his head to me—I mean he acted more like one intoxicated than one who is insane. I wonder if it couldn't have been that."

"Drink, hunh?"

"Intoxication, monsieur."

M. de Libertas seemed bent on making a fine distinction. His insistence, however, irritated the Count de Sacy who promptly buttoned his lips tightly and let it be seen that he was in no mood for triviality. He, more perhaps than anyone else present, had been insulted and outraged. He would have M. de Libertas know that responsibility for behavior such as they had witnessed went beyond the near-brutes who perpetrated it. A man charged with administering an estate like Bréda, like those administering the affairs of the whole island, was expected, among other things, to maintain discipline.

Suddenly there was commotion on the wide, banistered stair, a rush of ascending feet and the flutter of silks. A moment later the announcement responsible for the flight reached the three men. Diron Desautels, in a state of wild excitement, rushed toward them.

"I've been on the balcony," he cried.

"What of it?"

"The judgment is set. The books are open. Come and see."

Curiously, all three of the men began to sulk. Nothing that might happen could shake them more than they had been shaken or add to their present bewilderment. Not one of them made a move to follow the crowd that now stampeded on the stairs.

"What was the fellow's name?" de Sacy inquired, his voice sick with fright. "The one who cracked."

"Baissou," Diron answered, almost jubilantly. "He has

a companion named Boukman, more terrible than himself; and if you knew what they were up to, you wouldn't be standing there. The Revolution is here."

"The dog was mad," Captain Frounier said. "I saw the froth on his mouth."

"Mad—yes, that's the word."

Diron laughed boisterously.

"You mention revolution," de Sacy said, his anger increasing. "Aren't you afraid?"

Diron had turned to leave the other men. The count's question halted him. He paused and regarded the men seriously.

"Afraid of an upheaval? On the contrary. Conditions could not possibly be worse in Saint Domingue. I welcome the prospect of change. Revolution appeals to me. In fact, I'm excited over the idea."

"You're a fool," de Sacy told him.

Ignoring the remark, Diron turned to M. de Libertas.

"Incidentally, monsieur," he said. "Your wife has fainted."

He left them with a bound, fairly galloping up the stairs in the hallway.

"He's over-excited," M. de Libertas said when Diron was gone.

"The boy's a wild liar," Captain Frounier suggested.

Both men watched the small nobleman, now regaining his poise if not his usual color. De Sacy sucked his teeth, gave the remarks of each of them an inconsiderate sneer.

"He's neither excited nor untruthful," he said. "Both

of you are stupid, politically. That boy is a Jacobin, and he isn't very prudent. He's in the wrong climate. He'll lose his head."

3. Flames from the parched countryside climbed fantastically against the wall of night. Great orange tongues seemed to kindle hundreds of feet above the earth and lap at the stars. It was as if the very vine of oppression, reaching from this planet to a higher one, had caught fire.

The part of the balcony to which Diron had returned when he left the men downstairs was crowded. Chairs were being brought out for the women of the group. A bit of blown ash was already reaching Bréda, though the blazes were at no point less than a mile away. Several of the belles had covered their flimsy white dresses with dark dust cloaks. The panic which Baissou's gesture had started was gradually subsiding. An attitude of despair took its place. The situation was far too grave for hysterics and shouting. Plantations were burning on every side. Barns and haystacks and greathouses, one after another, took fire with an explosive burst of flame and smoke and sparks. Distant fields were being ravished by a hungry, red-lipped monster that cavorted and wallowed over dried stalks of cane.

"There you have it."

The voice was hard and resentful, and Diron turned to Paulette angrily.

"We neither understand nor sympathize with each other," he told her, "but that is no point now. It's time to consider some means of saving our lives."

"Have we a chance?"

The trim-figured Angélique joined them, her teeth chattering.

"I still can't understand," she said tearfully. "What's wrong? Nobody seems to know what's happening."

Diron looked at her frankly and decided that it was too late to be indirect.

"They all know," he said. "The slaves have broken free. They're setting fires, and there's no telling what else they may be doing."

"I'm stupid, I know, but is it necessary for them to start fires?"

"The blacks have been treated damnably."

"I thought the bad feeling was between the *petits blancs* and the mulattos."

"A few of us knew the blacks had their feelings, too. Nobody'd listen to us, of course."

"That's why you're elated," Paulette insisted.

"I'm not elated, Paulette," he said. "It's gruesome of you to say so."

The flames were unabated along the edge of the sky. Drums kept up an unbroken throb. From the Bréda stables came the whinnying of horses and the sounds of scurrying grooms and coachmen. Captain Frounier came through the window, following the bored and supercili-

ous old belles, Claire and Annette. Diron noticed that
the count had not come with them.

"Ah," cried Claire. "Magnificent. That's really an idea.
They're burning the devilish island. Thank God. Wish
I'd thought of it."

"We had some fireworks of our own," Annette remembered.

"This is too much better. Ours would seem silly now."

Standing in shocked silence, the crowd on the balcony
regarded the two giddy old courtesans with horrified
faces. Suddenly disgusted, Diron returned to the window.
Paulette ran after him, but the others stood paralyzed.
He was inside and had started down the hall when he
felt the woman's hand on his sleeve.

"What are you going to do?" she asked.

"I'm not staying here."

"You're burning with anger."

"They're idiots. I do not like aristocrats. And their
playmates sicken me."

"Come to my arms, Diron. Take me. Quench that fire."

They were alone in the hallway. A confusion of voices
came up from the lower rooms. A rear door banged repeatedly. On the balcony there was still much talking.
The hall candles shed a rich though flickering mauve
light. Shadows quavered. No shadows sullied Paulette's
dark, lacquered beauty, however. Diron acknowledged
that she was a glowing creature, but he tightened his
lips. Tonight he knew as never before that love was another thing.

"If you leave immediately, you may save your life," he said.

"Is it that bad?"

"Perhaps worse. Demand your carriage—or at least a horse."

"Can I depend on you?"

"I'll try to help you," Diron said.

She left him hurriedly, ran down the stairs.

His heart softened when she was out of sight. Paulette had her points if one didn't look too deep and could withstand a certain insincerity. Diron didn't want to see her harmed. He felt a vague responsibility for her presence at Bréda. She had at first proposed staying away.

He turned quickly and entered a room in which a woman slave, wearing a nightmarish pair of red pantalets under a candy-striped dress, kept watch over the hats, coats and riding clothes of the gentlemen guests. Despite the panic, no one seemed to have preceded Diron to this room. Later, however, when he passed through the downstairs hall, the appearance of his hat and saddle whip became a signal to a dozen confused men who had just returned from the veranda. All of them dashed at once toward the coat room.

Diron had reached the veranda steps when he awakened to the sound of footsteps following him. He recognized the click of Céleste's small heels and halted abruptly, embarrassed by the recollection that he had been about to leave without speaking to her again. When she caught up, his brow darkened. The narrow pencil-mark mustache on his upper lip took a serious slant.

"Listen, Céleste," he said earnestly. "God willing, I'll meet you in Le Cap. I brought Mme Viard here today. I'm afraid I have a duty now."

"Oh."

"You don't mind, do you?"

"I despise Mme Viard," she answered.

"Yet she is alone, while you have Mme de Libertas and her husband; you have a chance with them."

"No doubt she's fascinating, too."

"That's unfair, Céleste."

She seemed so bewildered, so childish as he looked at her now that for a moment he reproached himself for having ever kissed her. The longer he stood, and the more he thought, the greater his confusion became. Several guests came through the tall entrance doors, men with high red heels clicking nervously on the veranda, graceful young women sick with despair and fright. They swayed and wavered on the steps, cried tragically for their horses and coaches. When they disappeared among the shadows on the path, Diron tried again to find words for his dilemma. Surely, he thought, there should be some grounds on which he could gain an understanding with Céleste, even in the midst of panic. But the moment was too intense, the rush of time too great. Words choked in his throat. He was actually relieved when a slave led two saddled horses through a clump of shrubbery, across the flower beds and up to the steps of Bréda.

"They are yours," Céleste said, squinting. "So good-by."

"Yes, one is mine. Good-by."

She clung to his hand until he pulled away. Then when Paulette Viard came hurriedly through the shadows, Céleste turned away with hurt pride and returned to the entrance door. Diron helped his companion to her saddle without speaking. When he had mounted also, he turned curtly.

"There isn't much time," he said. "Possibly not enough."

"Time enough to dally with a pullet," she answered.

He was impressed with the unusual hardness that had come to her mouth and eyes under the strain. Paulette had now a coolness that was almost terrifying. She had lost her color. The marble whiteness of her face, the polished blackness of her hair, both kept flashing before Diron as the horses gained speed in the drive. Each glimpse disturbed him strangely. For some unaccountable reason Diron was haunted by the absurd fancy that he was riding beside a woman capable of killing. Once or twice he actually shuddered in the darkness.

There was danger of becoming over-wrought, he thought. One had to fight off ludicrous notions at a time like this. Diron knew that this was a night that would require all his powers. Of course, as a number of persons suspected, there were shadows on the reputation of the hot-blooded Creole beauty who rode beside him tonight, but they were not such as to give one the shudders on a midnight ride. Her parentage had never been too clear. The disappearance of her young husband was a near-scandal. The mystery of her support was downright annoying.

One thing about her seemed crystal clear, however. Paulette's jealous fondness for Diron was certainly no secret. If at times her passion failed to ring true, no one beside himself seemed ever to question it.

The horses clattered over a tiny wooden bridge, wheeled abruptly and turned into a narrow side road.

CHAPTER FIVE

1. Within an hour after the confusion in the dining hall
the conclusion had been generally accepted by the guests
as well as by the household at Bréda that the only hope
for any of them was to reach Cap Français and the pro-
tection of the colonial arms. Screaming bands of slaves
crossed and recrossed the charred plain, following thun-
derous batteries of savage drums. Havoc and fire marched
with the furious blacks. They were running amok; and
if there was anyone who imagined that Bréda would be
spared, he held his breath.

The back door still banged repeatedly. In all parts of
the house there was wild scurrying. The time for words
had passed. What speaking there was came in gasps from
tremulous lips. In the room where she stood guard over
the coats and hats of the gentlemen guests the firm-
breasted young slave woman came to the end of her endurance. Abandoned by the other blacks, as much in the
dark as anyone in respect to what was happening, she
suddenly snatched the turban from her head, hoisted the
striped skirt and, her screaming pantalets exposed to the
hips, dashed through the door. Half way down the hall,
however, she halted abruptly.

Count Armand de Sacy, angered, fearful of the enraged slaves, but primed with drink, came through his own door in time to stop one of her bounding knees with his belly. The impact sent him to the floor; it also arrested the terrified female. Rolling over quickly, the little nobleman regained his feet, vastly nonplussed, and stamped the floor with terrier-like passion.

"Filthy slut!" he cried, raising his hand. "Here is something to help you see where you're leaping."

He slapped her with his open palm; the blow, landing flush and clean, spun her completely around. Moreover it unhinged her mind, for she sprang at him resentfully, her arms whirling windmill fashion, and poured blows on the man who had struck her. It made no difference now that she was a slave, her wits were too confused. She clawed, she butted with her forehead, and de Sacy found himself clinging to her to keep from falling. But there was no holding her. The tall girl rushed him against a wall, held him by the shoulders and again aimed her forehead at his head. *Mon Dieu,* what a female! No wonder the Creoles were fond of dallying with slave wenches. Such venom. Such relentless passion. But, God's teeth, there she was maneuvering his head into a position where she could crush it with her own skull. The count saw the thrust coming and protected himself by ducking, resting his face against her bosom and trying to hold her arms.

In another moment he was pommeling her body with his own fists and gaining an advantage which further enraged the wench. He struck her in the face but paid for it when she flew at him so furiously she hurled him to the floor. She tumbled with him and almost immediately fastened her teeth in the fleshy part of his cheek. He fought back desperately, grunted, kicked, rolled, attempting to gouge. She refused to relax her teeth. She clawed his face with her hands. Blood appeared. Then somehow finally her anger subsided. She released the ineffectual little man, rose to her knees, allowed him to cuff her in the face. The blows were weak and half-hearted. They bolstered de Sacy's pride, however, and he staggered to his feet, turned toward the stairs. The young savage got up slowly. She seemed to be suppressing an inclination to laugh.

Exhausted, scratched and bloody, his clothes torn, his rouge and mascara smeared grotesquely, Armand de Sacy wavered down the stairs and through the lower hallway, reached the back door and went outside on the gravel path. In the open air it occurred to him that a carriage was waiting. Because of the turmoil and panic he had asked that it be held in the shadow of a tree some distance from the drive. Others were waiting for him. He had been a fool to delay them. Now he was unable to hasten. He was tired and his breath came short. He simply couldn't explain to them what had kept him; he decided to tarry on the path till he could catch his wind.

Outside, with darting shadows and the continuous scuffing of unseen feet, the terror was even greater than within the house. De Sacy waited as long as he could endure the tension then crossed a plot of soft earth, thrashed his way through prickly shrubs and came to the sequestered carriage.

"Who's here?" he asked, touching a wheel of the vehicle.

Someone uncovered a carriage lantern in the darkness, held it obsequiously before the aristocrat. De Sacy recognized M. Solange by his voice, not by the over-sized coachman's coat he was wearing, nor by his blackened African-like face.

"I am to be your coachman, monseigneur," the Creole said. "Do I look the part?"

The count ignored his question.

"Who's inside?"

M. Solange swung the door open, held the lantern within to aid the count in seating himself. Captain Frounier, his eyes wild, his toothless old jaws twitching nervously, sat beside a smartly dressed copper-colored belle. The young woman's disguise failed to deceive the count. He had paid enough attention to those almond eyes to recognize them even after their owner had darkened her face as a precaution against being waylaid by the aroused blacks. Moreover, he was himself author of the suggestion that she share a carriage with himself and Captain Frounier.

The coach lumbered in the soft field, rolled perilously in a ditch, shook its occupants fairly out of their wits before it gained the road near the impressive entrance gate of Bréda. A small breeze rose and a gust of smoke filled the carriage. Ash was blowing, too. The almond-eyed girl sneezed. Captain Frounier and the count both barked to keep from choking.

"Your place appeared to be one of the first to burn, Captain," the girl said.

"I won't forget it either," the old man said, his voice faltering.

"What kind of settlement do you expect?" the count asked.

"We'll have to loose most of the slave stock," the captain suggested. "When a thing like this gets to going, it's like the plague. An awful lot of the stock will have to be killed. But the blame goes further than the Africans. The General Assembly has this to answer for. They've carried their 'rights of man' foolishness too damn far. Count, the only way they can put themselves right now is by giving Saint Domingue its unconditional independence."

"The smoke is choking me," de Sacy complained. "Is there a bottle in here?"

"Two of them," the girl said.

She ran her hand behind her skirts on the floor. Finding the rum, she uncorked one bottle and handed it to the count. He drank deeply then rested the bottle between his knees.

"You forget, Captain," he said gloomily. "You forget we've had a worse madness in Paris. Don't expect too much from the General Assembly."

"They can't ignore a thing like this, monseigneur."

"I'm afraid they can. They're insane. France is going to the dogs."

"Well, they won't carry Saint Domingue with them. Plague take them, this is too rich a colony for even France to wreck."

"I'd rather walk than listen to that," the girl observed, bored.

The count stiffened, took another drink from the bottle and dropped the subject. The prolonged excitement affected the old captain strangely. He dropped his chin on his chest, nodded.

In his coachman's seat outside, M. Solange gave the horses his whip. Presently they went into a gallop. The speed pleased the count. He expanded confidently as the flying dust sifted into the carriage.

A few moments later the heavy coach swerved on the road. The horses, abruptly halted, went to their haunches as the weight of the rolling carriage pressed against their hind legs. A dark clamour confronted and surrounded them in the road. M. Solange stood in his seat, drawing the reins with all his strength. Suddenly, without seeing, the count realized that someone had the animals by their bits. Voices were heard, an uncertain number of them. A moment of confusion and abject fright passed before someone emerged from the roadside clump with a flaming torch.

The count's blood froze in his veins. The girl beside him screamed tearfully, then tried to call back the outburst, if that were possible, by shrinking as small as possible between the two men and uttering no further sound. It added little, if anything, to the consternation when, a moment later, the door of the coach was flung open from without and the torch thrust before their faces.

"Out!" a gross voice bellowed from the darkness.

Already someone had commenced to cut the horses from their harness. In the glow of the flare de Sacy saw half a dozen little mouse-colored mules with scarlet blankets and fierce black riders. His mind working swiftly now, the small man stepped obediently to the ground. Instantly, he observed M. Solange, safe in his disguise, inching away from the coach unnoticed. Captain Frounier was clearly too terrified to move. His eyes blinked, but he sat as if paralyzed.

"Does that include me, too?" the girl asked, trying hard to achieve the patois of the slaves.

"Well, if it isn't the captain!" one of the blacks shouted, recognizing the old slaver. "Bring him out here."

The discovery seemed to give them all deep satisfaction.

"The one that brought us across?" one asked.

A chorus of drunken outbursts went up, outlandish shouts colored perhaps by memories that should have been buried.

"And what are *you* doing here?"

The question was directed at the almond-eyed girl. She winced visibly as the blacks, incredibly bold, put their heads inside the coach.

"I been with these gentlemen," she said, chewing her lips between words. "You know what love is, don't you?"

They lost interest in her amid the greater excitement of dragging the captain to the ground. Immediately the pack surrounded him, waving weapons and clenching fists. De Sacy stood beside the tall black who had taken him in charge, gasping for his breath and trembling like a palsied man.

The old captain was cuffed indiscriminately. Rows of slaves encircled him with ribald glee and began robbing him, piece by piece, of his clothes. A bold leader took his hat. Another snatched the coat. Captain Frounier swore steadily in a bitter monotone. He received a jolt when two half-grown boys tripped him up and began working the boots off his feet. In a moment they had won not only these but also his breeches.

Someone with a mind for dark merriment suggested that the old man now be given a chance to save his life by running. The crowd assented and quickly broke the circle, withdrawing to allow the crooked, nude figure opportunity to make a break. Captain Frounier undertook to run but a blow from behind promptly stopped him. A glittering machete hissed, and left him dying on his feet. Then a blunt weapon bashed his head so that he began to sink. As he went down, a dozen wild creatures, eager to multiply injury, rushed insanely, accompanied by frightful shouts, and tried to land at the same time. The frightened horses reared, attempted to run away.

Suddenly, witnessing the butchery of the old captain, a desperate thought seized de Sacy. He touched the savage at his elbow confidentially, his eyes twinkling with guile. Then leaning toward him he whispered.

"Look at that pullet again," he said slyly. "She's no mulatto. She's disguised herself with brown paint. Look at her legs. A luscious woman, too."

The African, dumbfounded by the betrayal, left the

count unguarded momentarily and returned to the girl in the coach. During the brief instant this required, having bought his chance by disposing of the almond-eyed girl, de Sacy slipped through the crowd, plunged into a thicket, darted, ran, faded among the shadows.

2. Among those who heard the scuffling of the count and his female antagonist was the old, soft-voiced coachman of M. de Libertas. Toussaint, trusted beyond his fellows and respected for his judgment, had been assigned to the wine cellar during the festivities. When the trouble broke in the dining hall, he was pleased to remain at his post where he was presently joined by Mars, major domo among the house servants.

"Baissou is theatrical," the coachman had remarked following Mars's description of the tumult at supper.

"He's not afraid, though."

"He makes himself conspicuous—foolishly conspicuous."

An hour had passed. The two old blacks, fastidiously clean and well-dressed, sat on stools in the flickering light of a candle. Half a dozen times they were visited by slaves who reported what was happening on the countryside and at various neighboring estates visible from the tree tops or from the roof of the stable. The insurrection of the blacks was indeed something more than a dream now, they declared. The slaves of Bréda, notoriously well-treated at the hands of M. de Libertas and his wife, had not yet joined, but a dozen or more of those who had been borrowed for this occasion had, like Baissou, scampered across the fields to join the batteries of drums, the rude cavalry detachments mounted on plow horses, oxen, mules, and donkeys, the horde of barefooted followers carrying torches and armed with machetes, pikes and clubs.

"When do we join?" Mars asked, stifling a cough.

"I'll give the word. Not now," Toussaint told him decisively.

A few moments later they put their heads together and tried to comprehend the scuffle on the second floor. When it was over and one of the antagonists stumbled down the stairs and out the back door, Toussaint decided to leave the wine cellar and get busy.

"I won't be here when you come back," Mars told him on the ladder.

Toussaint paused.

"Feeling weak?"

Mars nodded.

"I want to lie down," he admitted.

"Well, get better. Tell Suzette where I am."

When he reached the hall above, the girl was still on the floor, her naked breasts exposed, her skirt twisted around her hips, her face long with exhaustion. She had the look of one who had been ravished; but when Toussaint squinted questioningly, she quickly corrected him. It wasn't what he thought.

"I fought back," she said. "The count struck me in the face; what's going to happen, *vieux* Toussaint?"

"War is beginning," he told her. "The slaves are breaking free. They'll have to fight the army by morning."

"I'm already free," the girl suggested.

"Yes, you are—scuffling with the count. Go to your quarters now."

The hall was empty, save for these two; and when the girl left, Toussaint walked back and forth nervously. Through the window that led out on the balcony, he saw the burning fields, but there was now no one out there enjoying the spectacle. The rooms within seemed deserted, too. Still a few sounds could be heard. Several doors stood open. In each case the occupant had fled leaving the lamp burning. The gentleman's coatroom had been left with a great number of neglected hats and riding garments.

M. Bayou de Libertas opened his door and came into the hall, stood silently, hands behind him on the knob, as tears filled his eyes and began running down his face. Seeing tears in the comical eyes of the overseer touched Toussaint immediately. He stopped pacing; his pitifully rounded shoulders, his hands, his wiry pigtail, his protruding teeth, together these made him an inexpressibly forlorn figure.

"Sad, Toussaint?" the overseer asked. "Or just tired?"

"Joy, like sorrow, has its tears," the coachman answered. "But I have no joy."

"You want to be free, don't you?"

"Is there a chance?"

"You know there is. Everything is with you."

"I haven't joined them—yet."

M. de Libertas looked at the shrewd old black with the utmost candor and sympathy.

"Why?" he asked simply, his eyes still tearful.

"Because of you and Madame."

"You mean—"

"Our people are not ungrateful, monsieur. Knowing how our brothers have fared on other plantations has convinced us that you are not an ordinary master of slaves."

"That's flattery, Toussaint."

"At any rate, I shall not leave your side till you and Madame de Libertas are safe. The slaves are a lustful pack tonight."

"They're drunk—drunk with freedom. I suppose it's natural, after what they've been through."

"We can carry one trunk in the coach, monsieur. If you'll have Madame indicate what she'd like to save, I'll come back and make it ready after I've harnessed the horses."

"Toussaint, I hadn't thought of running away."

"It's your only chance, monsieur. There's been blood-letting tonight, and there may be more. I'm not sure I can stop them when they reach Bréda."

Fresh tears filled the blinking, round eyes of M. de Libertas.

"No, Toussaint, no! It's like quitting a ship. I'm a hired man on this place. There's no running away."

The door opened as M. de Libertas's voice rose. He was hysterical. His wife and Céleste, both pale as ghosts, came out and stood beside him.

"Don't shout," the older woman implored. "I can't stand to see you worked up."

"We'll have to stay and take our chances," he said more calmly. "It's our penalty for being blind while all this was brewing."

"But you have no right to risk danger for these ladies." Toussaint spoke with unusual firmness.

"We risk danger if we go or if we stay."

"Monsieur, we're wasting time. Tonight, if you please, I am the master of Bréda. You don't seem to realize that slavery ended this evening when the servants walked out of the dining room and returned to their quarters without permission."

The overseer was too shaken to answer.

"What are your orders, Toussaint?" Mme de Libertas asked.

"Lay out the things you wish to save," he told her. "I'll be back presently to pack them in a trunk. Be ready to leave promptly. I hope to get the three of you to Le Cap."

He had turned before he finished his remarks. On the stairs he fairly bounded. Toussaint had an old face, but his body was made of hard, vibrant muscles. He had resources of strength that one discovered with surprise after long acquaintance.

A moment later he was on the path, hastening toward the stables. A pair of old carriage lamps gleamed on either side of the door leading into the harness room. Toussaint entered, his heels thumping solidly on the clean wooden floor. A lighted lantern swayed from a cross beam. Bare feet frisked excitedly on the roof overhead, like rats in an attic—black youngsters, perhaps, watching the fires from the distance.

When he had rolled a sturdy coach out into the yard by hand, he found bridles and quickly laid hands on the horses he preferred. Less than five minutes had passed when he swung himself to the coachman's place and, standing with feet braced apart, cracked a whip over the nervous, eager teams.

He was tying up at a sapling near the back door when he realized that he had delayed almost too long. The horde had reached Bréda. A flurry of drum beating broke out among the trees of the grove. Toussaint rushed to the door, paused long enough to feel his own quaking, dashed through the lower rooms and up the stairs. A moment later he was pounding on the door of Mme de Libertas's room.

When the door was flung open, the old coachman was pleased to discover that the woman and the girl were already in their capes, the girl apparently wearing one that belonged to the larger woman. M. de Libertas, his sorrel hair in disorder, had plopped a hat heedlessly on his head. The room itself looked as if plunderers had already visited it. The trunk in which Mme de Libertas kept the mementos of her bellehood had been uncovered and drawn into the middle of the room. A square affair, its top had been thrown back and its contents hurriedly sorted. On the floor at one side was a heap of outmoded clothes that had been discarded. In their place was to go a stack of wearable garments, spread at the moment on the bed and chairs. A quantity of silver was at the moment being stuffed into a plush bag already tight with small table-pieces and metal ornaments. The task had been given to the girl who, as she worked, trembled so noticeably that the old black took it out of her hands.

"Are we too late?" the overseer asked.

Toussaint did not answer. Instead he pointed to the bottles on a table.

"Drink something, monsieur."

"That's all he's been doing since you left," the stout wife replied, pushing the discarded things aside with her foot.

"They're coming through the grove," Toussaint said unsteadily. "You'd better go down now. The horses are tied near the back steps. I'll finish with these things. Monsieur, I suggest you lead the team around the house and get the coach out of sight. It's the safest way."

The three responded swiftly, carrying only as much as their arms could manage. With M. de Libertas it was his squirrel gun, two sets of duelling pieces, a small ornamental pistol with a carved handle. Céleste carried two fragrant dress boxes; and tucked under an orange satin coat Mme de Libertas bore the heavy chestlike box that contained the gold they had on hand.

"Are we the last?" M. de Libertas asked, passing through the door.

Toussaint had already fallen on his knees before the

open trunk and begun with swift efficiency to complete
the job. He did not look up when he answered.

"Almost the last, I imagine, monsieur."

The overseer's wife was behind him now, however, and
there was no chance of his turning. Toussaint heard their
steps on the stairs a moment later. He heard the voices
of Claire, Annette and perhaps a third woman in another
part of the house. He felt, rather than heard, the soft
thunder of drums, the impact of which fired his blood
like a drug. But what, he wondered, gave him that tin-
kling unsteadiness? Why did his teeth chatter? Was he
afraid of Boukman or Baissou or the crowd they had been
able to assemble?

Scarcely. There was no fear left in *vieux* Toussaint.
Furthermore there was no time now for pointless questions
of that sort. His task was clear. Madame and Monsieur
had been kind and reliable friends to him and to many
others in a time when the rule was cruelty and inhuman-
ity toward slaves. When these were dispatched safely,
along with their young friend, then—then he could hurl
himself into the struggle. Toussaint lost none of his former care, but he completed his work with such deft speed
that he was a trifle astonished himself as he realized
that the jewel boxes, the corsets, the petticoats and pantalets, the morocco slippers, the bales of India silk turbans,
the camphor and the sachet were all inside and that the
trunk was full.

He was standing the box on end and securing it with
straps and a rope when bedlam broke in the rooms downstairs. Glass shattered, chairs and tables toppled in a suc-

cession of wanton crashes. At the same moment heavy feet stormed the stairway.

Toussaint, calmer than he had been since the trouble first broke, recognized some of the savage voices and promptly decided to plead with the infuriated blacks in behalf of Bréda. On second thought, however, he swiftly changed his plan. There was no stopping them now. For a black who wished to see discretion and sober wisdom play a part in this thrust for liberty, the best line to follow—perhaps the only one—was to stay out of the picture until the bloody intoxication, the pent-up fury, had been spent. There was no need forgetting that a powerful French army was garrisoned in Cap Français, that this force contained veterans who had fought under the Marquis d'Estaing at the Siege of Savannah on the soil of continental America. Battalions would be in the field by morning, and this night of jungle heroics and wild abandon on the part of the slaves would be sure to have its sequel in fighting of another sort. The second and more important phase would not be firing greathouses, turning on masters and pillaging. Permanent freedom would have to be won by tedious patience in a hard, prolonged campaign against armed forces. The chiefs of the blacks would be confronted with the near-impossible task of commanding this madness and transforming it into an organized force fit to cope with military arms and discipline. In that fighting old Toussaint was sure to have a part. A flash of benign confidence gleamed on the coachman's mask-like face. One could not be overconfident, knowing the odds and the chances of failure, but

Toussaint knew that in his own heart he had already accepted the challenge. He was not a great one for the sort of havoc this night was producing; his mind was offended by messiness, confusion and turmoil. He hadn't the power to draw a brawling sword. But he was ready and anxious to meet a military foe if by doing so he could strike a blow for the freedom of the blacks. In fact, the prospect thrilled him, and he was feeling drunk with it.

At the moment, however, with the wild element in control and the pack on the stair, his business was to drop the trunk with its treasures through the window and make way for the plunderers. He raised the box and, hurrying before the approaching steps, sent it hurtling through the pane and to the ground below. When he turned, he looked into the faces of slaves who knew him well.

"*Vieux* Toussaint!" one cried.

The old black straightened the kink in his back, made a dignified salute.

"*Vive la liberté!*" he replied embarrassed.

"*Vive la liberté!*" The second voice was as hoarse and untamed as a lion's. It belonged to the gigantic, barrel-bellied Boukman.

Presently the room was filled with the slave pack. The fruits of plunder dangled from them grotesquely. One wore a yellow satin coat. Another had evidently fallen upon a jewelry box. A chain of vivid stones glittered about his neck. A handsome plumed hat adorned a savage head. There was a girl in the group, a lean bronze tomboy in an orange turban, an abbreviated skirt and gleaming boots.

"You should be home," Toussaint told her, not unkindly. "The apron should work for the pantaloons."

"Tomorrow," she said. "Everyone is out tonight. I couldn't stay."

The crowd drifted out of the room and into the hall.

"The time is slipping," Boukman growled impatiently. "Dig in. We've got to move along."

"Bréda deserves a better fate than the other estates," Toussaint suggested.

"You're soft, *vieux* Toussaint. You've been petted. See, your back is smooth. Look at these scars. I say spare none."

The burly giant gave the others his back, tore off his shirt and showed them the record of his servitude. Even Toussaint winced at the sight. Boukman had been more badly used than any beast. He snorted with ribald laughter as the others became pop-eyed with amazement.

"There is no answer to that," Toussaint remarked sadly.

The crowd quickly divided, breaking into the empty rooms like hungry jackals. Here and there a door had to be forced. This was followed each time by a resounding crash. Machetes and pikes, pirate sabers and rude spears, brandished overhead, smote one against the other in awkward confusion. A vast ravishment of curtains and hangings, of canopies and beds, of dressing tables and mirrors began. In the midst of it Claire and Annette suddenly appeared in the hall, their eyes bright with rum.

"Wait," Claire said, running after one of the wildest

insurgents and slapping him on his shoulder. "Give me a machete," she cried through the din.

The slave, so surprised he seemed frightened, raised his spear before her.

"What's this?"

"I've been waiting twenty years for something like this. Give me a weapon. I can fight, too. You can't leave me out."

"Nor me," Annette insisted. "I'll help."

The slaves shook them off but refrained momentarily from running them through with their blades.

"They aren't very playful," Toussaint told the women.

He turned and slipped swiftly down the stairs. From the bottom, he saw the enchanted Claire persuading Annette to slide down the banister.

A moment later, dragging the trunk across a flower bed, he reached the coach where M. de Libertas had secluded it in a clump of tall shrubbery and low trees.

"There is no peace, Toussaint," Mme de Libertas whimpered, drowsy with long excitement. "No peace anywhere. Turmoil, turmoil, turmoil—one fight after another."

"Each hour wounds," the coachman replied. "The last kills."

"We sent a word for Mme Jacques Juvet, this child's grandmother," the overseer's wife reminded. "Have you heard whether or not it was delivered?"

"A stable boy carried it," Toussaint assured her. Reluctantly he added, "It was too late."

"No. Oh, no. You don't mean—"

"The excitement, perhaps. Her heart."

He touched the horses and the coach moved heavily on the soft earth. Inside the carriage sobs broke. Toussaint was unable to distinguish between the voices.

3. When Diron discovered a company of people ahead, his first inclination was to stop, to turn back or perhaps strike vaguely through a grove. Second thought raised another question, however. Was it likely, or possible, that a band of inflamed slaves would huddle together in the manner of this slinking crowd? Could the Africans hold their tongues and walk their horses under these circumstances?

"Well," Paulette whispered, stopping her horse beside his.

"We've overtaken someone."

"You are not capable of treachery, are you, Diron?"

"There were others you might have ridden with, if you imagined so."

"I have a weapon," she said, bringing a small pistol from the bosom of her dress. "I won't be betrayed. I know you are a Friend of the Blacks, Diron."

His eyes flashed angrily, but he continued to regard the company ahead.

"Follow me, if you wish," he said, a hardness creeping into his voice.

The young woman made no answer but kept up as

he pushed his horse forward. As the two drew nearer a hush came over the already subdued voices. In another instant a hooded, dark-clad figure separated itself from the group, stood before the two riders in the rude cart path and halted them with a menacing wave of his hand. Presently, though the words came hoarsely, the figure emitted the cultivated voice of an educated man.

"Who's there?"

Another hush ensued. Then—

"It is I, *Oncle* Philippe," Diron said, relieved.

The company was predominantly male, fifty or more of them flanking a string of carts in which elegantly gowned women rode on boxes and chests containing treasures hurriedly snatched in the fearful confusion.

There was a shortage of horses, the stables of the aristocrats having been rifled, but the fastidious gentlemen faced the ordeal with grim courage. They were armed with hunting pieces, duelling pistols, old-fashioned long rifles and a few up-to-date flintlocks. Their clothes were too fine, their manners too soft, but they were ready to make a desperate stand if attacked.

Still smarting under Paulette's sting, Diron angrily considered how he might rid himself of her for the remainder of the journey. Slowly, over the dull jogging of his mare, a mood of self-loathing came to him. For the first time the full meaning of the woman's words reached his understanding. She knew him to be a Friend of the Blacks, of course. But it was only too clear also that she had interested herself in that fact far more than she had pretended. Paulette had been spying on him. Like a sudden revelation light broke. He groaned audibly. Lord, how could he ever have been so blind? It was as plain as day. Paulette was involved in politics.

Didn't that explain all the mystery? It was almost too simple. Paulette Viard's sinister character loomed before him like a ghost. He shuddered, recalling the dull luster of the weapon with which she had threatened him. The sight of her drawing it from her bosom with such cool deliberation now caused his blood to run cold as his mind dwelt upon the implications. If in morbid moments one could enjoy a certain fascination for a dark and deadly woman, it was quickly dispelled when one awakened to find he had been duped. There were no words for the horror Diron felt. Of one thing he was assured. He and the widow of Sylvestre Viard were enemies; they had always been opposed to each other. The fact that she was a vivid creature accounted for a bit of past dallying that he would give much to forget now that weapons were virtually drawn between them, but it only intensified his hatred. Had it been a man—but that was absurd. No man could change his colors so fantastically. No man could possibly refine deceit so thoroughly. Still, had it been a man, he'd have words for what he felt. He would know exactly what to do.

Figures in the procession seemed abnormally small and shrunken as the column swept into the shadows of a towering hedge. Fires were still visible. Smoke covered the sky, reddened the young moon. Drums, faint and firm like the pulse of the earth, kept the air vibrating. A host of distressed birds, rudely awakened to the judgment of fire, sent up scream after scream from the black thickets.

Drawn into the conversations of the other women, Paulette was led to join a group that filled one of the foremost carts, yielding her horse to an armed man. Diron walked his mare alongside long enough to avoid a conspicuous withdrawal, then began inching his way to the head of the procession. Out of her sight, he gave a sigh of great relief. Barring an unhappy incident, he would count himself rid of the sleek, unreliable woman.

They crossed the stony bed of a famished stream, worked their way up a slope and entered a wilderness of mangroves. Here shadows appalled them, but the carts lumbered on; the men, mounted and on foot, kept their cautious gait. Diron had just concluded that the actual peril was less than it seemed when, wheeling their horses behind a clump, a band of blacks crossed the cart path, sighted the company of whites, circled, shouted threateningly and fired a gun. Leaves were whipped from the trees. A twig snapped. Someone with a low, sick voice, feeling his chest thumped sharply, groaned aloud. The crowd continued to move. A moment later, deeply touched, Diron realized that he was passing within a few feet of the fallen figure. Mortally hurt, choking rapidly, the wounded aristocrat continued to cry. The company moved more rapidly than before. No one could afford to stop. There was no time to commiserate. The loss of the first member was taken without a comment from anyone.

Other shots blazed from the shadows, aimed at the steadily moving line. One broke the leg of a horse. Another, nipping a woman's breast, produced a shrill scream as well as some confused jostling of beasts and riders in the path. Much of the hot fire went astray. Diron saw that a clearing was near. Reaching that, he might have occasion to return some of this lead, but it was absurd to consider doing so at present. The slaves were all hidden behind trees. There was no indication of a target. The aim now was to rush toward the clearing. There, on equal terms, the company might exchange a few rounds with their attackers with an even chance of success. To fire now would only provoke more heated blasts from the shadowy figures among the mangroves.

The path was winding downward when the carts left the clump of trees, and the procession came into the open at top speed. They did not halt till the Africans followed them out of the shadows. Then, as one man, the band of fleeing aristocrats turned and scorched their antagonists with a blast that came so unexpectedly it utterly dismayed the blacks. Like indigo ghosts they faded in the grove.

Diron had a momentary feeling of sick revulsion. His pistol still smoked in his hand. He, the Friend of the Blacks, had fired along with the others. Of course, there were ways to rationalize his action. The slaves had leveled their aim against him as well as the others. He might just as well have been one of those struck. Moreover, the company might have been exterminated had they not resisted. It was his misfortune that he was in bad company. But, God willing, it wouldn't happen again. He absolutely would not be a party to another such mix-up. The blacks were entitled to their freedom. Slavery was a barbarism. It was a vestige of an age that had faded. The thing for him to do was to pull ahead of the others, spur his mare, meet the slaves alone, if he must encounter them at all, take his chances as an individual and not become involved with a company of people who represented precisely the things for which he did not stand. His duty to Paulette, if he ever had any, had been cancelled. There was, indeed, no reason why he should not out-distance the line, make peace with his own convictions at least, if he failed to do as well with the furious Africans.

Half an hour later, riding well ahead of the company, he was halted by a second detachment of blacks. These were on foot. They carried torches, and many of them wore the harvest of their plunder on their backs, in their ears, around their necks, arms and ankles. With one it was an orange satin cape. With another an impressive plume. With many it was the jewelry of their former owners.

"Who is it that rides alone tonight?"

"I am Diron Desautels, Friend of the Blacks."

"Dismount and prove yourself a friend."

"Here is my horse. And here my pistol. *Vive la liberté.*"

"Why does the Friend of the Blacks hasten to join our enemies?"

"There is someone I must meet. She is young and shiny like a star."

"Take our word, monsieur. Le Cap is no place for a Friend of the Blacks tonight."

"You know that for the truth?"

"We have our ears in their bed chambers. Pass, if you must."

He walked with zest when he left them. In his conscience he felt purged. The hills were just ahead.

4. Toussaint's coach reached the crest of the surrounding ridge by another way. Twice it had been halted by savage bands, but the authority of the familiar coachman had on neither occasion been challenged. Now, looking down upon the lights of the dismayed Creole city, he checked the horses of his own accord. Presently he was at the door of the coach, bowing sadly.

"Well, monsieur—"

"*Vieux* Toussaint."

There was fondness in each voice.

"With your leave, madame, and yours, monsieur—"

"You're leaving us?"

"There's no other way, madame."

The overseer stepped to the ground, his eyes blinking rapidly in the shadows. In time they were bright with moisture.

"I never expected to leave Saint Domingue again," he said. "I like the climate and the fruit. It's good for me."

"You plan to leave the island?" Toussaint asked.

"I hate war."

"Only one thing is worse," Toussaint said.

The former master nodded.

"Slavery is worse," he agreed. "I never doubted it."

"You're a kind man, monsieur."

"Kindness is not enough. I know now I should have done something."

"The Revolution in Paris was fought by Friends of the Blacks. Tonight the blacks take up arms, such arms as they have. This is a continuation, not a new conflict. You and I are not opposed."

"Never."

"And you will return?"

"Not as a master of slaves."

"Well, remember us."

The old coachman, twitching with electrical energy now, ran to the head of the team, swiftly cut two of the four horses from their traces. With almost simian nimbleness he leaped to the back of one, still holding the bridle of the other. His stiff, wiry queue bobbed against his neck. The dust-covered madras handkerchief which he wore on his head rose at the ends as the breeze struck it. Sweet-mannered and thoughtful, compassionate and meditative by nature, the pleasant old coachman seemed to catch fire at that instant. His duty done, his friends dispatched, a visible fierceness came to his face. It was as if he had suddenly laid claim to vast, half-forgotten resources of physical and mental strength. He slapped his horse savagely. A moment later, failing to hear the soft voices from the coach, he was riding through groves, crossing fields and leaping fences like the very god of insurrection.

Blacker and blacker grew the night into which his horses galloped, a night peopled by demons and witches, a night charged with jungle sorceries and voodoo incan-

tations, a night haunted by frightful masks and screaming ghosts, a night throbbing with drums. Once, at least,
Toussaint had the strange feeling that time itself was
slipping past him as his horses raced. Now again he
was in tune with things. The black wonders, the mysterious shades, were with him, not against him. It was as if
he had returned to the sweet age in which leaves were
born.

5. Meanwhile Diron, swinging his empty arms, hum-
ming a rousing air, approached the edge of the city. A
moment later he discovered that his hat was gone, but
he was unable to recall whether he had left it at Bréda
or lost it on the road. One way or the other was equally
unimportant now, however. His hat was gone. His hands
were empty. He was horseless and unarmed. Well, so
much the better for the lover of the people, the friend
of the blacks and the champion of liberty. Ah, better
indeed. This way, his feet kicking up dust, he could sense
a certain kinship with the half-naked slaves.

But there were also a few less joyous considerations
pressing upon him, considerations that could no longer
be forced aside now that Le Cap was within sight. Bloodshed was certainly not a pleasant thing to witness, even
when the cause seemed to demand it. Only a few minutes past Diron had listened to death groans as the party
with which he was identified met the fire of a band of

armed slaves. He had seen faces clearly marked with the lust to kill. Since the scene in the Bréda dining hall he had seen the whirlwind of passion gather force till it had become a hurricane of destruction on the countryside. Now, in the midst of the ravishment, the former masters and the people of their class were fleeing from their own slaves, attempting to reach the safety of Cap Français. With them went some who were as blameless as the slaves. Diron thought of Céleste and assured himself that she was safe. Toussaint would manage that successfully.

It was curious how the feeling that Toussaint was equal to any situation that might arise had taken hold of Diron since the trouble broke. Perhaps the impression had been in the back of his mind all the while and had simply waited for the proper occasion to bring it forward. Perhaps it was the affection of the other blacks for the coachman that suggested it, or perhaps the confidence M. de Libertas placed in him. Diron was not sure. He knew that he had never previously thought of Toussaint in connection with revolutionary activity; and he knew that now, for some inexplicable cause, everything seemed to rest upon the grave, slightly rounded shoulders of that melancholy old person. The safety of Céleste and her companions, the orderly direction of the wild forces at work among the slaves tonight, the calm wisdom necessary to wage a prolonged war for liberty in the island, the god-like authority required to weld miserable, ignorant and disunited savages into a fighting force—everything seemed to rest upon Toussaint. Diron turned the situation in his mind two or three times, wondering how

affairs could be resolved, whether or not the mild Toussaint would eventually manage to get in his hands the
reins that were at present held by Boukman and Baissou,
wondering even whether the personality of the coachman himself was sufficiently powerful to bring this colossal undertaking off successfully. At any rate, the spectacle would be worth watching. It was a pity to have
to leave just as things were beginning to happen. It was
a pity indeed, and possibly it was a mistake. Perhaps the
friend of the blacks should have remained with the
blacks and taken his chance with those he wished to
arouse. But the great disadvantage there, for the moment
at least, was the blacks themselves. Slavery had not failed
to leave its mark; the slaves had come to distrust all
whites.

Diron reached the city streets. It was two hours past
midnight. The news from the plantations of the plains
had reached Le Cap ahead of him, but the only effect
Diron saw was bewilderment. It was as if those who were
still awake refused to believe their ears and their eyes.
From this distance the sky was appallingly red. Half a
dozen distracted survivors, tongue-tied with terror, their
eyes haunted, had preceded Diron and made their reports. Still the only result he saw was people on verandas
in their night clothes holding lamps in their hands, shadowy figures darting from door to door and running along
the narrow streets, a small group of gendarmes consult-
ing together in the entrance to a tavern.

At first Diron purposed in his mind to go directly to
the home of his fellow member of *Les Amis des Noirs,*

M. Sylvain, the printer, but second thought changed that intention. If things took a certain turn, it was conceivable that the friends of the blacks would be called upon to defend themselves, or at least to furnish proof of their innocence in the present uprising. In such an eventuality it might be better if members of the group were not found together. Detection of one might lead to suspicion and detection of another and so on.

A few moments later he decided on the *Hôtel de la Couronne*. There he would be as comfortable and presumably as safe as anywhere. Moreover he would there be in a position to hear things, to learn the latest developments and to find his uncle and his friends from Bréda as soon as they reached the city.

The entrance gate was closed when he reached the inn, but two porters were on hand to open it instead of the usual one. Inside lights burned brightly. Windows and doors were thrown wide open. Apparently no one was asleep here.

"Walking, monsieur?" the regular porter inquired with agitation.

"My horse was taken. At that, I was fortunate."

"Is it indeed as bad as they are saying?"

"I'm afraid I'm too exhausted to describe it. Give me a chair on the veranda."

He sank into the seat that was provided, accepted a glass of rum and began to realize for the first time that he was near the end of his endurance. He felt dull, almost drowsy. The prolonged excitement, the danger and the chills of fear had finally drugged his senses. He emptied his glass and called for another drink. He had taken a sip from this when he noticed that a man was sitting in the chair beyond, half hidden in the shadows.

"Has something happened?" a miserable, alcoholic voice asked eventually.

Diron did not raise his head or turn his eyes.

"Did they tell you something's happened?"

"I've had two or three drinks," the other apologized. "I may have forgotten, monsieur."

"Don't think about it," Diron told him. "It'll just make you wretched."

"I'm quite all right now," the man protested. "You can tell me, monsieur, if you don't mind."

Diron did not answer at once. While he waited, the host came out, welcomed the newcomer and assigned him a room.

"Look at the sky toward Milôt," Diron said finally.

The man got up and walked to the other end of the veranda.

"A cane fire," he said, returning.

Diron was about to speak impatiently when he recognized that he had been talking to Hugo Juvet, Céleste's father. The boy's manner mollified immediately, and he gave his former neighbor a simple account of what had transpired during the past hours.

"So that's why they were so upset," Hugo Juvet said vaguely. "They've quieted down now, but before you came the guests and the servants were running about, making noise and acting terribly stupid. But you mentioned the child."

"Yes, she's with Mme de Libertas and her husband."

"You didn't by any chance see the old woman, did you?"

Hugo had a broken, tearful voice; but his drunken sentimentality had in it a touch of the ridiculous.

"Mme Juvet? No, I haven't seen her tonight."

"She was alone," Hugo reflected. "She's always alone. Do you suppose she needs help?"

"I'm sure she does, but there's no way to help her, unfortunately."

Hugo responded by crossing himself, his eyes raised toward the red night sky.

Presently the sound of galloping feet reached the inn. A moment later a shadowy horse and rider swept past on the cobbles of the narrow street, between the high stone fences on either side. This flying courier was followed directly by another not more than a hundred yards behind. A stable boy carrying a lantern let himself through the heavy gate of the inn and hurried away in the darkness. Lamp light appeared in the bell tower of the cathedral. In another moment bells were ringing.

Hearing the noise, the host came to the veranda again. A dapper man, he was beginning to show strain and sleepless tension, but he had not lost his admirable poise.

"They have decided to arouse the town," he observed.

"Perhaps it's the only thing to do," Diron told him.

"But the city is in no danger," the other insisted. "There's no reason to frighten the people. Even if there were an army, organized and equipped with field pieces and muskets, encamped on the Plain du Nord, we shouldn't be terrified in Le Cap. The harbor is open. Scores of ships are always on hand. The garrison in the barracks here could hold the passages between the hills without calling on more than a fifth of its men. They know how to handle insurrections, too. Three or four hundred troops took care of Chavannes and Ogé in their attempt; and those were mulattos, intelligent, educated and skilled in the use of arms. The slaves have only their machetes. We shouldn't be frightened of savages with sticks and cane knives."

"The Bastille was taken by a crudely armed mob, M. Coidevic," Diron reminded him.

"But you're pessimistic, monsieur."

"Not at all," Diron answered obliquely. "Not at all."

"Let me assure you, nothing will happen to Le Cap."

"But the plantations," Hugo Juvet lamented. "Think of the desolation, the burning of the mansions and the cane fields. Think of the murders."

"No, I'll get you a drink of rum. Don't brood, M. Juvet." M. Coidevic left the other two, entering the establishment through one of the numerous windows from the veranda. Diron heard him calling a *garçon* inside.

Before Hugo Juvet's drink arrived, however, a fresh clamor had broken in the street. The tattered company led by M. Philippe Desautels reached the entrance gate of the *Hôtel de la Couronne*. They were accompanied by gendarmes who had met them outside the city and by a host of half-dressed, panic-stricken townsfolk who followed to learn more about the terror that had taken the plains.

In the excitement the host, M. Coidevic, rushed down the steps of the inn, accompanying his porters to the gate. As the noise increased, guests of the inn came out of their rooms and stood on the upper veranda in their sleeping gowns, holding lamps and candles above their heads and peering down over the banister.

The carriage entrance was flung open, and through it lumbered the loaded carts one by one. The company of aristocrats, tragically reduced, came directly to the veranda. Diron stood beside the door, scarcely able to raise his eyes, and noted the survivors as they passed him, half a dozen unrecognizable women with wild hair and dust-caked evening dresses, twice as many men still cherishing to their bosoms the squirrel guns and duelling pistols which had brought them through. Scarcely one person in the entire company was without blood stains. Two or three, taken from the carts inside the gates of the inn, had to be supported when they walked. Among these was M. Philippe Desautels who had bound his bleeding arm with his coat, but who was so weakened now he seemed ready to faint.

Seeing his uncle's condition, Diron swiftly pulled himself together, took the older man's arm.

"Mother of God," the wounded man whispered hopelessly.

"But it isn't like you to groan, *Oncle* Philippe," Diron said, chiding affectionately as they reached the stair. "There now—my shoulder. Lean against me. It could have been worse."

"Oh, I doubt it," M. Desautels insisted miserably. "We are less than half the company that started, and some of us—well, some of us are wounded."

The stairway was crowded now, newcomers and innsfolk all going up or coming down at the same time. At the top Diron discovered for the first time that Paulette Viard was among the survivors. She was standing under a hall lamp. Her mouth was still vividly red, and her hair had not entirely lost its gleaming luster, but she was as disheveled and grimy as anyone in the company. A shoulder strap was broken on her dress. She stepped forward and offered to help support the bleeding man.

"Thanks. We can make it," Diron replied frigidly.

"You're angry," she said.

Unmoved by his refusal, she came up and put her arm around M. Desautels from the other side.

"We owe you everything," she told the elderly man, "everything, monsieur."

"I hope you got a chance to use that toy of yours," Diron told her resentfully.

She insisted on laughing it off.

"I did, really, but I can't imagine which way the shot went. I nearly perished of fear when I pulled the trigger."

"It was all beastly," the old man said in a half-daze.

They reached the room, and Paulette stood like a portrait in the door frame till Diron had assisted his uncle to the side of the bed. Then when the wounded man was stretched out on top of the bed covers, she put her face in her hands, shook her head miserably and tried to cry.

The performance seemed insincere to Diron. He waited, unwilling to close the door in her face, and presently she looked up.

"I want to talk to you, Diron," she said. "I'm afraid you despise me. I must talk to you."

"Not now, please." He indicated the suffering man; but as he did so, he could see that she was not going to be content with such an answer, so he added, "Perhaps when I've made *Oncle* Philippe comfortable here."

She smiled, but there were ghosts and demons in her eyes.

"Thanks," she answered. "There'll be a servant waiting for you at my gate."

Diron closed the door behind her and began swift preparations to bathe his uncle's wound.

6. Half an hour after the company of survivors came to the *Hôtel de la Couronne,* Hugo Juvet was still sitting on the lower veranda. He was a sentimental man when he was drinking, and tonight he was drinking even more than usual. He was a little vague on the precise nature of the calamity that had struck the plains beyond Le Cap. but he was fully convinced that something woeful had fallen upon the island. He kept thinking of his mother, the vulgar old saint with a corkscrew cane in one hand, in the other a coil of rope with one end stretching back to horns of the family cow. Then there was his child.

By now she was a lady, of course, and perhaps—yes, quite likely, there were young men waiting around, peeling their eyes.

Hugo fell into a puddle of melancholy reflections. A few moments later he was crying, tears slipping down his face. He wiped them aside with the back of his hand, took another sip from his glass.

The tumult in the streets had not abated since the company came. There were scores of gendarmes going and coming in disorderly arrangement. Riders bearing messages raced their horses on the cobblestones. Most of these seemed to go or come from the barracks on the side of the town away from the waterfront. In the streets larger and larger crowds milled. If anyone was still asleep, the peopled verandas and balconies, the lighted houses, gave no indication of it.

But it was not the panic about him that distressed Hugo Juvet. He was troubled because he imagined his mother's modest house to be among those that blazed on the plain. He was tearful because he couldn't bear to think of his dear ones in misery and death. Hugo bowed his head, covered his eyes with his hand. His sorrow was as vast as the sea.

But now there was a hand on his shoulder. He roused himself gloomily, looked up into the face of Diron Desautels.

"Do you know where Mme Sylvestre Viard lives, monsieur?" the boy asked.

The drinker consulted his glass, searched through his mind.

"Paulette, you mean—I know."

"I have a note for her," Diron said. "She's expecting me at her house, but I can't leave my uncle. He's still bleeding."

"Are you her fancy now?" Hugo inquired.

"Well, I hope not, monsieur. Would you mind delivering my note, or perhaps sending a *garçon?*"

"I'll go myself, and gladly, my young man. My respects to M. Philippe Desautels."

"Thank you very much indeed."

The other was standing. Rum did not rob him of his physical powers, though he swayed faintly in the dim light.

"So it's you she loves now, hunh?"

"Tell her I'll see her later tonight if it's urgent. Otherwise tomorrow."

The father of Céleste made his way down the steps, out through the gate and into the street.

He had been walking several minutes, oblivious to the confusion around him, when he reached the gate that he recognized and turned to enter. No servant waited to admit him, and no light burned out of doors. He did notice, however, that a coach with horses stood a few paces ahead; and when he tried the gate, he found that it was open. Inside the yard on the flagstones he paused, felt for the letter in his pocket and started toward the steps.

Suddenly he heard noises in the flower bushes. Hugo took a step or two and saw two ponderous shadows emerge from the dark clumps. In the next instant the two were upon him, their arms raised, clubs swinging. One of the blows fell across Hugo Juvet's head and instantly the light of his thought went out like a blown candle.

Still he did not go down at once. He stood swaying while a shower of crushing blows bashed his head. Then he toppled heavily to the ground.

The two who had done the foul business were about to pounce upon the helpless form when a door opened allowing a shaft of lamplight to fall upon the flagstone walk. With this they both became uncertain and paused foolishly. A moment later Paulette came stealthily down the steps, looked upon the unconscious man and gave a cry of astonishment and horror.

"*Mon Dieu!*" she gasped. "This is not he."

The two brutal giants looked at one another strangely. "There may still be some life in him," one of them ventured.

Paulette didn't appear to hear. Frightfully pale, wrapped in a black cape, she stood like a pillar of salt.

"Hugo Juvet," she whispered in deep anguish. "You, of all people."

7. Meanwhile, high in his coachman's seat, M. Bayou de Libertas was thrashing the very hair off the two horses that Toussaint had left him. That not all the peril was passed was becoming increasingly plain, though Toussaint

had evidently believed the three would be able to make the remainder of the journey without hindrance. Now M. de Libertas knew that the bands of blacks were roaming the section between their coach and Le Cap. It was even likely, he now feared, that they had the carriage road blocked some place up ahead. In that case there would be much indeed to worry about.

Suddenly, for no discoverable reason, the overseer found himself quoting scripture. It was as if the blood throbbing at his temples had started a refrain.

"Awake, awake," he cried loudly to his horses. "Put on strength; awake as in the ancient days, in the generations of old." The sweat-drenched beasts, hearing the voice behind them and feeling the whip that burned their flanks between periods, raced wildly. "Oh, who is this that cometh with dyed raiment?" M. de Libertas caught his breath when this had escaped him. He was not a pious man, but neither was he an admirer of M. Voltaire and that crowd of skeptics. He reproached himself soundly for this senseless talk. But now there was an answering echo which the overseer couldn't even pretend not to hear.

"I am he that tread the winepress."

The driver put a hand over his eyes to ward off the disagreeable hallucination.

"Yes, they are the ones," he said aloud. "The slaves. They're waking up. They dwell in dust, and they're singing a bloody song tonight. They're singing it to the accompaniment of machetes and pikes and scythe-swords. And the name of their song is Liberty."

Inside the coach Céleste and Mme de Libertas had

ceased their weeping. When the overseer allowed his
horses to slacken their pace for a brief stretch, the older
woman leaned her head out, called to him in a kindly
voice.

"Oh, don't be upset," she urged. "My poor dear. The
strain is too much. But we are not in a bad way now.
Take command of yourself. I can't stand to hear you
carrying on like that."

"I'm sorry," M. de Libertas said, suddenly sobered.
"I'm quite all right. I sort of forgot myself. Don't fret,
little pigeon."

A few minutes passed. Lashing his horses again, M. de
Libertas brought the coach reeling around a turn. He
looked ahead and lost his breath when he discovered that
the road was filled with shadowy figures a few hundred
yards away. They were in a state of confusion and clamor
when the overseer saw them, but it was instantly clear
that the chances of passing them with a team and a coach
were not promising. M. de Libertas felt his hands quaking. Toussaint had left his friends too soon. Here they
were within sight of a savage, maddened horde. Surely
everything was lost.

Still he would not give up while there was strength
in his limbs and breath in his body. The road was closed.
That way lay certain attack. A possible alternative was to
plunge through the roadside thickets and then undertake
to drive across the fields and the tangled hedges beyond.
A part of the land was wooded. The thought of traversing
it in a coach was a wild notion, a desperate choice that
did not become a man in his senses. Yet M. de Libertas

made it without hesitation. Standing in his seat, he put his weight against the bits of the horses, sawed the reins back and forth a moment or two, finally got the team into the dark clump. A moment later the coach was lumbering drunkenly, jolting the occupants almost out of their senses, making a path of its own over furrowed land, across ditches and through broken fences. Still lumbering wretchedly, the coach reached a wooded slope and M. de Libertas covered his head and face with his arms to avoid switches and pendulums of hanging vines. He closed his eyes and allowed the horses to take their own way.

Inside Céleste emitted little frightened outcries at every jolt, and Mme de Libertas wept steadily in a miserable voice. All cries ceased presently, however; for the carriage, rolling perilously fast on a downward slope, suddenly crashed into a stump, tore off a wheel, sent both horses sprawling and hurled the driver into a clump of wild coffee bushes.

Numb and half out of his wits, M. de Libertas recovered his strength, regained his feet and tried to make out what had happened. The horses lay on their bellies, unable to rise. The carriage, hopelessly broken, still managed to remain upright, but it was rocking on the stump that had caused the crash and seemed on the verge of toppling on its side as soon as the horses should be released. Alert and nervous again, the overseer flung the door open.

"What has happened now?" his wife cried. "Where are we? Where are we?"

Trembling and pale, the girl sat with her cloak drawn tight, unable to utter a sound.

"You must get out at once," M. de Libertas told them. They obeyed without question. On the ground the two withdrew a few steps and waited beside the trunk of a dim tree. Neither of them spoke. They showed no more emotion now than women might show in a trance. Céleste's hair had a certain brightness in the darkness, but her eyes gave no shine. Noticing the women as he stood beside the entangled horses, M. de Libertas thought that the girl's eyes seemed white, while his wife seemed to have no eyes at all. Only the places where eyes might have been. But this was no time for fancies. They had still to reach Cap Français, if that were possible.

When he had cut the beasts from their harness, M. de Libertas discovered with sharp excitement that both the horses were able to rise of their own power. Then, holding them by their bridles, he led them a little space and found that both could walk without limping too badly. Reassured, he returned to the tree where the women stood.

"Thank God, we still have the horses," he said.

"Where are we, monsieur?" Céleste asked hopelessly.

The overseer pointed toward Le Cap.

"That's our direction," he said. "Here, child, let me put you on the horse's back."

"But the traveling boxes," she protested. "What about the things we're carrying?"

The words were scarcely uttered when the sounds of voices reached the hillside.

"We're near a road," Mme de Libertas observed.

"Don't speak," her husband whispered. "Come now. You will mount first. I'll ride with you. We can carry nothing but ourselves—and perhaps the gold."

Mounting wasn't simple for Mme de Libertas. A large woman and unaccustomed to physical activity, she would have had her difficulties even with a saddle and stirrups. With nothing more than the bridle harness and the horse's mane for support, she was at a colossal disadvantage.

"I can't make it, Bayou," she said tearfully. "I'll have to walk."

"Do you want to be murdered?" the man snapped impatiently. "Try to help yourself for God's sake. Hoist your skirts. Higher. You can't be too graceful under circumstances like these. There now, use my hands as a step. Cling to the mane. Throw the other foot over the creature's back. Up now. Don't spare the brute. Heave."

It required half a dozen efforts, but eventually the stout woman got herself astride the animal. By that time her husband was so exhausted he could scarcely stand on his feet. He went to the carriage, however, and began to plunder the treasures which had been left on the floor. Finding the chest which contained the gold, he took the heavy affair in his hands and began to shake his head in despair. The chances of reaching the city with such a burden were slight indeed in M. de Libertas's opinion. He set it down again and began another search for a strong bag he remembered. Having found this, he opened the chest and quickly poured most of the treasure into the more easily managed bag. Then, securing the mouth with a cord, he hastily put it into his wife's hands. The trunk, the guns, the ornaments of silver, the clothes, all these he kicked aside and abandoned with the coach. In another moment he had swung himself to a position in front of his wife on her horse and taken the reins in his hands. He beckoned to Céleste, clucked to his own beast and started out through the thickets and the banana trees.

They had not proceeded far when for the third time the clamor of wild voices reached their ears. This time the direction of the sounds was vague. For a moment it seemed to be directly ahead. In another instant it seemed to come from the left. In both cases the voices were definitely nearer than they had been before. Some words could be distinguished. They were spoken in the Creole patois of the slaves.

"They seem to be everywhere," the man remarked, trying to appear unperturbed. "Stay near behind us, child. I intend to follow a semicircle, swinging to the right and later returning to the direction of the road."

He looked around as he spoke and saw the girl transfigured by fear, sitting pale and rigid on her horse and paying little if any attention to the words he had just uttered.

At his back the overseer felt the bag of gold pressed solidly against his spine as his wife, holding it to her bosom with one hand, clung to him with the other.

M. de Libertas had been misguided by his sense of sound, however, and a moment later he stopped his horse with a jolt when he saw that he had ridden almost into the very circle of the aroused slaves.

"Look where you're taking us," his wife groaned.

He summoned all his strength suddenly, wheeled the tired horse, lashed the beast without mercy, plunged into the darkest part of the wooded slope, lowered his face against the switching twigs, fled like a man pursued by death. His wife continued to cry aloud and shout admonitions into his ear, but he heard none of them for several seconds. Then, looking up, he saw that they were being followed. He had gone too far in the wrong direction. The blacks had seen them. Now the horde was following.

"Céleste," he finally heard his wife shouting. "Oh, what'll become of her?"

M. de Libertas saw the other horse galloping desperately toward an open field. It was being followed, as was his own beast, but there was one important difference. He was headed for Le Cap. Every step his horse took brought him nearer and nearer the safety of the city and the military forces of the colony. But Céleste—God only knew where she hoped to arrive by traveling back toward Bréda as she was doing in her confusion. The man's heart sank. He was gaining on his pursuers, but not enough to allow him to be of help to the poor girl. He was sure now that he could not be overtaken so long as his horse held out, but he could entertain no such hopes for poor Céleste.

CHAPTER SIX

1. When morning came, the sun saw a bewildered, hysterical city at Cap Français. Streets were alive with carriages, carts and saddle horses. Refugees in sad, disheveled companies, in groups of two and three, stumbled down hillsides, entered the city by every unguarded approach. Grenadiers strolled the waterfront but had little success in regulating the feverish rush to get aboard ships. Many vessels had been in the midst of taking on cargoes of indigo and sugar and hard woods. Now they were busily unloading to make room for additional passengers. A weird procession moved toward the harbor. Women wore the evening dresses in which they had made their sudden flights. One was accompanied by a pair of faithful servants, armed with sword and parasol respectively. A child sat on the shoulders of a tall grenadier, playing with the plumes of his helmet. A fat matron, heavily jeweled and perhaps demented, was being lowered into a boat in her chair, having refused to go aboard of her own will despite the pleadings of her family. Detachments of soldiers, reconnoitering in the narrow streets of the city, expecting an attack upon the city itself, seemed as confused as anyone.

The throng in the *Hôtel de la Couronne* prompted a note of sad merriment in one of the guests.

"We are like a masquerade ball at the *Opéra*," he lamented.

Diron, looking drawn and tall against the door frame, turned. Seeing that no one had paid the gentleman any attention, he nodded unsmilingly.

"Yes," he answered.

In the crowd were faces from which the black disguise had not yet been removed. Men as well as women showed the results of hasty dressing. Their clothes were out of keeping. Especially was this true of an agitated figure that appeared to be an old white-haired woman with curls. Scrutiny revealed the buckled shoes of a man beneath the skirts and petticoats.

Failing to discover those whom he sought in the crowd, Diron went out into the street and walked hurriedly toward the edge of the city. A column of soldiers was marching on the Milôt road, the *vivandière* of the battalion running far ahead. The Friend of the Blacks waited for an opportunity to cross, then continued toward a grove through which no road passed. He wandered here like a distracted poet, his mind in turmoil. Suddenly he was impressed with the seeming unreality of things. He had always thought of the struggle for liberty as something intensely real. Now it was hard to accept what his eyes saw.

He had been walking half an hour among the trees when he spied a horse stumbling along miserably on the uneven ground, burdened with two full-sized riders, carrying its head so low it seemed to obstruct its own knees. As soon as he recognized M. de Libertas and his wife, Diron drew near and greeted them wistfully. The man dismounted, rubbed his aching legs, then proceeded, leading the horse while he himself walked beside the younger man.

An awkward silence fell between them immediately. In time Diron, laying a hand on his companion's arm, spoke softly.

"What became of her?" he asked.

The overseer's comical, lashless eyes had lost all traces of mirth. His wife, biting her lips, bowed her head tearfully.

"Toussaint meant to see us through," M. de Libertas explained. "He thought we were past danger when he left."

"You were not?"

"We turned off the road to avoid a band of slaves. We wrecked the coach." He paused as if he had lost his thread. "The girl got lost from us," he added. "She was on the other horse."

Diron, who had anticipated the conclusion, was himself lost by now, lost in an abstraction which the other two could in no wise penetrate. He had no wish to hear more. Neither did he think it worth while to try to imagine how Céleste had fared since the others last saw her. A young girl, scarcely more than a child—such a girl alone in a tempest like the present one must certainly rely on her stars.

For a few moments Diron had a black feeling of despair, a painful sense of emptiness and ashes. His physical powers were still intact and his mind was much too active to support the idea of weakness, but Diron felt his strength as hopelessly ineffectual. He was now sure he had blundered tragically when he left Céleste at Bréda. But a man had so many obligations—courtesy, loyalty, self-respect, all these made demands. Into the complication and strife created by diverse allegiances another element was introduced in the case of men like himself: a sense of mankind as a whole. Finally a girl with round golden arms, green morocco slippers and a becoming Creole turban appeared, to throw all loyalties, all convictions into a state of chaos.

They reached the inn. Outside the entrance the two men helped the stout woman to the ground and supported her, one on either side, as the porter swung the gate open and took charge of the horse. On the veranda they led her to a chair. The sun was up strong, but Diron had not yet been conscious of the heat; it surprised him to see that Mme de Libertas was perspiring, trickles running from her hair and down the sides of her face. He found a palmetto leaf and began to fan her. The exhausted overseer sank into another chair and called for refreshments.

Later when the newly arrived couple were given a room, Diron went upstairs to his uncle and sat with the wounded man in chairs drawn out on the balcony from their own room. For once there was little regard anywhere for the perilous mid-day heat. Frenchmen of all classes were in the streets. Fires continued on the Plain du Nord, and the sky retained a certain haze, but the sun was not obscured. A small gray ash fell occasionally.

"I don't think I shall remain in Saint Domingue," the older man reflected with disappointment.

The remark brought Diron's head up sharply.

"Paris?"

There followed another period of reflection.

"No, that's impossible," M. Desautels said finally. "I've thought of New Orleans."

"M. de Libertas will return to France if he can get passage."

"That's very well for him. No political complications. What about yourself, Diron?"

"I'm trying to decide," the boy said.

"You're not compelled to leave, of course. The house is gone, but the trouble won't last. A fortnight, perhaps. Maybe three weeks or a month, if it is worse than we imagine."

"A year of fighting wouldn't surprise me, *Oncle* Philippe."

"Don't be sentimental. Soldiers are already in the field. I know your feelings about slavery, but be realistic for once."

Diron was in no mood for argument. His thoughts were inclined to wander; an unbecoming sadness could be detected in his voice. A sense of bewilderment clouded his eyes.

"Well," he said at length. "Nothing is the same, at any rate. Nothing can ever be the same again. I hope I can come to a conclusion by evening."

"I can't see that you have many alternatives. If there is to be fighting out here, one may run away or he may stay and fight."

"It isn't that simple for me. I don't think I'd run from a fight if I knew positively which side to join."

M. Desautels turned his head to see if Diron's face actually revealed a serious intent. Unable to comprehend the boy, he fell into a silence. A few moments later Diron rose and began to pace the balcony.

"You mean you could fight for the blacks actually—under circumstances like these?" the uncle asked eventually.

"But for one thing I'd be certain of it," Diron admitted. "Yet I'm afraid I won't be able to say till I find what has become of Céleste."

"Would it change your convictions to learn that she had not been spared?"

"No," the boy answered directly. "Still it would be too gruesome to fight with them after a thing like that. I couldn't do it."

Whether or not M. Desautels found Diron's position comprehensible he did not state. He was plainly tired of the subject, however, and indicated it by falling asleep presently, his wounded arm lying across his bosom. Diron kicked off his own boots, removed his coat and stretched across a bed. In time he too fell into an uncomfortably warm and tortured mid-day nap.

He did not leave the room again till time for supper. The evening meal was served beneath swinging lamps; and when Diron had finished eating, he went out and made inquiries among his acquaintances. He was determined to find Céleste if she had reached Le Cap. An hour later, having assured himself that she was nowhere to be found within the city, he entered a tavern and began to drink. He had started on his second tumbler when a *garçon* from the *Hôtel de la Couronne* came to his table with a message. Mme Sylvestre Viard had been trying to reach him. Would he come to her house or let her know where she and he could meet?

For the first time it occurred to Diron that he had had no answer from his message to Paulette the night before.

"Tell her to come to the *Couronne*," he told the boy petulantly.

When the messenger was gone, Diron repented of his words. There was no reason to act boorish with Paulette now, he reasoned. The boy was by now well on his way, but the memory of his own words still rankled within Diron. Perhaps, he would send another boy a few moments later, tell her to disregard the first. But that seemed unnecessarily complicated. Half an hour later Diron rose from his place and went himself directly to Paulette's house.

Admitted by a servant, he was shown directly into a room to the right of the entrance. Paulette, plainly exasperated by his message, was engaged in writing him a note as he entered. She looked up and changed her mood perceptibly.

"Pardon me, Paulette," he said. "The boy who brought your message got on my nerves."

"Shame on you. He's a lovely boy."

"I know. I'm a beast."

She rose and cleared away the writing things.

"You won't need to see this now," she said, destroying the half-written note. "It wasn't a pleasant one."

"I'm sure it wasn't. I'm not capable of pleasantness either, tonight."

"Isn't it all too dreadful?"

"Worse than you imagine."

"No, I've heard about the girl. But what could you expect?"

"I don't understand."

"It was stupidity on her part."

"She was frightened," Diron said. "She isn't stupid."

Paulette's tone changed swiftly.

"But must we discuss her?"

"No, certainly not."

"Still, if one doesn't mind plumpness, she isn't bad."

"That's terribly inappropriate tonight," Diron said with unexpected sharpness. "You're callous, Paulette. That's what I dislike about you."

She pretended to disregard his words.

"Had you and she made promises already?"

He showed angry embarrassment.

"Does it make any difference?"

A moment later she was looking up into his face.

"Do you realize that you have never at any time said a kind thing to me, Diron?"

"That's absurd."

"Why, Diron? Why? Why do you loathe me?"

"I don't. There are some things I don't understand. Perhaps I'm a little afraid of you."

"Afraid of me? I don't believe it. Afraid of yourself. Afraid of the beast behind that soft voice."

She put a pale hand on his arm, a hand with long fingers, rings and vivid nails. Diron thought less of her words than of her perfume. He couldn't recall that he'd ever given much attention to it before. A more agreeable scent was hard to imagine.

"You puzzle me, Paulette. You have always puzzled me. You stand for things which I do not approve. You raise questions. Besides—"

"I know what you think," she interrupted. "I don't blame you for disliking me. You've heard things. Maybe, of course, I'm not as black as I'm painted. You've never heard my side."

"Well, don't tell me now," he said. "I'm sick of petty contention. Great conflicts interest me—war and the rumor of war—not these quarrels."

"Am I petty, Diron? Tell me that."

Her voice was tired, but Diron marveled to see her holding up as well as she was.

"No," he admitted reluctantly. "Not really."

"Would you mind kissing me?"

He tilted her face, paused. An enormous sense of confidence and power rose in him. He watched the long lashes of her eyes come together as the lids fell. He felt her fingers in his hair. Fascinated, confused, he kissed her bright lips. Almost immediately he felt duped, began to reproach himself.

"Of course, I'm not in my senses tonight," he explained, "but for the moment I don't seem to mind."

"Well, at least you're not half-hearted. Thanks awfully."

"Laughing at me?"

"Absurd. How could I laugh, adoring it as I do? I was just thinking how right I've always been about you."

"Right in what way?"

"You *are* afraid of yourself."

"Have it your way. It doesn't matter."

"You don't really dislike me, do you?"

"Perhaps not. It's more like war. I'm against your side. Much more so, since last night. It isn't altogether personal."

"You felt that you couldn't afford to treat me too well?"

"I have always felt just as I do now. But I've never wanted to tell you that I don't trust you. Now you might as well know."

She stiffened immediately.

"Thanks. I'm glad to know it." She spoke through firmly locked teeth.

"I hope I've made it plain."

She became at once cold, distant and hard. A moment later she twisted her shoulders to wrench herself from Diron's grasp. He let his hands slide down her arms to her wrists, held her hands in his.

"You're a Jacobin and a Friend of the Blacks."

"Have I denied it? This is the second time you have reminded me. I invite you to make the most of it."

When she began to jerk and pull to free herself from his grip, he took a firmer hold and allowed her to struggle. His clinging infuriated her. She summoned all her strength. Her hair fell out of order as a result of the activity. Blazes came into her eyes. Diron could literally feel the heat of her anger.

"Release me," she cried.

"I never imagined you were capable of scuffling," he said with obvious ridicule.

"You aren't so smart. You'll answer for what happened to poor Hugo Juvet. I suspect there are those who'd like to know *Les Amis des Noirs* about now."

"Tell me about M. Juvet. I haven't heard."

His coolness exasperated her afresh. She struggled like an enraged child. Diron was amazed to see that she was capable of biting, scratching and kicking. Curiously, however, his own mind became unusually active. Never before had he felt so sure of his ground with Paulette.

"Never mind about Hugo," she said. "That was a mistake. Take care that *you* don't get what you've earned."

"And about my friend Sylvestre Viard? You tell me so little, Paulette."

His irony went deep. She tried to fly at his face, but he held her securely.

"You suspect me in connection with my husband's death, do you? Well, help yourself."

"I intend to turn you loose, but wait."

"Why should I wait? Let me go now. You're a swine."

"But you've complicated things completely," he said. He paused, taking stock. "You make it so very hard. Yet in another sense you make it easy. At any rate, you'll have to go with me when I leave."

She sneered.

"I'm not so helpless as I seem."

When she opened her mouth to scream for help, he quickly muffled her cry with the palm of his hand, swung her from the floor with the other arm, rushed out through the windows and along the veranda carrying her in his arms, raced down the steps as she kicked and struggled. Dismayed servants came to the windows, bewildered by the noises they had heard, peered blankly into the darkness but understood nothing.

"I can't leave you just now," he explained, hurrying through the gate and into the narrow street. "After what you've said, I'd better keep you with me till I can leave the city. I couldn't trust you out of my sight a minute."

2. At Bréda Toussaint had made his decision, but he did not believe the time had come for him to take a conspicuous part in the insurrection of the blacks. The frenzy had not yet spent itself. The mad element was still in command. Both Boukman and Baissou were stupid in Toussaint's opinion. Like many others, naturally strong and capable, they had been degraded by slavery. Certainly the most optimistic observer could see no final success for these two. As eager as any to have a hand in the freedom of the slaves, Toussaint saw too clearly what might happen if he tried to subordinate himself to such chieftains.

Instead he would give himself to thought for the present. He could spend time reading in his volumes of Abbé Grégoire's *Histoire des deux Indes*. He could work out plans for fighting an organized, trained and equipped colonial army with ignorant, demoralized and crudely armed slaves. That was the challenge held out to some black man of destiny. Toussaint never doubted for a moment that fate had selected him. For years he had known it in his heart. Now it was as clear as day. He would be the first of the blacks. He, Toussaint Bréda, coachman and rude practitioner of medicine, called in childhood *fatras bâton* because of his skinniness, known at forty-five as *vieux* Toussaint because of his round shoulders and his thoughtful melancholy habits, was sure to wear a brighter name than anyone yet guessed—anyone, that is, beside himself. He would call himself the opener when the time came, *L'Ouverture*. Ah!

But one need not be idle to think. There was still much to be done at Bréda. The mansion, ravished and gutted of its handsome furnishings, had been miraculously preserved from fire during the fury of the two preceding nights. With his white friends safe in Le Cap, Toussaint felt greatly relieved where Bréda was concerned. He stood in the gray light of another dawn, his back against an impressive mango tree, his hands in his pockets, and saw the swift morning sun make its way.

The fires seemed to have added to the dryness of the season. That which was not parched was in ashes. The fruit trees in many cases had not been badly damaged; and while the cane fields were lost, Bréda's stables, out-buildings and slave quarters had been protected from the flames.

Sleepless nights had begun to tell on the rank and file of the blacks, too. Scarcely anyone was stirring as Toussaint's eye covered the scene. A near-by corral of plow oxen was in a temporary uproar, an uproar caused by the smell of blood. One of the animals had just been butchered for food. The scent of blood maddened the living beasts. They seemed ready to charge the fences of their enclosure.

Next time meat was slain, Toussaint told himself, he would see to it that the quartering was done at a safe distance from the corrals. Even the brutes knew the cry of blood. A vague, sorrowless protest rose in them, a protest against the slaughter of their kind. But unlike the slaves, swayed by similar instincts, the brutes were incapable of direct action.

Stiff-legged from standing so long in one position, Toussaint left his tree and walked toward the carriage shed. He had always carried responsibilities at Bréda. Besides his duties as coachman he had long been in charge of all animals on the place, an unheard of authority for a slave. Now, the whole estate was his to command; and with the sun coming up, he suspected it might not be a bad idea to busy himself. He reached the carriage room and found the doors open.

The shed, usually accommodating three or four coaches, was empty. Mars had drawn a grindstone to the center of the floor and sat at the wheel, operating it with his foot as he sharpened the kitchen knives.

Toussaint entered, murmuring a soft greeting.

"You don't mean to say they left all those knives when they sacked the place?"

"They didn't find these," Mars explained with a twinkle.

"You're a shrewd man, Mars." Toussaint patted his shoulder. "If you don't let that cough get the best of you, you'll be my *aide de camp* when we join the blacks."

Mars smiled his gratitude.

"But I'm impatient," he added.

"I know. I know. I wish it were different," Toussaint assured him. "There's nothing else we can do, though. We must take time and keep our wits about us. We mustn't waste strength. The gendarmes have decided to take offensive positions around Le Cap. That's the best thing that could happen at the moment. It gives us time to think. More important still, it gives us time to see what attitude the mulatto *affranchis* will take. They are experienced in bearing arms. All the men have served in the army. Then there are those people in the great house. We have to do something about them."

Mars looked up and shook his head following the last remark.

"They're a curse on us, Toussaint. Why don't you send that group away?"

The coachman locked his hands behind his back, walked back and forth.

It was true that the Bréda mansion still housed whites, a fact which not only annoyed Mars, who had to serve them, but also perplexed the other blacks of the plantation. In fact, the report of it had gone beyond Bréda, but the rumor that crossed the walls of the estate was a carefully distorted one, the guile of which might conceivably have been traced to old Toussaint himself. At any rate, it was being said on every side that Toussaint was harboring Mme de Libertas, the wife of his old master. Toussaint knew that nobody in the northern department enjoyed a greater reputation for humane dealings with slaves than M. Bayou de Libertas. He also knew that the big, charitable heart of the overseer's wife was often given credit for that gentleman's generosity and kindness. He felt sure that the blacks would tolerate a little expression of sentiment on his part toward his former master and mistress. He was not the only grateful slave. Dozens of others were intervening to save the lives of masters who had used them well.

The danger lay in the fact that neither Mme nor M. de Libertas was at Bréda. And if Toussaint had not really given a false report, at least he had failed to correct an error he might easily have corrected had he considered it wise to do so. He had personally dispatched the old couple. He had heard of their arrival in Le Cap, their separation from Céleste. Now he had taken it upon himself, with Mars and a few others as confederates, to save Claire and Annette, the discarded females who had been stranded when the others fled. Angélique, the count's latest, was with them now, having turned back when her group was attacked and scattered on the way to the city.

"There's nothing else we can do," Toussaint repeated after some length. "This was unexpected, but we have to do such things when we have occasion. We won't be forgiven for killing wantonly."

"I don't say kill them," Mars protested. "But is it necessary to detain them?"

"It amounts to the same thing," Toussaint assured him calmly. "If they go, they will not reach safety under present conditions. Besides, we're not ready to fight. We might as well look after these women while we're waiting. It gives us something to do."

Mars was not in complete agreement, but he had no wish to urge his view further. He trusted the coachman fully. Moreover, he was not anxious that the new master of Bréda should conclude that he was shirking the little work that waiting on the women entailed. Toussaint seemed definitely eager to keep things going at Bréda, to keep the slaves as busy as they had been when M. de Libertas was there. Mars had to admit that the slight black man had a handsome way of imposing his will on the hundreds of slaves at Bréda. Toussaint had done nothing to put himself at their head. It had just worked out naturally. When M. de Libertas and the others left, there Toussaint was. The slaves began to look at him, and he began telling them what they should do.

When Mars finished grinding his knives, the two walked to the kitchen shed together. A few moments later, having satisfied themselves that breakfast was under way, they continued around the house and down the sweeping driveway. From the front it could be seen that the house had undergone changes. Windows and doors had been boarded up on the lower floor. Even above, looking from the windows that were occupied, rude drapes hung before the openings, adding to an air of desolation. The spectacle depressed Toussaint. He could not have felt worse had he seen pigeons flying from the windows. In fact, chickens and pigs had already made a horror of the front steps. As the coachman and his companion passed, three small goats came around from the side, leaped upon the out-door chairs and tables.

The two did not stop. Eventually they reached the entrance gate and passed out to the public carriage road. Except for Toussaint's drive with the overseer's family, neither of them had been beyond this gate since the trouble broke. Now in the early hours of the morning they felt drawn to the scenes beyond.

Less than half a mile away they stumbled upon their first mutilated body. The head was gone, as were also the hands. Even the sex of the corpse was uncertain. They came upon others presently. Insane anger had inspired many of the killings. The bodies had been hideously marred. Reaching scenes of resistance, Toussaint and Mars discovered that the blacks had here been repaid better than man for man for their attacks. Carrying arms, the fleeing aristocrats had retaliated vigorously. But numbers had been against them. They had been overwhelmed.

"Shall we go further?" Toussaint asked.

Mars shook his head.

"I've seen enough."

"It's a dreadful world, Mars," Toussaint said, indicating the disfigured corpses. "You and I need stronger stomachs. We must become dreadful men."

"Could you, *vieux* Toussaint? Could you?"

"I'm not sure," the coachman whispered. "I wish I knew."

They turned directly, retraced their steps part of the way, then cut across a field and reached the kitchen shed behind the great house by walking through the grove of shade trees. The strapping black girl Zoune was entering the house by a back door, carrying morning coffee and small cups. When she saw the men, she paused, beckoned to them.

The two old fellows approached, both looking grave and apprehensive.

"There's another one this morning," she told them. "That makes four."

"Another?"

Toussaint showed unusual astonishment.

"The young girl—you know her. Mademoiselle Céleste."

3. She had lost consciousness on reaching the house; but now, with Angélique and the other two standing over her, Céleste began to see light and to regain her senses. What had happened? Had it been a week, a month or a year since she left this room last? Or had she been away at all? Céleste was far from certain. It might have all been a nightmare. Surely it was hard to believe that so much calamity could be crowded into a short period of actual

living. Yet here she was in her torn clothes. Her body ached with the bruises she had suffered. There was scarcely a spot she could touch that did not remind her of mad, demon-pursued flight on horseback, of being thrown from the horse, of walking and running till she fell exhausted in the grove, and finally of a ghastly encounter among the trees.

Yes, it had been real enough, she reflected, much too real. Especially the encounter. She covered her face with her hands as she thought of it now, and the three women looked at her with mingled sympathy, exasperation and puzzlement. In their opinion the girl had undoubtedly passed a wretched night, but why she did not make an effort to talk more sensibly they failed to understand. They would gladly help her if she would allow them. Céleste understood their confusion; still she was unable to get herself together well enough to help them minister to her.

"Go away," she urged them finally. "Please. Please."

They all obeyed, leaving the door half open, and Céleste lay undisturbed till the slave girl came with coffee. Céleste had no taste for anything, but she made a special effort to hold a cup and drink a few sips anyway. This done, she kicked the ruined slippers from her feet and lay down again.

Immediately the face of Count Armand de Sacy loomed before her. She opened her mouth to cry aloud, but instead thrust the knuckles of her hand between her teeth. In just such a way he had come upon her in the grove where she lay spent, bruised and almost out of her senses.

Consternation, flight and the prospect of death had completed his degeneration. He had crouched like a beast in frayed and soiled clothes. Discovering the miserable girl, his eyes had grown bright. And instantly his gross intention had become clear to Céleste.

Rising to her feet, she had made an effort to flee. The rest was blurred in her mind by her remembrance of the struggle that followed, a struggle which she rather hoped than believed had been unsuccessful on his part. She knew that eventually she had seen him stumbling away in the shadows, that soon thereafter she had fainted. She knew, too, that regaining consciousness, she had seen the sun in the morning sky, had risen with a profound effort and made her way toward Bréda. To her utter amazement the great house was still standing.

Céleste lay on the bed now, tortured by ghosts of the past two nights. After another long interval the trim Angélique, whose face when examined closely still seemed older than her body, came with the slave girl who served them, poured warm water into a bowl, began to unfasten the girl's remaining hooks and to remove the shreds of her clothes. Wearing only a night cap and a soiled petticoat, Angélique knelt beside the bed and bathed the girl's bruised legs and thighs.

This completed, Céleste began to weep softly.

"There now," Angélique said. "You'll be all right, my dear. Don't work yourself up all over again."

She bent over and kissed the unhappy girl tenderly on the cheek.

"Everything seemed so wonderful two days ago,"

Céleste reflected. "But it wasn't real. I can't understand, Angélique. What is it all about? Is it the final judgment?"

"I know no more than you, child. Rest yourself."

"Do you suppose I could have brought it on—wanting him as I do?"

"Nonsense. I've been in love," Angélique said, smiling sweetly. "But nothing like this happened."

"Oh, what's going to become of us here?"

"Wait," the other said, moving toward the door. "Don't be impatient. We'll find out if we wait."

4. Count Armand de Sacy had gone his way when the sun rose, a tiny lost man struggling through the tall green shrubbery of a tropical grove. He knew he was no longer himself. The impulses that came to him were not natural under such circumstances. He recalled his escape from an angry pack at the expense of the almond-eyed belle, but he was now incapable of remorse. In fact, the trickery that had come to his rescue was simply funny in retrospect. The count laughed aloud among the palm trees. A moment later he was bewildered again, staggering, pulling at his hair, groaning painfully.

A beast had risen in him at the sight of the languishing Céleste. Now, he vaguely felt, he was paying for it. A mind tortured and perhaps unhinged made a mockery of every decent impulse that came to him. Nothing appealed to his present mood but hideous defilement and molestation. Fear had gone. He had even forgotten the exact nature of the peril that sent him thrashing like a wild thing through the tall grasses. His destination was equally obscure.

Falling eventually into a bed of leaves, he suddenly realized that his strength was gone. Exhaustion, as much as tension and danger, had contributed to his frenzy. Now, sprawled upon his face and lacking the will to rise, he gradually fell asleep.

He woke to the unreality of lacy shades and the fantastic loveliness of Caribbean moonlight. He had slept throughout the long day without an interruption; now he roused himself painfully from earth softened only by leaves and responded strangely to the paradise of palms about him. Where was he?

It all occurred to him in time. His goal was Le Cap. The night before, during the worst of the madness, he had failed to reach safety by following his own instinct through the tangled thickets and groves. He was now sure that he must follow the road, keep his wits and dart into the hedges only when actual danger approached. He must find a creek and moisten his throat. A banana or two would give him strength. Above all else, however, he would have to be nimble.

Finding a banana tree, the count eagerly tore half a dozen of the ripe fruit from the bunch. These he did not eat at once, preferring to wait till he had first had a drink of water. Not until he had walked half a mile, turned into a carriage road and proceeded as far again did he discover a creek, however. Without a second's delay, he left the drive, fell upon his belly and filled his stomach. Walking again, he began to peel and eat the bananas. Belching lustily, feeling strong enough to walk all night if necessary, he gradually gained an illusion of security and well-being. Certainly all was not lost. A cunning and capable man, particularly if well-born, was certainly not to be taken in a snare by easy means. It would indeed require more than maddened slaves to out-maneuver the Count Armand de Sacy.

He chuckled with satisfaction. Well, he hoped they had enjoyed the almond-eyed belle. Too bad it had been necessary to throw her to the pack, especially when he had just begun to speculate on her charms himself, but Le Cap was not exactly destitute of warm, golden Creoles. Moreover, he had been stung by other bees, too. He could not forget the apricot-colored Manoune and her thin, swaying walk. He had heard in Paris about Saint Domingue's thousands of rose-lipped mulattresses. On previous trips he had paid these passing notice. Never before, however, had he seen one so disturbing as the mistress of the drunken poet. Then there was that savage black wench with the scarlet pantalets. The count visualized a great deal of amusement for himself after the troops had quelled the present disorders. Fortunately he was still a lusty man. He felt equal to almost any enterprise, including a tussle with a tall black girl; even if she had a penchant for biting and scratching, he felt capable of holding his own.

Again he turned his attention to the witchery of moonlight on banana leaves. Then suddenly cries broke in a thicket. Instantly the count was waylaid by slaves. The little terrified man bounded. A huge black figure loomed before him, blocked the way. The count turned and collided with another like the first. He then made a third dash, desperately determined to break through the circle that had commenced to form around him. This time he found himself hurled backwards so forcibly he went to the ground. In the next instant the blacks were upon him, binding his hands behind his back.

Recognition began to dawn upon the slaves.

"This is the foxy one," someone remarked.

"What are you doing?" the count cried, feeling the clothes torn from his waist downward.

"Just inserting a little gun-powder," a slave replied.

"No," the tiny man shrieked. "No, for God's sake. Please."

The cool ocean air chilled his naked buttocks. The slaves were grimly determined now. The sky-splitting outcries of the helpless victim moved them not at all. The count felt himself half torn apart by crude implements devised to help accommodate the charge. A moment later, fainting away, he ceased to struggle or to protest.

The slaves were beyond mercy or compassion. A leaping, screaming circle of them, intoxicated with their desperately won freedom, driven wild by the imaginings of their own hearts and the examples of cruelty they had learned from their masters, made a frightful circle in the carriage road. Torches flared. The moon silvered the tips of coconut palms. Finally, the preparations finished, silence fell upon the group. Someone bent over and touched a flame to the paper fuse. Then all withdrew a safe distance, waited breathlessly. A few seconds elapsed. Then the dull thud of the exploding powder aroused them to a second noisy demonstration. An unseen spatter of blood, tiny bits of flesh and particles of dung filled the air.

5. Meanwhile Diron, sitting at a garret window, looked down into the dark alley-like passage below. Lamps, flickering in a few of the houses that overlooked the way, cast queer spangles of light upon the filthy cobblestones.

The hour was growing late. Sinister figures crept along the walls, indicating that the crisis on the plains had not yet disrupted the celebrated night life of Le Cap. A carriage or two went by; even a few well-dressed men passed on foot, stepping gingerly to avoid dead cats, offal and other abominations of Cap Français' by-streets.

There was no light in the garret window where Diron waited; none, at least, that the moon did not furnish. Still it was not too dark for him to see Paulette lying across the bed, her hands securely bound. He watched the street below, but his gaze darted back and forth. Never for more than a second did he neglect his prisoner. And now that this had lasted nearly twenty-four hours, he was beginning to feel uneasy.

Presently, however, a familiar figure down below

caught his attention, and Diron whistled lustily. The astonished man paused, raised his eyes upward. It was Arsenne Brieux, Friend of the Blacks and lover of Manoune. Diron leaned far out the window, waving his arms vigorously in the moonlight, but Arsenne appeared to be unable to recognize him from that distance. Finally, throwing caution away, Diron spoke loudly enough to be heard in the street.

"Knock at the door, Arsenne," he said. "They will let you in. I want to see you."

The other nodded, disappeared in the entrance. A few moments later the steps were creaking beneath his uncertain tread. Diron crossed the room, let the poet into the chamber. Arsenne had been given a candle downstairs. With this in his hand he surveyed the room, tried to make sense of what he saw.

"This is absurd," he said, finally. "Is this your contribution to the freedom of the blacks, Diron?"

"It is," Diron assured him.

Paulette rose to a sitting position. She glared angrily at the two young men.

"But you two have been fighting," Arsenne added. "Frankly, Diron, I thought she loved you."

Paulette sneered.

"It's complicated, Arsenne," Diron said. "Don't try to make any sense of it. Even if you hadn't been drinking, you'd find it difficult. I'm compelled to keep Paulette near me till I can leave Le Cap."

"He's a coward," Paulette said calmly. "He's afraid of a woman."

"Yes, that's true. I'm afraid of a woman. Particularly when she is out of my sight. You see, I still remember poor Sylvestre Viard. More recently, Arsenne, something has happened to Hugo Juvet. Of course, I'm assured that that was a mistake. I am left to imagine who was really marked for that particular attack." He paused, drawing himself erect and fastening his eyes upon the woman who returned his stare. "While I do not intend to personally revenge these friends, where Paulette is concerned, I am nevertheless obliged to obstruct, so far as I am able, any further plans of the same nature which she might entertain."

"You don't mean—"

"It's ridiculous, Arsenne," Paulette interrupted. "Don't believe a word of it."

Diron shrugged.

"That's up to you. What I want is a weapon, if you have one, and some news about the progress of the gendarmes."

Arsenne parted his coat.

"A pistol and a sword," he said. "I'll divide with you. Take your choice."

Diron considered a moment, settled upon the sword.

"Thanks," he said, adjusting his own belt to accommodate the weapon.

"Nothing much has come through from the Plain du Nord, so far as I know," Arsenne told him. "They are saying that the commander of the garrison has decided on defensive tactics. He proposes to defend the city if it is attacked, but has chosen to let the blacks exhaust themselves rather than have his small detachments of soldiers follow them into the hills."

"I see," Diron nodded. "Nothing else?"

"Yes, one other thing." Arsenne looked suspiciously at Paulette, wondering whether or not to say what he knew in her presence.

"We might step outside the door," Diron suggested, seeing his gesture.

Outside, standing at the head of the dark stairway, they put their heads together quietly.

"Manoune says the mulattos will probably throw their strength with the slaves if the blacks can hold out till Beauvais, the mulatto leader, arrives. Word is being sent to him. Oh, yes, M. Sylvain, the printer, has just left the city secretly. He hopes to reach Port-au-Prince. Several others of us who are against slavery are staying out of sight till we can secure a boat to take us around by water. Manoune's relatives live near there."

"Why Port-au-Prince?"

"The free mulattos are very strong there. While we can't be sure they will fight on the side of the slaves, we can be quite certain they will not fight against them. It will be more comfortable there for those who hold views like ours. M. Sylvain has it in his mind to organize whites to fight on the side of the slaves, provided Beauvais and the mulattos decide to do the same."

Excitement instantly put a lump in Diron's throat. Not a second was required for his personal decision. Céleste came to his mind. He hoped desperately that the blacks would not make it necessary for him to charge them with her fate. In such a case his heart could never be as fully in their cause as it had been in the past. However that might be, he would leave immediately.

"One more favor, Arsenne," he said breathlessly. "The girl Céleste failed to reach Le Cap. I haven't given up hope, however. If I find her, I shall try to overtake M. Sylvain. My problem now is Paulette. If she were released immediately, I might not get outside the city safely. I want to ask you to keep her here till I have time to make a start. Half an hour, say?"

Arsenne nodded.

"See you in the west," he said as they shook hands.

"Give me half an hour," Diron repeated.

He was off in a rush, stumbling noisily on the dark stair. When he reached the bottom, he heard scuffling overhead. He knew what it meant. Paulette was attempting to break free. A cold perspiration came to his forehead. Somehow he could not be confident of Arsenne's ability to restrain the tempestuous woman. But be that as it might, he could not return to the scene now. He must reach the livery stable, secure a horse, leave a word for his uncle at the *Hôtel de la Couronne,* then make his dash. There would be no time to spare, particularly if Arsenne should fail at his task. Diron fairly ran when he reached the narrow street.

Approaching the stables of the riding academy, he halted his pace. It would not be well to arouse suspicions by coming into the place breathless. There were dozens of reasons why he should appear casual as he bargained for a saddle horse. But this was no occasion to enumerate them, even secretly to himself; time was precious. He must think rapidly. For example, he had not yet formulated a plan of search. Where was he to seek the girl who had last been seen fleeing on the back of a coach horse? Who could answer his inquiries? Assuming that the slaves would be cordial, what would the soldiers say to him as he passed them on his way out of the city?

Ten minutes later he was leaving the stables of the academy on one of their most spirited beasts. At a hitching stone around the corner from the inn he dismounted and tied up. Making the knot secure, he quickly walked around to the entrance gate where a porter admitted him promptly.

On the steps he thought of Paulette and Arsenne. He could not forget the sound of aroused heels on the garret floor as he had left the house in which he had detained the young woman. Surely Arsenne had given up the struggle by now, if indeed she had not immediately fought her way past him when Diron left. The thought of her being free to plot against him, to set rough scoundrels in his path, to commission them to pursue him, left Diron limp. Paulette was remarkably resourceful, and there was no longer need to deny that her intentions were vicious.

Diron swung the door of his room open and bluntly announced to M. Philippe Desautels that he was leaving immediately.

"Sailing?" the older man inquired without surprise.

Diron shook his head.

"I have a good horse," he said. "Good-by, *Oncle* Philippe."

"Well, I know better than to attempt to change your mind. You've never been notably sensible, Diron."

"Wish me luck, anyway."

"Perhaps it's your age."

"No, it's a girl, *Oncle* Philippe. Céleste."

"But even if you found her, Diron, what would you do? You couldn't return to Le Cap. You'd be suspected."

"There is the Western Province and Port-au-Prince," Diron suggested. "Some have gone that way."

The older man rose, embraced his nephew with his good arm, then turned toward the little starry balcony. Diron, gloomily handsome in the dim room, moved toward the door, let himself out and walked directly to the stairs. Unaccustomed recently to a sword against his leg, the thing got in his way. He shifted it further to the side, began to walk more rapidly as he crossed the veranda and descended the outside steps.

He had reached the street and proceeded halfway to the corner when he was accosted from behind. He threw a nervous glance over his shoulder. Two heavy, menacing figures approached. Diron spun swiftly as they drew nearer. Back to the wall, he confronted them so suddenly both seemed taken aback. With the same motion he brandished his steel.

"So you're the cat's paws?" he cried, feinting with an upward motion of the weapon.

Two hoarse grunts answered him, and a blade struck

the stone wall near his head. Holding his position to keep both of them before him, Diron snarled back savagely and retaliated with a succession of short, vicious thrusts all of which were executed with lightning swiftness. He rose on his toes to get the full advantage of superior height and a longer blade and settled himself grimly for a stand against death.

They were not fancy swordsmen. Instead the two men faced Diron with heavy brawling knives as long as a man's arm. The rogues came at the young man by turn, chopping downward with powerful swings.

A lunge on Diron's part would have been fatal. Off balance for a single instant, his chance would certainly vanish. A quickened mind told him that much at the start. Eyes growing steadily sharper in the half-dark street revealed the gross features of the murderous pair Paulette had sent against him. She had been swifter than he expected. A great rage rose in Diron as the sword darted back and forth before him. Even without Paulette's clear hint he would have recognized these men as the ones who had set upon Sylvestre Viard. Perhaps in that particular affair a former lover of the dark-haired belle had played a part, too, a politically prominent lover known for his hatred of Jacobins. In any case, Diron felt angry enough to fight a dozen men.

No longer content to stand against the wall and fight defensively while waiting till either he or his antagonists became exhausted, he suddenly leaped into the middle of the road. There, dancing fiercely, lurching, taking advantage of every opening, he quickly changed the character of the contest. His opponents came at him with a flicker of broad blades while Diron sliced and pecked them with a waspish sword point.

The fight wore on; in time it attracted a group of timid spectators who watched from a safe distance, trying at the same time to efface themselves in the shadows of the wall. The encounter threatened to degenerate into a stand-off. Then, quite abruptly, Diron realized that one of his adversaries was growing weak from the loss of blood. For several moments he watched the fellow, noted sluggish reactions. Finally, well-assured, Diron began to maneuver craftily for a position. A second later the opening came, and Diron, fairly bursting with rage, stung the rogue with a thrust that went a full six inches between the man's ribs.

The second individual commenced to fade as soon as his partner was dispatched. Diron began to leap about the ponderous, heavy-footed ruffian with a superiority of footwork and dexterity that completely confused the fellow. A moment later, having taken a vicious slice across the face, the man deliberately turned his back and fled into the darkness of the narrow street.

Diron walked to the corner, conscious of the shy but fascinated spectators, untied his horse and swung himself into the saddle. Not until he had ridden a hundred feet did it occur to him to replace his blade. This, however, was not an easy operation in the boy's present state. His hand trembled miserably. The strain had been great.

6. Another night came to Bréda, and the four women sequestered in the upper rooms of the greathouse slipped their dresses over their heads and prepared to retire. Clad in petticoats, the barefoot Claire and the uncorsetted Annette put their heads together, lighting cigars at the same time over the single candle flame that served their room.

"If you were more alluring," Claire suggested, "somebody might be interested in rescuing us."

"In that case *you'd* still be left. Think of some other way," Annette told her impatiently.

"We have the girl, fortunately."

"That sounds like the remark of a scheming old devil with a marriageable daughter."

"Only because the situation is similar."

Annette pondered a moment.

"Do you think we could really interest one of the slave leaders in her?"

"It's something to think about. Angélique is attractive, too."

"We can't stay here forever. That's certain."

"Oh, I'll work out a plan if worse comes to worst."

"While you're working it out, don't forget to find out what Céleste and Angélique think of the arrangement."

"They *are* inclined to be difficult sometimes, both of them."

The two smoked in silence for a long while. The house itself was remarkably still. Claire settled herself in a chair, leaned backwards and flicked ashes on the floor. Annette sat on the side of a bed, crossed her heavy legs lugubriously.

"I can't help thinking of the count sometimes," she said.

Claire let her chair down violently.

"Mon Dieu!"

"You're just bitter," Annette said.

Claire found the chamber pot and spat into it with resounding emphasis.

"Well, my opinion of you certainly gets no better, mademoiselle."

"Forget about him then. Shall we talk to Céleste and Angélique?"

"Yes. Have them come in here."

Annette's hair had not been combed in days. It gave her a desperate appearance as she shuffled out of the room and down the hall. A few moments later she returned alone.

"They'll come," she said, leaving the door open.

While the two delayed, Claire went to the window and looked down upon the shadows of the driveway. Arching her back and squinting, she tried to penetrate the darkness. The effort was wasted, however. Nothing, so far as she could discern, moved in that blackness.

"Thought I heard something," she said, returning to her chair.

"Like what?"

"I don't know. Maybe I'm imagining things. But they'll come back and burn the place eventually. Even if Toussaint does keep them fooled about Mme de Libertas, making them believe she's still here, they'll get tired of looking at this awful house. It can't last long."

"I can depend on you to be dismal. But remember we still have a good chance. Céleste is a neat trick. If we can interest the slave ringleaders in her and Angélique, you and I can at least go along as sort of mothers-in-law."

"I refuse," Claire said with irony. "But maybe I can be persuaded."

A sound of footsteps in the hall silenced them. Annette chewed on the stump of her cigar. The footsteps suggested one person rather than two. A firm, heavy tread was also indicated. A moment later the two women, breathlessly amazed, saw Diron Desautels standing at their door. He seemed taller than usual and more melancholy. His clothes were in a bad state, but his hair had not lost its shine, and he had an angry, fighting face that they had never seen before. He seemed spent and roughly used, but he also appeared hardened and ready for more.

"Toussaint told me she was here," he announced.

They nodded stupidly like a couple of abandoned lunatics, unable to believe their eyes.

"Yes, stay here," Claire said, rising. "I'll call her."

Diron stepped aside to let her pass. Then he stood inside the room, waiting for her return.

The girl finally came in, starry-eyed and pale. Her hair was loose; the strings in her shoes dangled. Her dress had not been hooked. Without speaking, Diron fell upon one

knee and began lacing Céleste's shoes. Claire and Angélique followed the girl into the room and watched Diron
with bewilderment. He rose, finally, pressed the girl's
hands a moment and then turned to the others.

"Aren't the rest of you coming?" he asked.

"We don't know. May we?" Angélique said with feeling.

"Some of the whites are making an effort to reach
the West Province, particularly the Friends of the
Blacks," Diron explained. "Some may continue as far as
Port-au-Prince. Toussaint has provided mules. His brother
Paul and others from Bréda will accompany us a part
of the way."

Suddenly, and unaccountably, the tenseness of the first
night of the insurrection returned. The women flew from
room to room. Holding Céleste's hand firmly, Diron went
out and waited in the dark hall, overlooking the greater
darkness of the stairway. Doors banged open and were
left standing. A cape, a hood, a few hastily snatched personal items occupied the women for a moment or two.
Then, neglecting the candles in their rooms, the three
followed the young couple down the stairs, sliding their
hands on the banister rail as they descended.

A score of Bréda blacks stood in the tense darkness
outside. Some of them held the bridles of the tiny mules
that had been secured. Others darted about like shadows
or ghosts. Still they were not hostile. Most of them had
expected to see Mme de Libertas and perhaps the girl
emerge. This revelation astonished and amused them. It
did not make them angry.

The company of whites, mounting, followed their escort around the great house, across the ruined gardens of the estate, through a thicket of odorous shrubs and came into the driveway near the entrance gate.

The air was fine, though cooler than usual. There was a dampness in it, too, a dampness which suggested that perhaps the dry spell was near an end. A few clouds lay near the horizon. Across the dim countryside there was no indication of strife. All was now remarkably quiet. Having decided not to follow the bands of blacks, the armed forces had taken positions outside Le Cap, waiting for the rumored attack upon the city by the slaves. The blacks, on the other hand, having broken free, having pillaged and burned and put their masters to flight, were equally bewildered. Divided into two bands under their chiefs Baissou and Boukman, they became more eager and confident every hour, but they had no idea what to do next, and their leaders had no idea what to suggest.

The sweet-scented night saw no turmoil.

"We were making plans of our own when you came," Claire said to Diron as they rode.

He did not seem interested.

"I'm sorry I had to spoil them," he answered.

"Forget that," Annette protested to her companion. "This way will be better if it works."

Curiously the count came into her mind again. She couldn't help hoping that the little man had reached Le Cap safely. To be sure, she held much against him, but she was willing to forget some things now. At that moment her beast stumbled over some parts of a badly demolished body lying in the road. She did not like to be morbid, but the shame, the disfigurement, the utter humiliation of death did create a certain gloom. She simply couldn't help wondering how she would feel if it had been someone she knew lying there mutilated—the Count Armand de Sacy, for example.

The young pair ahead had not seen the roadside horror. It was plain, even in the darkness, that neither of them was too preoccupied with their wretched state to be in love. Suddenly Annette heard the girl burst into tears.

"Where have you been, Diron?" she cried. They were almost her first words since leaving Bréda, and she uttered them much as one might speak on awakening from a trance. "How did you get here?"

Drawing his beast close beside hers, the boy gave her his arm for support. She seemed as if she would fall without his help.

"I came to find you," he told her. "I got here by killing rogues, bribing men of God on the way and bargaining with demons. I had to find you."

The girl crossed herself surreptitiously, delighted and horrified by his bold irreverence. Annette, riding directly behind them, began to feel tearful on her own part. She averted her face, however, rather than allow Claire to see her show of sentiment.

The road was growing steadily darker. Presently a few drops of rain fell.

By daybreak the company had reached the summit of a mountain that looked down on a drenched plain. In consternation they discovered that the slopes below were alive with hordes of near-naked blacks. Later, detachments of the colonial army came into view, pouring through a divide with cavalry, field pieces and infantry. Diron and his companions were fascinated by the spectacle, but they continued to move along the ridge. In time, however, thunder broke on the plains below, and the company halted abruptly to watch the outcome.

The mass of slaves had gone wild. An unorganized pack, thousands in number, swarmed toward the cannon and fortified positions beyond the slope. They were armed with cane knives, hoes, scythe-swords and picks. Among them went the demented boy Hyacinth, who had convinced thousands that he possessed authority over death and the ability to wing the spirits of the fallen blacks to their native Africa. He waved above his head the tail of a bull, shouting unintelligibly above the tumult, and walked unharmed through a rain of shells. As he leaped before the host, the slaves went into a frenzy.

Splitting the sky with their shrieks, they swarmed over the army's position. They clutched at the bridles of rearing horses. They pulled the gaudy dragoons to the ground. They reached their arms down the barrels of the field pieces. The discharged cannon destroyed them, tore their ranks unmercifully. Others came on, climbing over the guns, strangling the gunners, taking the iron balls out of the mouths of the cannon.

For hours it continued. Then a turn came. The field was abandoned. A hundred soldiers lay dead—two thousand slaves. But the army was fleeing in disorder.

The dreamy-eyed slave called Paul, brother of Tous-saint, clung to the halter of Diron's beast.

"Half of you may return now," Diron said. "Most of the danger is passed."

"Merci, monsieur."

The black man bowed gravely.

"One request before you leave, however. Can you get a message through to Le Cap for me?"

"Very easily, Monsieur Desautels. There are many blacks in Le Cap. I can go myself. Everyone knows that at Bréda we're still behaving well."

The little company huddled together closely, the three women listening as Diron instructed the messenger.

"Tell my uncle you saw us past the dangers of this region. Tell him the girl Céleste is at my side, also the other women. We should reach Port-au-Prince in a few days."

Half of the escort returned with the dreamy-eyed slave. The rest continued with Diron's tired company, moving toward Gonaïves in the intolerable sunlight. From that city the way would be quite safe; the blacks could be allowed to return home.

7. Meanwhile the day passed drowsily in Le Cap. In the cool of the afternoon, however, reports of the route spread new terror. A new rush for passage on the boats

lying in the harbor commenced. M. Bayou de Libertas
was fanning his wife with a palmetto leaf on the veranda
of the *Hôtel de la Couronne* when he saw M. Philippe
Desautels totter down the path and up the entrance steps.
The elderly man's arm was still in a sling.

"You've been walking, monsieur?" the former overseer observed.

"I'm afraid Diron was right," M. Desautels said. "This
thing is not going to be settled as easily as we imagined.
I've been negotiating for passage."

"My wife feels the same way. She's just fainted again,"
the other said.

"I'm quite all right now," the woman insisted, sniffing
at her bottle of salts.

"Take my seat, monsieur. You're weak," M. de Libertas urged.

"Thank you."

"Did you succeed with arrangements?"

"We sail in a few hours," the tired man answered.
"There was room for a few others. Do you know anyone
else who might be interested in a vessel going to New
Orleans by way of Port-au-Prince?"

M. de Libertas wrinkled his forehead.

"How about your nephew?"

The older man shook his head gloomily.

"Diron had other ideas," he said. "He left on horseback."

"Well, there's Mme Viard," M. de Libertas suggested.
"Why don't you ask her?"

"If you would be so kind," M. Desautels said, "I'd appreciate your sending the word. I'm afraid it will require all my strength to reach the boat."

"Certainly, monsieur. I'll carry her the message myself, immediately. We are returning to Paris. Otherwise it might be pleasant if Madame and I could sail with you, too."

Blinking rapidly, M. de Libertas placed the fan in his wife's hand, left the other two on the veranda as he went to find Mme Sylvestre Viard. A few moments later he was within her gate, walking rapidly up the path. There was no answer to his knock; and when he walked around the veranda and called from room to room, no servant responded. He continued out to the stables, shouting and receiving no response. Then he returned and tried the doors and windows.

All were unlocked. M. de Libertas concluded that Paulette Viard had been deserted by her servants. The overseer turned to leave. Second thought, however, impressed him to enter the house. He went in and glanced through the rooms of the lower floor. There was no noticeable disorder. It was difficult to explain Mme Viard's leaving her house open like this, assuming that she knew there were no servants on hand. The only possible answer for M. de Libertas was that she had left before the servants. But even that was strange. Deeply puzzled, he went to the staircase and hurried up to the second floor. A moment later he staggered, throwing his hand before his eyes.

Doors had been flung wide in the upper rooms. In one of the sleeping chambers directly ahead he saw the raven-haired young woman sitting half-clad in a chair before her dressing table. She was facing the mirror, her back to the door. The face that M. de Libertas saw reflected was masked by loose hair. The chin rested on the breast. The arms hung stiffly downward . . . An ugly knife projected from a shoulder blade.

M. de Libertas tried to think.

It was evident that Mme Viard had failed to endear her servants to her, just as she had failed to endear others. The man turned in confusion, his heart thumping wildly, and hastened back to the inn.

"She won't be leaving," he told the two on the veranda. Both of the others seemed to notice his paleness, but neither commented. After a brief pause the overseer looked at his wife with woe in his eyes. "Need that detain us, my dear?" he asked. "Don't you think we'd better get our things together?"

"Toussaint's brother Paul was here," his wife said. "Diron found Céleste. They've crossed the hills."

"Diron will join me at Port-au-Prince—you may count on that," M. Desautels ventured confidently. "I'm sure I can make the boy talk sense now that he's found Céleste." He paused, observing the stunned look on the overseer's face as he stared at his wife. A moment later he added, "Maybe it's just as well Mme Viard wasn't interested in coming, monsieur."

Neither M. de Libertas nor his wife answered.

Bewildered, the stout woman rose and followed her trembling husband into the entrance hall.

M. Desautels remained in his chair till he saw another company of exhausted, fleeing troops pass before the inn. Then he rose and called a mulatto porter to assist him with preparations for the voyage that lay ahead.